P9-CSW-316

BEHIND CLOSED DOORS

BEHIND CLOSED DOORS

B. A. PARIS

ST. MARTIN'S PRESS ≋ NEW YORK

This is a work of fiction. All of the characters, organizations, and events portrayed in this novel are either products of the author's imagination or are used fictitiously.

BEHIND CLOSED DOORS. Copyright © 2016 by B. A. Paris. All rights reserved. Printed in the United States of America. For information, address St. Martin's Press, 175 Fifth Avenue, New York, N.Y. 10010.

www.stmartins.com

Designed by Steven Seighman

The Library of Congress Cataloging-in-Publication Data is available upon request.

ISBN 978-1-250-12100-4 (hardcover)
ISBN 978-1-250-12216-2 (international edition)
ISBN 978-1-250-12101-1 (e-book)

Our books may be purchased in bulk for promotional, educational, or business use. Please contact your local bookseller or the Macmillan Corporate and Premium Sales Department at 1-800-221-7945, extension 5442, or by e-mail at MacmillanSpecial Markets@macmillan.com.

First published in Great Britain by MIRA/Harlequin, HarperCollins UK

10 9 8 7 6 5 4 3 2

For my daughters
Sophie, Chloë, Céline, Eloïse, Margaux

ACKNOWLEDGMENTS

I have so many people to thank, not least my wonderful agent, Camilla Wray. I feel so lucky to have found you! Huge thanks also to Naomi, Mary, Emma, Rosanna and everyone else at Darley Anderson.

In the UK, I am very grateful to my fantastic editor, Sally Williamson, and to Alison, Jennifer, Clio, Cara and the rest of the team at HQ. And in the US, to Jennifer Weis, Lisa Senz, Jessica Preeg and Sylvan Creekmore at St Martin's Press.

Eternal gratitude to Gerrard Rudd, who had faith in me right from the beginning, long before I had faith in myself, and to Jan Michael, for her generous and invaluable help. Thank you both, from the bottom of my heart.

Special thanks to my wonderful daughters, for all their help and encouragement and to my husband, for giving me the space to write. To my parents, for being determined to walk into a bookshop and buy my book, to my lovely friends Louise and Dominique, for never failing to ask how my writing is going. To Karen and Philip, for the same reason and to my sister, Christine, for reading every word of everything I write.

BEHIND CLOSED DOORS

PRESENT

The champagne bottle knocks against the marble kitchen counter, making me jump. I glance at Jack, hoping he won't have noticed how nervous I am. He catches me looking and smiles.

'Perfect,' he says softly.

Taking my hand, he leads me to where our guests are waiting. As we go through the hall, I see the flowering lily Diane and Adam brought us for our garden. It's such a beautiful pink that I hope Jack will plant it where I'll be able to see it from the bedroom window. Just thinking of the garden makes tears well up from deep inside me and I swallow them down quickly. With so much at stake tonight, I need to concentrate on the here and now.

In the sitting room, a fire burns steadily in the antique grate. We're well into March but there's still a nip in the air and Jack likes our guests to be as comfortable as possible.

'Your house is really something, Jack,' Rufus says admiringly. 'Don't you think so, Esther?'

I don't know Rufus or Esther. They are new to the area and tonight is the first time we've met, which makes me feel more nervous than I already am. But I can't afford to let Jack down, so I fix a smile on my face, praying that they'll like me. Esther doesn't smile back, so I guess she's reserving judgement. But I can't blame her. Since joining our circle of friends a month ago, I'm sure she's been told over and over again that Grace Angel, wife of brilliant lawyer Jack Angel, is a perfect example of a woman who has it all—the perfect house, the perfect husband, the perfect life. If I were Esther, I'd be wary of me too.

My eyes fall on the box of expensive chocolates she has just taken out of her bag and I feel a flicker of excitement. Not wanting her to give them to Jack, I move smoothly towards her and she instinctively holds them out to me.

'Thank you, they look wonderful,' I say gratefully, placing them on the coffee table so that I can open them later, when we serve coffee.

Esther intrigues me. She's the complete opposite of Diane—tall, blonde, slim, reserved—and I can't help respecting her for being the first person to step into our house and not go on about how beautiful it is. Jack insisted on choosing the house himself, telling me it was to be my wedding present, so I saw it for the first time when we came back from our honeymoon. Even though he'd told me it was perfect for us I didn't fully realise what he meant until I saw it. Set in large grounds at the far end of the village, it gives Jack the privacy he craves, as well as the privilege of owning the most beautiful house in Spring Eaton. And the most secure. There is a complicated alarm system, with steel shutters to protect the windows on the ground floor. It must seem strange that these are often kept shut during the day, but as Jack tells anyone who asks, with a job like his, good security is one of his priorities.

We have a lot of paintings on the walls of our sitting room but people are usually drawn towards the large red canvas that hangs above the fireplace. Diane and Adam, who have already seen it, can't help going over to have another look, and Rufus joins them, while Esther sits down on one of the cream leather sofas.

'It's amazing,' Rufus says, looking in fascination at the hundreds of tiny markings that make up most of the painting.

'It's called *Fireflies*,' Jack offers, untwisting the wire from the bottle of champagne.

'I've never seen anything quite like it.'

'Grace painted it,' Diane tells him. 'Can you believe it?'

'You should see Grace's other paintings.' Jack eases the cork from the bottle with only the slightest of sounds. 'They really are quite something.'

Rufus looks around the room with interest. 'Are they here?'

'No, I'm afraid they're hanging elsewhere in the house.'

'For Jack's eyes only,' Adam jokes.

'And Grace's. Isn't that right, darling?' Jack says, smiling over at me. 'For our eyes only.'

'Yes, they are,' I agree, turning my head away.

We join Esther on the sofa and Diane exclaims in pleasure as Jack pours the champagne into tall glasses. She looks across at me.

'Are you feeling better now?' she asks. 'Grace couldn't make lunch with me yesterday because she was ill,' she explains, turning to Esther.

'It was only a migraine,' I protest.

'Unfortunately, Grace is prone to them.' Jack looks over at me sympathetically. 'But they never last long, thank goodness.'

'It's the second time you've stood me up,' Diane points out.

'I'm sorry,' I apologise.

'Well, at least you didn't just forget this time,' she teases. 'Why don't we meet up next Friday to make up for it? Would you be free, Grace? No dental appointments for you to suddenly remember at the last minute?'

'No, and no migraines either, I hope.'

Diane turns to Esther. 'Would you like to join us? It would have to be at a restaurant in town because I work.'

'Thank you, I'd like that.' She glances over at me, maybe to check that I don't mind her coming along and, as I smile back at her, I feel horribly guilty, because I already know I won't be going.

Calling everyone to attention, Jack offers a toast to Esther and Rufus, welcoming them to the area. I raise my glass and take a sip of champagne. The bubbles dance in my mouth and I feel a sudden flash of happiness, which I try to hang on to. But it disappears as quickly as it came.

I look over to where Jack is talking animatedly to Rufus. He and Adam met Rufus at the golf club a couple of weeks ago and invited him to join them in a game. On finding Rufus to be an excellent golfer, but not quite excellent enough to beat him, Jack invited him and Esther around for dinner. Watching them together, it's obvious that Jack is out to impress Rufus, which means it's important I win Esther round. But it won't be easy; whereas Diane is simply admiring, Esther seems more complicated.

Excusing myself, I go through to the kitchen to fetch the canapés I made earlier, and to put the last touches to the dinner. Etiquette—Jack is pedantic about it—means I can't be gone for long, so I quickly whisk the egg whites that are waiting in a bowl into peaks, and add them to the soufflé base I made earlier.

As I spoon the mixture into individual dishes, I glance nervously at the clock, then put the dishes into a bain-marie and place it in the oven, noting the exact time. I feel a momentary wave of panic that I might not be able to pull everything off, but reminding myself that fear is my enemy I try to remain calm and return to the sitting room with the tray of canapés. I pass them around, accepting everybody's compliments gratefully, because Jack will have heard them too. Sure enough, with a kiss to the top of my head, he agrees with Diane that I am indeed a superb cook, and I breathe a silent sigh of relief.

Determined to make some headway with Esther, I sit down next to her. Seeing this, Jack relieves me of the canapés.

'You deserve a rest, darling, after all the hard work you've done today,' he says, balancing the tray on his long elegant fingers.

'It wasn't hard work at all,' I protest, which is a lie, and Jack knows it, because he chose the menu.

I begin to ask Esther all the right questions: if she has settled into the area, if she was sorry to leave Kent behind, if her
two children have settled into their new school. For some
reason, the fact that I am well informed seems to irk her, so I
make a point of asking the names of her son and daughter,
even though I know they are called Sebastian and Aisling. I
even know their ages, seven and five, but I pretend that
I don't. Aware of Jack listening to my every word, I know
he'll wonder what I'm playing at.

'You don't have children, do you,' Esther says, making it a
statement rather than a question.

'No, not yet. We thought we'd enjoy a couple of years on
our own first.'

'Why, how long have you been married?' Her voice regis-
ters surprise.

'A year,' I admit.

'It was their anniversary last week,' Diane chips in.

'And I'm still not ready to share my beautiful wife with
anyone else,' Jack says, refilling her glass.

I watch, momentarily distracted, as a tiny splash of champagne misses the glass and lands on the knee of his pristine
chinos.

'I hope you don't mind me asking,' Esther begins, her curi-
osity getting the better of her, 'but were either of you married
before?'

She sounds as if she wants the answer to be yes, as if to
find a disgruntled ex-husband or wife lurking in the background would be proof that we're less than perfect.

'No, neither of us were,' I say.

She glances at Jack and I know she's wondering how someone so good-looking managed to stay unattached for so long. Sensing her eyes on him, Jack smiles good-naturedly.

'I must admit that at forty years old, I'd begun to despair of ever finding the perfect woman. But as soon as I saw Grace, I knew she was the one I'd been waiting for.'

'So romantic,' sighs Diane, who already knows the story of how Jack and I met. 'I've lost count of the number of women I tried to set Jack up with but no one would do until he met Grace.'

'What about you, Grace?' Esther asks. 'Was it love at first sight for you too?'

'Yes,' I say, remembering. 'It was.'

Overwhelmed by the memory, I stand up a little too quickly and Jack's head swivels towards me. 'The soufflés,' I explain calmly. 'They should be done now. Are you all ready to sit down?'

Spurred on by Diane, who tells them that soufflés wait for no one, they drain their glasses and make for the table. Esther, however, stops on the way for a closer look at *Fireflies* and, when Jack joins her rather than urge her to sit down, I breathe a sigh of relief that the soufflés are nowhere near ready. If they were, I would be near to tears with stress at the delay, especially when he starts explaining some of the different techniques I used to create the painting.

When they eventually sit down five minutes later, the soufflés are cooked to perfection. As Diane expresses her amazement, Jack smiles at me from the other end of the table and tells everyone that I am very clever indeed.

It's during evenings like this that I'm reminded of why I fell in love with Jack. Charming, amusing and intelligent, he knows exactly what to say and how to say it. Because Esther and Rufus are newcomers, he makes sure that the conversation as we eat our soufflés is for their benefit. He prompts Diane and Adam into revealing information about themselves that will help our new friends, such as where they shop and the sports they play. Although Esther listens politely to their list of leisure activities, the names of their gardeners and babysitters, the best place to buy fish, I know that I am the one who interests her, and I know she's going to return to the fact that Jack and I have come relatively late to marriage, hoping to find something—anything—to tell her it is not as perfect as it seems. Unfortunately for her, she's going to be disappointed.

She waits until Jack has carved the beef Wellington and served it with a gratin of potatoes, and carrots lightly glazed with honey. There are also tiny sugar peas, which I plunged into boiling water just before taking the beef from the oven. Diane marvels that I've managed to get everything ready at the same time, and admits she always chooses a main course like curry, which can be prepared earlier and heated through at the last minute. I'd like to tell her that I'd much rather do as she does, that painstaking calculations and sleepless nights are the currency I pay to serve such a perfect dinner. But the alternative—serving anything that is less than perfect—isn't an option.

Esther looks at me from across the table. 'So where did you and Jack meet?'

'In Regent's Park,' I say. 'One Sunday afternoon.'

'Tell her what happened,' urges Diane, her pale skin flushed from the champagne.

I hesitate a moment, because it's a story I have told before. But it's one that Jack loves to hear me tell, so it's in my interest to repeat it. Luckily, Esther comes to my rescue. Mistaking my pause for reticence, she pounces.

'Please do,' she urges.

'Well, at the risk of boring those who have already heard it before,' I begin, with an apologetic smile, 'I was in the park with my sister Millie. We often go there on a Sunday afternoon and that Sunday there happened to be a band playing. Millie loves music and she was enjoying herself so much that she got up from her seat and began to dance in front of the bandstand. She had recently learnt to waltz and, as she danced, she stretched her arms out in front of her, as if she was dancing with someone.' I find myself smiling at the memory and wish desperately that life was still as simple, still as innocent. 'Although people were generally indulgent, happy to see Millie enjoying herself,' I go on, 'I could see that one or two were uncomfortable and I knew I should do something, call her back to her seat perhaps. But there was a part of me that was loath to because—'

'How old is your sister?' Esther interrupts.

'Seventeen.' I pause a moment, unwilling to face reality. 'Nearly eighteen.'

Esther raises her eyebrows. 'She's something of an attention seeker, then.'

'No, she's not, it's just that . . .'

'Well, she must be. I mean, people don't usually get up and dance in a park, do they?' She looks around the table triumphantly and when everyone avoids her eye I can't help feeling sorry for her.

'Millie has Down's syndrome.' Jack's voice breaks the awkward silence that has descended on the table. 'It means she's often wonderfully spontaneous.'

Confusion floods Esther's face and I feel annoyed that the people who told her everything else about me didn't mention Millie.

'Anyway, before I could decide what to do,' I say, coming to her rescue, 'this perfect gentleman got up from his seat, went over to where Millie was dancing, bowed and held out his hand to her. Well, Millie was delighted and, as they began to waltz, everybody started applauding and then other couples got up from their seats and started to dance too. It was a very, very special moment. And, of course, I fell immediately in love with Jack for having made it happen.'

'What Grace didn't know at the time was that I had seen her and Millie in the park the week before and had immediately fallen in love with her. She was so attentive to Millie, so utterly selfless. I had never seen that sort of devotion in anybody before and I was determined to get to know her.'

'And what Jack didn't know at the time,' I say in turn, 'was that I had noticed him the week before but never thought he would be interested in someone like me.'

It amuses me when everybody nods their head in agreement. Even though I am attractive, Jack's film-star good looks mean that people think I'm lucky he wanted to marry me. But that isn't what I meant.

'Grace doesn't have any other brothers and sisters so she thought the fact that Millie will one day be her sole responsibility would discourage me,' Jack explains.

'As it had others,' I point out.

Jack shakes his head. 'On the contrary, it was the knowledge that Grace would do anything for Millie that made me realise she was the woman I'd been looking for all my life. In my line of work, it's easy to become demoralised with the human race.'

'I saw from the paper yesterday that congratulations are in order again,' Rufus says, raising his glass in Jack's direction.

'Yes, well done.' Adam, who is a lawyer in the same firm as Jack, joins in. 'Another conviction under your belt.'

'It was a fairly cut-and-dried case,' Jack says modestly. 'Although proving that my client hadn't inflicted the wounds herself, given that she had a penchant for self-harm, made it a little more difficult.'

'But, generally speaking, aren't cases of abuse usually easy to prove?' Rufus asks, while Diane tells Esther, in case she doesn't already know, that Jack champions the underdog—more specifically, battered wives. 'I don't want to detract from the wonderful work you do, but there is often physical evidence, or witnesses, are there not?'

'Jack's forte is getting the victims to trust him enough to tell him what has been going on,' Diane, who I suspect of being a little in love with Jack, explains. 'Many women don't have anybody to turn to and are scared they won't be believed.'

'He also makes sure that the perpetrators go down for a very long time,' adds Adam.

'I have nothing but contempt for men who are found to be violent towards their wives,' Jack says firmly. 'They deserve everything they get.'

'I'll drink to that.' Rufus raises his glass again.

'He's never lost a case yet, have you, Jack?' says Diane.

'No, and I don't intend to.'

'An unbroken track record—that's quite something,' muses Rufus, impressed.

Esther looks over at me. 'Your sister—Millie—is quite a bit younger than you,' she remarks, bringing the conversation back to where we left off.

'Yes, there are seventeen years between us. Millie didn't come along until my mother was forty-six. It didn't occur to her she was pregnant at first so it was a bit of a shock to find she was going to be a mother again.'

'Does Millie live with your parents?'

'No, she boards at a wonderful school in North London. But she'll be eighteen in April, so she'll have to leave it this summer, which is a shame because she loves it there.'

'So where will she go? To your parents'?'

'No.' I pause for a moment, because I know that what I am about to say will shock her. 'They live in New Zealand.'

Esther does a double take. 'New Zealand?'

'Yes. They retired there last year, just after our wedding.'

'I see,' she says. But I know she doesn't.

'Millie will be moving in with us,' Jack explains. He smiles over at me. 'I knew it would be a condition to Grace accepting to marry me and it was one that I was more than happy to comply with.'

'That's very generous of you,' Esther says.

'Not at all—I'm delighted that Millie will be living here. It will add another dimension to our lives, won't it, darling?'

I lift my glass and take a sip of my wine so that I don't have to answer.

'You obviously get on well with her,' Esther remarks.

'Well, I hope she's as fond of me as I am of her—although it did take her a while once Grace and I were actually married.'

'Why was that?'

'I think the reality of our marriage was a shock to her,' I tell her. 'She had adored Jack from the beginning, but when we came back from our honeymoon and she realised that he was going to be with me the whole time, she became jealous. She's fine now, though. Jack is once again her favourite person.'

'Thankfully George Clooney has taken my place as Millie's object of dislike,' Jack laughs.

'George Clooney?' Esther queries.

'Yes.' I nod, glad that Jack has brought it up. 'I had this thing about him . . .'

'Don't we all?' murmurs Diane.

'. . . and Millie was so jealous that when some friends gave me a George Clooney calendar for Christmas one year, she scrawled on it "I don't like George Clooney", except that she spelt it phonetically—J-O-R-J K-O-O-N-Y—she has a bit of trouble with the "L",' I explain. 'It was so sweet.'

Everyone laughs.

'And now she never stops telling everyone that she likes me but she doesn't like him. It's become a bit of a mantra— "I like you, Jack, but I don't like George Cooney".' Jack smiles. 'I must admit that I'm quite flattered at being mentioned in the same breath,' he adds modestly.

Esther looks at him. 'You know, you do look a bit like him.'

'Except that Jack is much better looking.' Adam grins. 'You can't believe how relieved we all were when he married Grace. At least it stopped the women in the office fantasising about him—and some of the men too,' he adds laughingly.

Jack sighs good-naturedly. 'That's enough, Adam.'

'You don't work, do you?' Esther says, turning back to me.

I detect in her voice the thinly veiled scorn that working women reserve for those who don't, and feel compelled to defend myself.

'I used to, but I gave up my job just before Jack and I got married.'

'Really?' Esther frowns. 'Why?'

'She didn't want to,' Jack intervenes. 'But she had a high-powered job and I didn't want to come home exhausted and find that Grace was just as exhausted as I was. It was perhaps selfish of me to ask her to give up her job but I wanted to be able to come home and offload the stress of my day rather than be offloaded onto. She also travelled quite a lot and I didn't want to come home to an empty house, as I already had done for many years.'

'What was your job?' Esther asks, fixing me with her pale-blue eyes.

'I was a buyer for Harrods.'

The flicker in her eyes tells me she's impressed. The fact that she doesn't ask me to expand tells me that she's not going to show it yet.

'She used to travel all over the world first class,' Diane says breathlessly.

'Not all over the world,' I correct. 'Just to South America. I sourced their fruit, mainly from Chile and Argentina,' I add, largely for Esther's benefit.

Rufus looks at me admiringly. 'That must have been interesting.'

'It was.' I nod. 'I loved every minute of it.'

'You must miss it, then.' Another statement from Esther.

'No, not really,' I lie. 'I have plenty here to keep me occupied.'

'And soon you'll have Millie to look after.'

'Millie is very independent and anyway, she'll be working most of the time at Meadow Gate.'

'The garden centre?'

'Yes. She loves plants and flowers so she's very lucky to have been offered the perfect job.'

'So what will you do all day long?'

'Much the same as I do now—you know, cooking, cleaning, gardening—when the weather permits.'

'You'll have to come for Sunday lunch next time and see the garden,' says Jack. 'Grace has green fingers.'

'Goodness,' says Esther lightly. 'So many talents. I'm so glad I was offered a post at St Polycarp's. I was getting quite bored being at home all day.'

'When do you start?'

'Next month. I'm replacing a teacher on maternity leave.'

I turn to Rufus. 'Jack tells me you have a huge garden,' I prompt and, while I serve more of the beef Wellington, which, along with the vegetables, has been keeping warm on a hotplate, the conversation around the table revolves around landscaping rather than me. As everyone laughs and talks together, I find myself looking wistfully at the other women and wondering what it must be like to be Diane, or Esther, to not have someone like Millie to consider. I immediately feel guilty because I love Millie more than life itself and wouldn't change her for the world. Just thinking about her gives me new resolve and I get purposefully to my feet.

'Is everyone ready for dessert?' I ask.

Jack and I clear the table and he follows me through to the kitchen, where I place the plates neatly in the sink to be rinsed off later while he tidies the carving knife away. The dessert

I've made is a masterpiece—a perfect un-cracked meringue nest three inches high, filled with whipped Devon cream. I fetch the fruit I prepared earlier and place slices of mango, pineapple, papaya and kiwi carefully onto the cream and then add strawberries, raspberries and blueberries.

As I pick up a pomegranate, the feel of it in my hand transports me back to another time, another place, where the warmth of the sun on my face and the chatter of excited voices were things I took for granted. I close my eyes briefly, remembering the life I used to have.

Conscious of Jack waiting, his hand outstretched, I hand the fruit to him. He slices it in half and then I scoop out the seeds with a spoon and sprinkle them over the rest of the fruit. The dessert complete, I carry it through to the dining room, where the exclamations that greet its arrival confirm that Jack was right to choose it over the chestnut and chocolate gateau I would have preferred to make.

'Would you believe that Grace has never done a cookery course?' Diane says to Esther, picking up her spoon. 'I'm in awe of such perfection, aren't you? Although I'm never going to get into the bikini I bought,' she adds, groaning and patting her stomach through her navy linen dress. 'I shouldn't really be eating this considering that we've just booked to go away this summer but it's so delicious I can't resist!'

'Where are you going?' Rufus asks.

'Thailand,' Adam tells him. 'We were going to go to Vietnam but when we saw the photos of Jack and Grace's latest holiday in Thailand, we decided to keep Vietnam for next year.' He looks over at Diane and grins. 'Once Diane had seen the hotel they stayed in, that was it.'

'So are you going to the same hotel, then?'

'No, it was fully booked. Unfortunately, we don't have the luxury of being able to go on holiday out of term-time.'

'Make the most of it while you can,' Esther says, turning to me.

'I intend to.'

'Are you going back to Thailand this year?' Adam asks.

'Only if we can go before June, which isn't likely with the Tomasin case coming up,' says Jack. He looks meaningfully across the table at me. 'After that, well, Millie will be with us.'

I hold my breath, hoping no one will suggest that if we wait, we'll be able to take Millie along too.

'Tomasin?' Rufus raises his eyebrows. 'I heard something about that. Is his wife one of your clients?'

'Yes, she is.'

'Dena Anderson,' he muses. 'That must be an interesting case.'

'It is,' Jack agrees. He turns to me. 'Darling, if everyone's finished, why don't you show Esther the photos of our last holiday in Thailand?'

My heart sinks. 'I'm sure she doesn't want to see our holiday snaps,' I say, keeping my voice purposefully light. But even that slight suggestion of discord between the two of us is enough for Esther.

'I would love to see them!' she exclaims.

Jack pushes his chair back and stands up. He takes the photo album from the drawer and hands it to Esther. 'Then Grace and I will make coffee while you look at the photographs. Why don't you go through to the sitting room—you'll be more comfortable there.'

By the time we come back from the kitchen with a tray of

coffee, Diane is exclaiming over the photos, although Esther doesn't say much.

I have to admit that the photos are stunning and, in those where I can be seen, I am shown to my advantage: beautifully tanned, as slim as I was in my twenties, and wearing one of my many bikinis. In most of the photos, I'm standing in front of a luxurious hotel, or lying on its private beach, or sitting in a bar or restaurant with a colourful cocktail and a plate of exotic food in front of me. In each one I am smiling up at the camera, the epitome of a relaxed and pampered woman very much in love with her husband. Jack is something of a perfectionist when it comes to taking photographs and takes the same shot over and over again until he is happy with the result, so I have learnt to get it right the first time. There are also some photographs of the two of us, taken by amenable strangers. It is Diane who points out teasingly that in those photographs, Jack and I are often gazing adoringly at each other rather than at the camera.

Jack pours the coffee.

'Would anyone like a chocolate?' I ask, reaching as casually as I can for the box that Esther brought.

'I'm sure we've all had quite enough to eat,' Jack suggests, looking around at everyone for confirmation.

'Definitely,' says Rufus.

'I couldn't eat another thing,' Adam groans.

'Then I'll put them away for another day.' Jack holds his hand out for the box and I'm just resigning myself to never tasting them when Diane comes to the rescue.

'Don't you dare—I'm sure I can fit in a chocolate or two.'

'I suppose there's no point mentioning your bikini,' Adam sighs, shaking his head in mock despair at his wife.

'Absolutely no point at all,' Diane agrees, taking a chocolate from the box Jack has handed her and passing it to me. I take one, pop it in my mouth and offer the box to Esther. When she declines to take one, I take another before passing the box back to Diane.

'How do you do it?' Diane asks, looking at me in wonder.

'Sorry?'

'Eat so much and never put on weight.'

'Luck,' I say, reaching over and taking another chocolate. 'And control.'

It's only when the clock strikes half-twelve that Esther suggests making a move. In the hall, Jack hands out the coats and, while he helps Diane and Esther on with theirs, I agree to meet them in town the following Friday at 'Chez Louis' for lunch at twelve-thirty. Diane hugs me goodbye and when I shake Esther's hand I tell her that I'm looking forward to seeing her again at the lunch. The men kiss me goodbye and, as they leave, everybody thanks us for a perfect evening. In fact, there are so many 'perfects' ringing round the hall as Jack closes the door behind them that I know I've triumphed. But I need to make sure that Jack knows I have.

'We need to leave at eleven tomorrow,' I say, turning to him. 'To get there in time to take Millie for lunch.'

PAST

My life became perfect eighteen months ago, the day Jack danced with Millie in the park. Some of what I told Esther was true—I'd seen Jack in the park the previous Sunday but hadn't thought he'd be interested in someone like me. First of all, he was exceptionally good-looking and back then I didn't look as good as I do now. And then there was Millie.

Sometimes I told my boyfriends about her from the beginning, sometimes—if I liked them a lot—I said that I had a younger sister who was away at school but only mentioned that she had Down's syndrome a few weeks into the relationship. Some, when I told them, didn't know what to say and didn't stay around long enough to say anything much at all. Others were interested, supportive even, until they met Millie and were unable to classify her spontaneity as wonderful, as Jack did. Two of the best were still there long after they met her, but even they had trouble accepting what a huge part of my life Millie was.

The clincher was always the same; I'd told Millie from the beginning that when the time came for her to leave her wonderful but highly expensive school she would come and live with me, and I had no intention of letting her down. It meant that six months previously I'd had to let go of Alex, the man I thought I would spend the rest of my life with, the man who I'd lived very happily with for two years. But when Millie had turned sixteen, the imminence of her arrival began to weigh heavily on him—which is why I found myself, at thirty-two years old, single once again and seriously doubting that I would ever find a man who would accept both Millie and me.

In the park that day, I wasn't the only one who noticed Jack, although I was probably the most discreet. Some—mainly the younger women—smiled at him openly, trying to catch his attention, while teenage girls giggled behind their hands and whispered excitedly that he had to be a film star. The older women looked at him appreciatively and then, more often than not, at the man walking beside them, as if they found him wanting. Even the men looked at Jack as he walked through the park, as there was a casual elegance about him that couldn't be ignored. The only one who remained oblivious to him was Millie. Engrossed in the card game we were playing, there was only one thought in her mind—winning.

Like many others that day in late August, we were picnicking on the grass not far from the bandstand. Out of the corner of my eye, I saw Jack head for a nearby bench and, when he took a book from his pocket, I turned my attention back to Millie, determined not to let him see me looking at him. As Millie dealt the cards for yet another game, I decided he was probably a foreigner, an Italian perhaps, in London for the weekend with his wife and children who were visiting some monument or other and would join him later.

As far as I was concerned, he didn't even look my way that afternoon, unperturbed, it seemed, by Millie's loud cries of 'Snap!' We left soon after because I had to get Millie back to her school by six o'clock, in time for dinner at seven. Even though I didn't think I'd ever see him again, my mind returned again and again to the man I'd seen in the park and I found myself pretending that he wasn't married, that he had noticed me and had fallen in love with me and planned to return to the park the following Sunday in the hope of seeing me again. I hadn't fantasised about a man in such a way since I was a teenager and it made me realise how much I was beginning to despair of ever getting married and having a family. Although I was devoted to Millie, I had always imagined that by the time she came to live with me I would have children of my own, so she would become a part of my family rather than my sole family. I loved her dearly, but the thought of the two of us growing old together on our own filled me with dread.

The following week, the day the band was playing in the park, I didn't see Jack until he walked up to where Millie was dancing by herself in front of the bandstand, her arms around a partner only she could see. At such times, the emotions

Millie provoked in me were often hard to deal with. While I was fiercely proud of her, that she had managed to master the steps she was performing, I was also fiercely protective, and when I heard someone laughing behind me I had to remind myself that their laughter was probably kind and that even if it wasn't, it wouldn't affect Millie's enjoyment of what she was doing. But the urge to stand up and bring her back to her seat was so strong that I hated myself for it, and for just about the first time I found myself wishing that Millie was ordinary. Images flashed through my mind of how our lives—my life—could have been and it was as I was quickly blinking away the tears of frustration which had filled my eyes that I saw Jack making his way towards Millie.

At first, I didn't recognise him and, thinking he was going to ask Millie to sit back down, I got to my feet, ready to intervene. It was only when I saw him bowing to her and holding out his hand that I realised he was the man I'd been dreaming about all week. By the time he brought Millie back to her seat two dances later, I'd fallen in love with him.

'May I?' he asked, indicating the chair next to me.

'Yes, of course.' I smiled at him gratefully. 'Thank you for dancing with Millie, it was very kind of you.'

'The pleasure was all mine,' he said gravely. 'Millie is a very good dancer.'

'Nice man!' Millie said, beaming at him.

'Jack.'

'Nice Jack.'

'I really should introduce myself properly.' He held out his hand. 'Jack Angel.'

'Grace Harrington,' I said, shaking it. 'Millie's my sister. Are you here on holiday?'

'No, I live here.' I waited for him to add 'with my wife and children' but he didn't, so I stole a look at his left hand and when I saw that he wasn't wearing a wedding ring I felt such a rush of relief I had to remind myself it didn't mean anything. 'And you? Are you and Millie visiting London?'

'Not really. I live in Wimbledon but I often bring Millie here at weekends.'

'Does she live with you?'

'No, she boards at her school during the week. I try and see her most weekends, but as I travel a lot for my job it's not always possible. Fortunately, she has a wonderful carer who steps in when I can't be with her. And our parents do, of course.'

'Your job sounds exciting. Can I ask what you do?'

'I buy fruit.' He looked at me quizzically. 'For Harrods.'

'And the travelling?'

'I source fruit from Argentina and Chile.'

'That must be interesting.'

'It is,' I agreed. 'What about you?'

'I'm a lawyer.'

Millie, bored with our conversation, tugged at my arm. 'Drink, Grace. And ice cream. I hot.'

I smiled apologetically at Jack. 'I'm afraid I have to go. Thank you again for dancing with Millie.'

'Perhaps you would let me take you and Millie to tea?' He leant forward so that he could see Millie sitting on the other side of me. 'What do you think, Millie? Would you like some tea?'

'Juice,' Millie said, beaming at him. 'Juice, not tea. Don't like tea.'

'Juice it is, then,' he said, standing up. 'Shall we go?'

'No, really,' I protested. 'You've been too kind already.'

'Please. I'd like to.' He turned to Millie. 'Do you like cakes, Millie?'

Millie nodded enthusiastically. 'Yes, love cake.'

'That's decided then.'

We walked across the park to the restaurant, Millie and I arm in arm and Jack walking alongside us. By the time we parted company an hour later, I had agreed to meet him the following Thursday evening for dinner, and he quickly became a permanent fixture in my life. It wasn't hard to fall in love with him; there was something old-fashioned about him that I found refreshing—he opened doors for me, helped me on with my coat and sent me flowers. He made me feel special, cherished and, best of all, he adored Millie.

When we were about three months into our relationship, he asked if I would introduce him to my parents. I was a little taken aback as I'd already told him that I didn't have a close relationship with them. I had lied to Esther. My parents hadn't wanted another child and, when Millie arrived, they definitely hadn't wanted her. As a child, I had pestered my parents so much for a brother or sister that one day they had sat me down and told me, quite bluntly, that they hadn't really wanted any children at all. So when, some ten years later, my mother discovered she was pregnant, she was horrified. It was only when I overheard her discussing the risks of a late abortion with my father that I realised she was expecting a baby and I was outraged that they were thinking of getting rid of the little brother or sister I'd always wanted.

We argued back and forth; they pointed out that because my mother was already forty-six, a pregnancy at that age was risky; I pointed out that because she was already five months pregnant, an abortion at that age was illegal—and a mortal sin, because they were both Catholics. With guilt and God on my side, I won and my mother went reluctantly ahead with the pregnancy.

When Millie was born and was found to have Down's—as well as other difficulties—I couldn't understand my parents' rejection of her. I fell in love with her at once and saw her as no different from any other baby, so when my mother became severely depressed I took over Millie's general day-to-day care, feeding her and changing her nappy before I went to school and coming back at lunchtime to repeat the process all over again. When she was three months old, my parents told me that they were putting her up for adoption and moving to New Zealand, where my maternal grandparents lived, something they had always said they would do. I screamed the place down, telling them that they couldn't put her up for adoption, that I would stay at home and look after her instead of going to university, but they refused to listen and, as the adoption procedure got underway, I took an overdose. It was a stupid thing to do, a childish attempt to get them to realise how serious I was, but for some reason it worked. I was already eighteen so with the help of various social workers, it was agreed that I would be Millie's principal carer and would effectively bring her up, with my parents providing financial support.

I took one step at a time. When a place was found for Millie at a local nursery, I began working part-time. My first job was working for a supermarket chain, in their fruit-buying department. At eleven years old, Millie was offered a place at a school I considered no better than an institution and, appalled, I told my parents that I would find somewhere more suitable. I had spent hours and hours with her, teaching her an independence I'm not sure she would have otherwise obtained, and I felt it was her lack of language skills rather than intelligence that made it difficult for her to integrate into society as well as she might have.

It was a long, hard battle to find a mainstream school willing to take Millie on and the only reason I managed was because the headmistress of the school I eventually found was a forward-thinking, open-minded woman who happened to have a younger brother with Down's. The private girls' boarding school she ran was perfect for Millie, but expensive, and, as my parents couldn't afford to pay for it, I told them I would. I sent my CV to several companies, with a letter explaining exactly why I needed a good, well-paid job, and was eventually taken on by Harrods.

When travelling became part of my job—something I jumped at the chance to do, because of the associated freedom—my parents didn't feel able to have Millie home for the weekends without me there. But they would visit her at school and Janice, Millie's carer, looked after her for the rest of the time. When the next problem—where Millie would go once she left school—began to loom on the horizon, I promised my parents that I would have her to live with me so that they could finally emigrate to New Zealand. And ever since, they'd been counting the days. I didn't blame them; in their own way they were fond of me and Millie, and we were of them. But they were the sort of people who weren't suited to having children at all.

Because Jack was adamant that he wanted to meet them, I phoned my mother and asked her if we could go down the following Sunday. It was nearing the end of November and we took Millie with us. Although they didn't exactly throw their arms around us, I could see that my mother was impressed by Jack's impeccable manners and my father was pleased that Jack had taken an interest in his collection of first editions. We left soon after lunch and, by the time we dropped Millie back at her school, it was late afternoon. I had intended to head home, because I had a busy couple of days before leaving for Argentina later that week, but when Jack suggested a walk in Regent's Park I readily agreed, even though it was already dark. I wasn't looking forward to going away again; since meeting Jack I had become disenchanted with the amount of travelling my job required me to do as I had the impression that we hardly spent any time together. And when we did, it was often with a group of friends, or Millie, in tow.

'What did you think of my parents?' I asked when we had been walking a while.

'They were perfect,' he smiled.

I found myself frowning over his choice of words. 'What do you mean?'

'Just that they were everything I hoped they would be.'

I glanced at him, wondering if he was being ironic, as my parents had hardly gone out of their way for us. But then I remembered him telling me that his own parents, who had died some years before, had been extremely distant, and decided it was why he had appreciated my parents' lukewarm welcome so much.

We walked a little further and, when we arrived at the bandstand where he had danced with Millie, he drew me to a stop.

'Grace, will you do me the honour of marrying me?' he asked.

His proposal was so unexpected that my first reaction was to think he was joking. Although I'd harboured a secret hope that our relationship would one day lead to marriage, I'd imagined it happening a year or two down the line. Perhaps sensing my hesitation, he drew me into his arms.

'I knew from the minute I saw you sitting on the grass over there with Millie that you were the woman I'd been waiting for all my life. I don't want to have to wait any longer to make you my wife. The reason I asked to meet your parents was so that I could ask your father for his blessing. I'm glad to say he gave it happily.'

I couldn't help feeling amused that my father had so readily agreed to me marrying someone he had only just met and knew nothing about. But as I stood there in Jack's arms, I was dismayed that the elation I felt at his proposal was tempered by a niggling anxiety, and just as I'd worked out it was because of Millie, Jack spoke again. 'Before you give me your answer, Grace, there's something I want to tell you.' He sounded so serious that I thought he was going to confess to an ex-wife, or a child, or a terrible illness. 'I just want you to know that wherever we live, there will always be a place for Millie.'

'You don't know how much it means to me to hear you say that,' I told him tearfully. 'Thank you.'

'So will you marry me?' he asked.

'Yes, of course I will.'

He drew a ring from his pocket and, taking my hand in his, slipped it on my finger. 'How soon?' he murmured.

'As soon as you like.' I looked down at the solitaire dia-
mond. 'Jack, it's beautiful!'

'I'm glad you like it. So, how about sometime in March?'

I burst out laughing. 'March! How will we be able to orga-
nise a wedding in such a short time?'

'It won't be that difficult. I already have somewhere in
mind for the reception, Cranleigh Park in Hecclescombe. It's
a private country house and belongs to a friend of mine. Normally, he only holds wedding receptions for family members
but I know it won't be a problem.'

'It sounds wonderful,' I said happily.

'As long as you don't want to invite too many people.'

'No, just my parents and a few friends.'

'That's settled then.'

Later, as he drove me back home, he asked if we could
have a drink together the following evening as there were a
couple of things he wanted to discuss with me before I left
for Argentina on Wednesday.

'You could come in now, if you like,' I offered.

'I'm afraid I really need to be getting back. I have an early
start tomorrow.' I couldn't help feeling disappointed. 'I'd like
nothing more than to come in and stay the night with you,'
he said, noticing, 'but I have some files I need to look over tonight.'

'I can't believe I've agreed to marry someone I haven't
even slept with yet,' I grumbled.

'Then how about we go away for a couple of days, the
weekend after you get back from Argentina? We'll take Millie
out to lunch and after we've dropped her back at school, we'll
visit Cranleigh Park and find a hotel somewhere in the country for the night. Would that do?'

'Yes.' I nodded gratefully. 'Where shall I meet you tomorrow evening?'

'How about the bar at the Connaught?'

'If I come straight from work, I can be there around seven.'

'Perfect.'

I spent most of the next day wondering what Jack wanted to discuss with me before I went to Argentina. It never occurred to me that he would ask me to give up my job or that he would want to move out of London. I had presumed that once we were married we would carry on much as we were, except that we would be living together in his flat, as it was more central. His propositions left me reeling. Seeing how shocked I was, he sought to explain, pointing out what had occurred to me the day before, that in the three months since we'd known each other, we'd hardly spent any time together.

'What's the point of getting married if we never see each other?' he asked. 'We can't go on as we are and, more to the point, I don't want to. Something has to give and as I hope we'll be having children sooner rather than later . . .' He stopped. 'You do want children, don't you?'

'Yes, Jack, of course I do,' I smiled.

'That's a relief.' He took my hand in his. 'The first time I saw you with Millie I knew you'd make a wonderful mother. I hope I won't have to wait too long before you make me a father.' Overwhelmed by a sudden desire to bear his child, I found I couldn't speak. 'But maybe you'd rather wait a few years,' he went on, hesitantly.

'It's not that,' I said, finding my voice. 'It's just that I don't see how I can give up my job, not while Millie is still at school. I pay her fees, you see, so I won't be able to give up work for a year and a half.'

'There's absolutely no question of you working for another eighteen months,' he said firmly. 'Millie can move in with us as soon as we come back from our honeymoon.'

I looked at him guiltily. 'Much as I love Millie, I'd really like us to have a little time on our own first. And she's so happy at her school it seems a shame to take her out a year early.' I thought for a moment. 'Can we speak to her school and ask them what they think?'

'Of course. And maybe we should ask Millie what she thinks. I, for one, will be delighted if she chooses to move in with us at once. But if everybody thinks that it's best to leave her where she is for the moment, I insist on paying her fees. After all, she's going to be my sister soon.' He took my hand in his. 'Promise to let me help.'

I looked at him helplessly. 'I don't know what to say.'

'Then don't say anything. All you have to do is promise to think about handing your notice in. I don't want to never see you once we're married. Now, what sort of house would you like? I need to know because, if you'll let me, I'd like to buy you the house of your dreams as a wedding present.'

'I've never really thought about it,' I admitted.

'Well, think about it now, because it's important. Would you like a big garden, a swimming pool, lots of bedrooms?'

'A big garden, definitely. I'm not bothered about a swimming pool and as for the number of bedrooms, it depends how many children we're going to have.'

'Quite a lot then,' he smiled. 'I'd like to live in Surrey, near enough to London to make the commute each day bearable. What do you think?'

'Anywhere, as long as you're happy. What about you? What sort of house would you like?'

'I'd like it to be near a pretty town but far enough away for us not to be disturbed by noise. Like you, I'd like it to have a big garden, preferably with high walls around it so that nobody can see in. And I'd like a study, and a basement to keep things in. That's about it really.'

'A nice kitchen,' I said. 'I'd like a nice kitchen leading onto a terrace where we could have breakfast each morning, and a huge fireplace in the sitting room where we can have real log fires. And a yellow bedroom for Millie.'

'Why don't we draw up a plan of our dream house?' he suggested, taking a sheet of paper from his briefcase. 'Then I'll have something to work with.'

By the time he put me in a taxi two hours later, he'd made a drawing of a beautiful house, complete with landscaped gardens, a terrace, three reception rooms, a fireplace, a kitchen, a study, five bedrooms—including a yellow one for Millie—three bathrooms, and a little round window in the roof.

'I defy you to find such a house by the time I get back from Argentina,' I laughed.

'I'll do my very best,' he promised, before giving me a kiss.

The next few weeks passed in a whirlwind. When I got back from Argentina, I handed in my notice and put my house on the market. I had used my time away to think things over carefully and never doubted that I'd be doing the right thing if I did as Jack had asked. I knew that I wanted to marry him, and the thought that by the following spring I'd be living in a beautiful house in the country and maybe expecting our first baby, filled me with excitement. I'd been working non-stop for thirteen years and there'd been times when I'd wondered if I'd ever be able to get off the treadmill. And because I'd known that once Millie came to live with me I'd no longer be able to travel as I had, or work the long hours that I sometimes worked, I had been nervous about what sort of job I'd end up with. Suddenly, all my worries disappeared and, as I chose wedding invitations to send out to friends and family, I felt I was the luckiest person in the world.

PRESENT

Jack, meticulous as always, comes up to the bedroom at ten-thirty in the morning and tells me we'll be leaving at eleven o'clock precisely. I'm not worried that I won't be ready in time. I've already showered, so thirty minutes is long enough to dress and put on my make-up. The shower calmed me down a little as, since waking at eight, I've been in a continuous state of excitement, hardly daring to believe that I'll soon be seeing Millie. Ever cautious, I remind myself that anything could happen. Yet the face I present to Jack shows nothing of my inner turmoil. It is calm and composed and, as he stands back to let me pass, I am just an ordinary young woman about to go on a day out.

Jack follows me into the bedroom next door, where my clothes hang. I walk over to the huge wardrobe that runs the length of the wall, slide back the mirrored door, pull out one of the drawers and select the cream-coloured bra and matching knickers which Jack bought me last week. In another drawer I find some flesh-coloured stockings, which I prefer to tights. Jack watches from a chair while I take off my pyjamas and put on my underwear and stockings. Then I slide back the next door and stand for a moment, looking at all the clothes hanging neatly by colour. I haven't worn my blue dress in a long time and it is one that Millie loves because it is the same colour as my eyes. I take it out of the wardrobe.

'Wear the cream one,' Jack says. It's true that he prefers me in neutral colours so I put the blue dress back and put on the cream one.

My shoes are stored in clear boxes on shelves in another part of the wardrobe. I choose a pair of beige shoes with a heel. As we usually go for a walk after lunch, flat ones would be more practical, but Jack likes me to be elegant at all times, whether we're walking around a lake or having dinner with friends. I slip them on, take a matching bag from the shelf and hand it to Jack. I walk over to the dressing table and sit down. It doesn't take me long to do my make-up: a little bit of eye pencil, some blusher and a dash of lipstick. There are still fifteen minutes left so to fill in the time I decide to wear some nail varnish. I choose a pretty pink from the various bottles arrayed on the dresser, wishing I could take it with me and paint Millie's nails, something I know she would love.

When it's dry, I stand up, take my bag from Jack and go downstairs.

'Which coat would you like to wear?' he asks, as we reach the hall.

'My beige wool, I think.'

He fetches it from the cloakroom and helps me on with it. I button it up and turn out the pockets while Jack looks on. He opens the front door and, once he's locked it behind us, I follow him out to the car.

Although we are almost at the end of March, the air is cold. My instinct is to draw it in hard through my nose and gulp it down. Instead, I remind myself that I have the whole day in front of me, and rejoice in that thought. This trip out has been hard won and I intend to make the most of it. As we reach the car, Jack activates the remote control and the huge black gates that front our house begin to open. Walking around to the passenger side of the car, he opens my door for me. I get in and a man jogging past the house looks through the gates towards us. I don't know him but Jack wishes him a good morning and—either because he is too out of breath to speak or because he is saving his energy for the rest of his run—the man acknowledges the greeting with a wave of his hand. Jack closes my door behind me and, less than a minute later, we drive out through the gates. As they swing shut behind us, I turn my head for a glimpse of the beautiful house Jack bought for me, because I like to see it as others see it.

We begin the journey into London and as we drive along, my mind goes back to the dinner party we hosted last night. How I managed to pull it off is still a mystery when there were so many things that could have gone wrong.

'Your soufflés were perfect,' Jack says, telling me that I'm not the only one thinking about the previous evening. 'It was clever of you to predict a delay in getting to the table and allow for it in your calculations, very clever indeed. But Esther doesn't seem to like you very much. I wonder why that is?'

I know I need to choose my words carefully. 'She doesn't appreciate perfection,' I say.

It's an answer that pleases him. He begins to hum a little tune and, as I look at the passing landscape, I find myself thinking about Esther. Under other circumstances, I would probably like her. But her undoubted intelligence makes her dangerous to someone like me. It's not that she doesn't appreciate perfection, as I first thought, it's more that she's suspicious of it.

It takes the best part of an hour to reach Millie's school. I spend the time thinking about Dena Anderson, Jack's client. I don't know much about her apart from the fact that she recently married a wealthy philanthropist, well respected for his work with various charities and therefore an unlikely candidate in the wife-battering stakes. Still, I know only too well how appearances can be deceiving and if Jack has agreed to take her on as a client she must have a very strong case. Losing is not a word in Jack's vocabulary, as he never ceases to remind me.

We haven't seen Millie for a month so, impatient to see me, she's waiting on the bench outside the front door wrapped up in a yellow hat and scarf—yellow is her favourite colour—with Janice, her carer. When I get out of the car, she rushes over, her eyes bright with tears of relief and, as I hug her tightly, I'm aware of Jack watching us. Janice joins us and I hear Jack telling her that although we knew Millie would be disappointed, we hadn't dared to come and see her until I had completely recovered from the bout of flu that had laid me so low. Janice reassures him that we did the right thing, adding that she had explained to Millie why we couldn't come.

'But it was very hard for her,' she admits. 'She adores you both so much.'

'And we adore her,' Jack says, smiling fondly at Millie.

'Say hello to Jack, Millie,' I remind her quietly and, disentangling herself, she turns to Jack.

'Hello, Jack,' she says, giving him a big smile. 'I happy to see you.'

'And I'm very happy to see you too,' he says, kissing her cheek. 'You do understand why we couldn't come before, don't you?'

Millie nods. 'Yes, poor Grace ill. But better now.'

'Much better,' Jack agrees. 'I have something for you, Millie, for being so patient.' He puts his hand into his coat pocket. 'Can you guess what it is?'

'Agatha Christie?' Her brown eyes light up with pleasure, as there's nothing she loves more than listening to murder mysteries.

'Clever girl.' He takes an audio book from his pocket. 'I don't think you've got *And Then There Were None*, have you?'

She shakes her head.

'It's one of my favourites,' Janice says, smiling. 'Shall we start it tonight, Millie?'

'Yes,' Millie nods. 'Thank you, Jack.'

'It's my pleasure,' Jack tells her. 'And now I'm going to take my two favourite ladies out to lunch. Where would you like to go?'

'Hotel,' says Millie immediately. I know why she has chosen the hotel, just as I know why Jack is going to refuse.

'Why don't we go to the restaurant by the lake?' he says, as if she hadn't spoken. 'Or the one that serves those delicious pancakes for dessert?' Millie's face falls. 'Which would you prefer?'

'The lake,' she mutters, her dark hair swinging in front of her face.

Millie doesn't talk much on the way. She had wanted me to sit in the back of the car with her but Jack told her he would feel as if he was a taxi driver.

When we arrive at the restaurant, Jack finds a parking space and, as we walk up the path he takes our hands, so that we're on either side of him. The staff greets us like old friends because we often bring Millie here. They show us to the round table in the corner, the one that Jack likes, by the window. We sit as we always do, Jack facing the window and Millie and I sitting on either side of him. As we study our menus, I stretch my leg out under the table and find hers, my secret sign to her.

Jack chats away to Millie during the meal, encouraging her to talk, asking her what she did during the weekends when we didn't come to see her. She tells us that once Janice took her back to hers for lunch, once they went out for afternoon tea, and once they were both invited to her friend Paige's house, and not for the first time I thank God that Millie has someone like Janice to step in whenever I can't be with her.

'Grace come walk?' Millie asks once lunch is over. 'Round lake.'

'Yes, of course.' I fold my napkin neatly and place it on the table, my movements deliberately unhurried. 'Shall we go now?'

Jack pushes back his chair. 'I'll come too.'

Even though I didn't expect anything less, there is still a feeling of crushing disappointment.

'We go all way round,' Millie warns.

'Not all the way around,' protests Jack. 'It's too cold to be outside for long.'

'Then Jack stay here,' Millie tells him. 'I go with Grace.'

'No,' says Jack. 'We'll all go.'

Millie looks solemnly at Jack from across the table. 'I like you, Jack,' she says. 'But I don't like Jorj Koony.'

'I know.' Jack nods. 'I don't like him either.'

'He ugly,' says Millie.

'Yes, he's very ugly,' agrees Jack.

And Millie bursts into fits of laughter.

We walk a little way around the lake, Jack walking between me and Millie. Jack tells Millie that he's busy getting her room ready for when she comes to live with us and when she asks if it's going to be yellow, he says that of course it is.

He was right; it is too cold to be outside for very long and after about twenty minutes we head back to the car. Millie is even quieter on the way back to her school and I know she feels the same frustration that I feel. When we say goodbye, she asks if we'll be back to see her the following weekend and when Jack says he's sure we will be, I'm glad that Janice is within earshot.

PAST

When Jack and I told Millie that we were getting married, the first thing she asked was if she could be our bridesmaid.

'Of course you can!' I said, hugging her. 'That is all right, isn't it, Jack?' I added, dismayed to see a frown on his face.

'I thought we were having a simple wedding,' he said pointedly.

'We are, but I'll still need a bridesmaid.'

'Really?'

'Well, yes,' I said, feeling flustered. 'It's traditional. You don't mind, do you?'

'Don't you think it'll be a bit much for Millie?' he asked, lowering his voice. 'If you really need a bridesmaid, why not ask Kate or Emily?'

'Because I want Millie,' I insisted, aware of her watching us anxiously.

There was a moment's awkward silence. 'Then Millie you shall have,' he said, smiling and holding his arm out to her. 'Come on, let's go and tell your headmistress the good news.'

Mrs Goodrich and Janice were delighted to hear we were getting married. After sending Millie off to wash her hands in preparation for dinner, Mrs Goodrich agreed that it would be best if Millie stayed at school for another fifteen months, until she turned eighteen, as had been planned all along, despite Jack reiterating that he would be quite happy to have Millie move in with us at once. I was glad when Mrs Goodrich suggested it would be nice for us to have some time on our own and I wondered if maybe she'd guessed that we hoped to start a family straight away.

Soon after, we were on our way to Hecclescombe, where Cranleigh Park was every bit as beautiful as Jack had told me it was. It was the perfect setting for a wedding and I was grateful to Giles and Moira, Jack's friends, for allowing us to use their beautiful home. We didn't think any of our guests would mind the forty-minute drive from London to be able to spend the afternoon and evening in such a lovely setting, especially as Giles and Moira kindly offered to put up anyone who couldn't face the drive back to London once dinner was over. After a couple of hours spent deciding on a menu for fifty, which would be cooked and served by a catering company from London, we left for the hotel Jack had booked while I'd been in Argentina.

I couldn't wait for Jack to take me to bed at last, but dinner had to be got through first, because we only arrived in time for our reservation. The meal was delicious but I was impatient to be back in our room.

I went off to have a shower and, when I came out of the bathroom, eager to make love, I was dismayed to find Jack sound asleep on the bed. I didn't have the heart to wake him as I knew he was exhausted—he had confessed to me during dinner that he had almost cancelled our weekend away because of the amount of work he had on but hadn't wanted to let me down. When he eventually stirred a couple of hours later, he was mortified that he had fallen asleep and, gathering me in his arms, he made love to me.

We stayed in bed for most of the next morning and, after a lazy lunch, we headed back to London. Even though it meant that I didn't see Jack for the whole of the following week, I was glad we'd managed to take some time out from the frenzy our imminent wedding had precipitated us into. And not being able to see Jack gave me the chance to finish the painting I had started for him two months previously. Because I rarely had time to work on it I had resigned myself to giving it to him as a wedding present rather than for Christmas, as I had wanted to do, but with Jack busy in the evenings and my suitcases consigned indefinitely to the back of the cupboard, I managed to complete it in time for Christmas Day. I hoped that if he liked it, it would grace the walls of our new home—I could easily imagine it hanging above the fireplace we'd talked about having.

It was a large painting and, at first glance, it seemed to be an abstract design of different shades of red with tiny shots of silver running through it. It was only on closer inspection that one could distinguish the mass of red as hundreds of tiny fireflies—and only Jack and I would know that the mass of red had been created, not from paint, but from lipstick, which I had then sealed with a clear varnish before completing the painting.

I had never told Jack that I enjoyed painting, and even when he had admired one of the canvases that hung in my kitchen I hadn't mentioned that I was the artist. So when I told him on Christmas Day—once I was certain he liked the painting I'd given him—that not only had I painted *Fireflies* myself but that I had created it by kissing the canvas hundreds of times wearing different shades of red lipstick, he lavished so many compliments on me that I was pleased I had managed to surprise him. He was delighted that I could paint and told me that once we moved into our house, he would expect me to cover the walls with my work.

My house sold quickly. I wanted Jack to put the money I received from the sale towards the house he had found for us in Spring Eaton, but he refused, reminding me that it was his wedding present to me. He had discovered the sleepy village of Spring Eaton whilst driving back from Adam and Diane's one Sunday, and found its situation some twenty miles south of London ideal. Because there was some minor work to be done on the house before we moved in, he didn't want me to see it until we came back from our honeymoon. When I badgered him to tell me what it was like, he simply smiled and told me it was perfect. When I asked if it was like the one in the picture we had drawn up together, he replied solemnly that of course it was. I told him that I wanted to use the money from the sale of my house to furnish our new home as my wedding present to him and, after a lot of persuasion, he agreed. It was strange shopping for furniture for a house I had never seen but Jack knew exactly what he wanted and I couldn't fault his taste.

I left my job a month before we were due to be married and a week later, after I complained teasingly to Jack that the novelty of not having anything to do all day long was wearing off, he appeared on my doorstep carrying a box tied with a red bow. Opening it, I found a three-month-old Labrador puppy staring up at me.

'Jack, she's adorable!' I cried, lifting her out. 'Where did you get her? Is she yours?'

'No, she's yours,' he said. 'Something to keep you busy.'

'She'll certainly do that,' I laughed. I put her down on the ground and she ran around the hall exploring everything. 'But I don't understand what I'm meant to do with her while we're on honeymoon in Thailand. We could ask my parents to have her, I suppose, but I'm not sure they'd agree.'

'Don't worry, it's all arranged. I've found a housekeeper to look after our house while we're away—I don't want it lying empty and there's still some furniture to be delivered, so she's going to live in until we get back—and she's going to look after Molly for us.'

'Molly?' I looked at the puppy. 'Yes, it suits her very well. Millie will be so pleased, she's always wanted a dog. Millie and Molly—they sound perfect together!'

'That's exactly what I thought,' Jack nodded.

'Millie is going to love her.'

'And you? Will you love her?'

'Of course I will!' I scooped her into my arms. 'I already

do.' I laughed as she began to lick my face. 'I'm afraid I'm going to hate leaving her behind when we go to Thailand.'

'But just think how pleased you'll be to see her again when we get back. I can already picture your reunion,' he smiled.

'I can't wait to show her to Millie! You're so wonderfully kind, Jack.' Leaning towards him, I kissed him tenderly. 'Molly is exactly what I need to keep me company while you're at work all day. I hope there are some lovely places to walk in Spring Eaton.'

'There are plenty, especially along the river.'

'I can't wait,' I told him happily. 'I can't wait to see the house and I can't wait to be married to you!'

'Neither can I,' he said, kissing me back. 'Neither can I.'

With Molly to keep me on my toes, the final weeks flew by. On the day before the wedding, I picked Millie up from school and we dropped Molly off with Jack, who was taking her down to the house that evening to settle her in with the housekeeper. I hated leaving her, but Jack assured me that Mrs Johns, the lady he'd found to house-sit for us, was wonderfully kind and was happy to look after Molly until our return from Thailand. I'd moved into a nearby hotel a few days earlier, after I'd seen the last of my possessions disappear off to Spring Eaton in a removal van, so Millie and I went back there to prepare for the next day. We spent the evening making sure our dresses fitted perfectly and trying out make-up I had bought especially for the wedding. I hadn't wanted to wear a traditional wedding dress so I'd bought a cream silk dress that reached almost to my ankles and clung to my figure in all the right places, and Millie had chosen a cream dress too, but with a pink sash the exact colour of the bouquet she would carry.

When I put my dress on the next morning, I had never felt so beautiful. The wedding bouquets had arrived at the hotel earlier—pink roses for Millie and a cascade of deep red ones for me. Jack had organised a car to take us to the registry office and when there was a knock on the door at eleven the next morning I sent Millie to answer it.

'Tell them I'll be out in a minute,' I said, disappearing into the bathroom to check myself one last time in the mirror. Satisfied with what I saw, I went back into the bedroom and picked up my bouquet.

'You look stunning.' Startled, I looked up and saw Jack standing in the doorway. He looked so handsome in his dark suit and deep red waistcoat that my stomach flipped over. 'Almost as beautiful as Millie, in fact.' Next to him, Millie clapped her hands happily.

'What are you doing here?' I cried, anxious and delighted at the same time. 'Has something happened?'

He came over and took me in his arms. 'I couldn't wait to see you, that's all. And also, I have something for you.' Releasing me, he put his hand in his pocket and drew out a black box. 'I went to the bank this morning to fetch them.' Opening the box, I saw an exquisite pearl necklace lying on a bed of black velvet with a matching pair of pearl earrings.

'Jack, they're beautiful!'

'They belonged to my mother. I'd forgotten all about them until last night. I thought you might want to wear them today, which is why I came over. You don't have to, of course.'

'I'd love to wear them,' I told him, lifting out the necklace and undoing the clasp.

'Here, let me.' He took them from me and slipped them around my neck. 'What do you think?'

I turned towards the mirror. 'I can't believe how perfectly they match the dress,' I said, fingering them. 'They're exactly the same shade of cream.' I unclipped the gold earrings I was wearing and replaced them with the pearls.

'Grace pretty, very, very pretty!' Millie laughed.

'I agree,' said Jack gravely. He put his hand in his other pocket and drew out a smaller box. 'I have something for you too, Millie.'

When Millie saw the tear-shaped pearl on the silver chain, she gave a gasp of delight. 'Thank you, Jack,' she said, beaming. 'I wear it now.'

'You're so kind, Jack,' I told him as I put it around Millie's neck. 'But did you know it's supposed to be bad luck to see your bride on her wedding day?'

'Well, I guess I'll just have to take my chance,' he smiled.

'How's Molly? Did she settle in all right?'

'Perfectly. Look.' He took his phone out of his pocket and showed Millie and me a photograph of Molly curled up asleep in her basket.

'So the floor has tiles,' I mused. 'At least I know one thing about my future home.'

'And that's all you're going to know,' he said, pocketing his phone. 'Now, shall we go? The chauffeur was surprised enough when I asked him to pick me up on the way to collect you, so if we don't go out soon he might think I've come to call the whole thing off.' After offering me and Millie an arm each, he escorted us down to the car and we set off for the registry office.

When we arrived, everyone was there waiting for us,

including my parents. They had all but boxed up their house in preparation for their move to New Zealand and were set to leave a fortnight after we got back from our honeymoon. I'd been a bit surprised when they'd told me they were leaving so soon, but when I thought about it, they'd waited a long sixteen years. The previous week, Jack and I had met them for dinner, where they had officially signed Millie over to us, which meant that we were now her legal guardians. All of us were delighted by this arrangement and my parents, perhaps because they felt guilty about Jack shouldering the financial burden, told us that they would of course help out in any way they could. But Jack was adamant that he and I would be responsible for Millie and promised my parents that she would want for nothing.

Our guests were surprised to see Jack stepping out of the car alongside Millie and me, and as we set off up the flight of steps that led to the registry office, they teased him good-naturedly about not being able to resist riding in a Rolls-Royce. Dad was escorting me and Jack was escorting Millie and my Uncle Leonard, whom I hadn't seen for several years, had given Mum his arm. I was almost at the top of the steps when I heard Millie cry out and, spinning round, saw her tumbling down the steps.

'Millie!' I screamed. By the time she came to a stop in a crumpled heap at the bottom of the steps, I was already halfway there. It seemed an age before I managed to push through the throng of people gathered around her and I knelt down beside her, not caring that my dress was getting dirty, only caring that Millie was lying there motionless.

'It's all right, Grace, she's breathing,' Adam said reassuringly, from where he crouched on the other side of her, as I searched frantically for a pulse. 'She'll be fine, you'll see. Diane's phoning for an ambulance, it'll be here in a minute.'

'What happened?' I asked, my voice shaking, aware of Mum and Dad crouching down next to me. I stroked Millie's hair back from her face, not daring to move her.

'Grace, I'm so sorry.' I looked up and saw Jack, his face as white as a sheet. 'She suddenly stumbled—I think her heel got caught in the hem of her dress—and before I knew what was happening, she was falling. I tried to grab her but I couldn't reach her.'

'It's all right,' I said quickly. 'It's not your fault.'

'I should have held on to her more tightly,' he went on desperately, running his hand through his hair. 'I should have remembered that steps aren't always easy for her.'

'I don't like the way her leg is bent,' Dad said quietly. 'It looks as if it's broken.'

'Oh God,' I moaned.

'Look, she's coming round.' Mum took Millie's hand in hers.

'It's all right, Millie,' I murmured as she began to stir. 'It's all right.'

The ambulance arrived in minutes. I wanted to go to the hospital with her but Mum and Dad told me they would go, reminding me that I was meant to be getting married.

'I can't get married now,' I sobbed, as Millie was carried into the ambulance.

'Of course you can,' said Mum briskly. 'Millie's going to be fine.'

'She has a broken leg,' I wept. 'And maybe other injuries we don't know about.'

'I won't blame you if you want to call it off,' Jack said quietly.

'It's just that I don't see how we can go ahead with everything when we don't even know how badly injured Millie is.'

The paramedics were wonderful. Understanding what a difficult situation I was in, they examined Millie as thoroughly as they could in the ambulance and told me that apart from her leg there didn't seem to be any other broken bones and that if I wanted to carry on with my wedding, they were sure my parents would keep me informed of any developments. They also pointed out that as soon as Millie arrived at the hospital, she would be whisked away for X-rays so I wouldn't be able to stay with her anyway. Still torn, I looked over to where Jack was standing talking quietly to Adam and the look of desolation on his face decided me. I clambered into the ambulance and kissed a drowsy Millie goodbye. After promising I would go and see her the next morning, I gave my parents Jack's mobile number, because mine was in my case, and asked them to let me know as soon as they had any news.

'Are you sure you still want to go ahead?' Jack asked anxiously, once the ambulance had left. 'I don't suppose anyone particularly feels like celebrating after what's happened to Millie. Maybe we should wait until we know that she's definitely going to be all right.'

I looked at our guests, who were milling about, needing to know if our wedding was still taking place or not. 'I think they'll be fine with it if we are.' I turned him to face me. 'Jack, do you still want to get married?'

'Of course I do, more than anything. But, ultimately, it's your decision.'

'Then let's get married. It's what Millie would want,' I lied, because I knew Millie wouldn't understand why we had gone ahead and got married without her. The feeling that I was betraying her made fresh tears well in my eyes and I blinked them away quickly so that Jack wouldn't see, hoping I'd never have to choose between him and Millie again.

Everyone was delighted that we were getting married after all and when Mum phoned a couple of hours later to tell us that Millie was fine apart from a broken leg, I felt weak with relief. I wanted to cut the reception short and go to see her that evening, but Mum said that she was sleeping soundly and, with the painkillers the doctor had given her, she wasn't expected to wake until the following morning anyway. She added that she intended to stay at the hospital overnight, so I told her that Jack and I would stop off to see Millie the next morning, on the way to the airport.

Although I managed to enjoy myself for the rest of the evening, I was glad when the last of our guests had left and Jack and I were finally on our way to our hotel. Because Jack's car was still in London, Moira and Giles had lent us one of theirs so that we could get to the airport the next day and back to Spring Eaton when we returned from Thailand. With a garage full of cars, they insisted that they didn't need it and said we could drop it back whenever we had time.

When we arrived at the hotel where we were to spend our wedding night, I went straight to the bathroom and ran myself a hot bath, leaving Jack to pour himself a whisky while he waited for me. As I lay in the bath, my mind turned again and again to Millie, and I couldn't help being glad that the day was finally over. With the water beginning to get cold, I got out and dried myself hurriedly, eager to see Jack's face when he saw me in the cream silk camisole and knickers I'd bought specially for our wedding night. I slipped them on and, with a shiver of anticipation, opened the door and walked into the bedroom.

PRESENT

On the way home in the car from seeing Millie, I mention to Jack that I'm going to have to phone Diane sometime before Friday to tell her that I can't make lunch with her and Esther.

'On the contrary, I think you should go,' he says. Because he's said the same thing many times before I know it doesn't mean anything. 'After all, you've already cancelled twice.' Even those words aren't enough to get my hopes up. But on Friday morning, when he tells me to put on my prettiest dress, I can't help wondering if the moment I've been waiting for has finally come. My mind races so far ahead that I have to remind myself firmly of all the other times I've ended up disappointed. Even when I get into the car beside Jack, I still don't let myself believe that it might happen. But when we drive all the way into town I can't help but believe it, and I begin to plot feverishly, terrified that I'll let the moment slip through my fingers. It's only when Jack parks the car in the road outside the restaurant and gets out that I realise how deluded I've been.

Diane and Esther are already seated. Diane waves and I make my way over, a smile hiding my bitter disappointment, conscious of Jack's hand on my back.

'I'm so glad you could make it,' she says, giving me a quick hug. 'Jack, how nice of you to come and say hello. Is it your lunch hour?'

'I worked from home this morning,' he says. 'And, as I don't have to be in the office until later this afternoon, I was hoping you'd let me gatecrash your lunch—in exchange for me treating you, of course.'

'In that case, you can join us with pleasure,' she laughs. 'I'm sure it won't be any trouble to add an extra place, especially as it's a table for four.'

'Except that we won't be able to talk about you now,' Esther jokes. As Jack purloins a chair from another table, it occurs to me that had she wanted to say anything more damaging, she wouldn't have been able to. Not that it really matters any more.

'I'm sure you've got far more interesting things to talk about than me,' Jack smiles, placing me opposite Esther and signalling to the waitress to bring another place setting.

'And Grace would only have nice things to say about you anyway, so it wouldn't be much fun,' Diane sighs.

'Oh, I'm sure she'd be able to find a few little imperfections.' Esther looks at me challengingly. 'Wouldn't you, Grace?'

'I doubt it,' I say. 'As you can see, Jack is pretty perfect.'

'Oh come on, he can't be that perfect! There must be something!'

I furrow my brow, making a show of giving it some thought, then shake my head regretfully. 'No, sorry, I really can't think of anything—unless buying me too many flowers counts. Sometimes it's hard to find enough vases to put them in.'

Beside me, Diane groans. 'That is not a fault, Grace.' She turns to Jack. 'I don't suppose you could give Adam a few tips on how to spoil one's wife, could you?'

'Don't forget that Grace and Jack are practically newlyweds compared to all of us,' Esther points out. 'And they don't have children yet. Gallantry tends to fly out of the window once familiarity and babies install themselves in a relationship.' She pauses a moment. 'Did you live together for long before you got married?'

'We didn't have time to live together,' Jack explains. 'We got married less than six months after we met.'

Esther raises her eyebrows. 'Gosh, that was quick!'

'Once I knew Grace was the one for me, there didn't seem to be any point in hanging around,' he says, taking my hand.

Esther looks over at me, a smile playing at the corner of her mouth. 'And you didn't find any skeletons in the closet once you were married?'

'Not a single one.' I take the menu the waitress holds out to me and open it eagerly, not only because I want to stop Esther's interrogation of my relationship with Jack but also because I'm hungry. I scan the dishes on offer and see that their fillet steak comes with mushrooms, onions and French fries. Perfect.

'Is anybody having anything remotely fattening?' Diane asks hopefully.

Esther shakes her head. 'Sorry. I'm going for a salad.'

'I'm having the fillet steak,' I tell her. 'With fries. And I'll probably have the chocolate fudge cake for dessert,' I add, knowing that is what she wants to hear.

'In that case, I'll join Esther in a salad and you in the fudge cake,' she says happily.

'Would anybody like wine?' Jack asks, ever the perfect host.

'No, thank you,' says Diane, and, regretfully, I resign myself to an alcohol-free lunch because Jack never drinks during the day.

'I'd love some,' says Esther. 'But only if you and Grace have some too.'

'I won't,' says Jack. 'I have a lot to do this afternoon.'

'I will,' I tell Esther. 'Would you prefer red or white?'

The conversation, while we're waiting to be served, turns to the local musical festival, which takes place every July and draws people from miles around. We agree that where we all live, we're near enough to be able to attend the festival easily yet far enough away to not be disturbed by the thousands of people that descend on the town. Although Diane and Adam always go to the festival, Jack and I have never been and we're soon drawn into Diane's plans for all of us to go together. In talking about music, we learn that Esther plays the piano and Rufus the guitar and when I admit to not being at all musical, Esther asks me if I like reading and I tell her I do, although I do very little. We talk about the sort of books we like, and Esther mentions a new bestseller that has just come out and asks if we've read it. It turns out that none of us have.

'Would you like me to lend it to you?' she asks, as the waitress puts our meals on the table.

'Yes, please.' I'm so touched that she has offered to lend her book to me rather than to Diane that I forget.

'I'll drop it round this afternoon,' she offers. 'I don't teach on Fridays.'

Now I remember. 'You might have to leave it in the letter box. If I'm in the garden, which I probably will be, I won't hear the bell.'

'I'd love to see your garden sometime,' she enthuses. 'Especially after what Jack said about you having green fingers.'

'There's no need for you to drive over,' says Jack, neatly sidestepping the massive hint she's just dropped. 'Grace can buy the book for herself.'

'It's really no problem.' Esther eyes her salad appreciatively. 'Gosh, this looks lovely.'

'In fact, we'll go and buy a copy as soon as we've finished here. Smith's is just around the corner.'

'Is it just on Fridays that you don't work?' I ask, wanting to change the subject.

'No, I don't work Tuesdays either. One of the other teachers and I job-share.'

'I'd love to be able to do that,' says Diane wistfully. 'It's hard working full-time when you've got children. But I'd hate to give up working altogether, which is the only alternative because my firm haven't heard of job-sharing yet.'

Esther looks over at me. 'I can't believe you don't miss working. I mean, you had a pretty exciting job before you got married.'

I busy myself cutting a piece of steak, because it's hard being reminded of the life I used to have. 'Not at all—I have plenty to keep me occupied.'

'So what are your other hobbies, apart from painting, gardening and reading?'

'Oh, a bit of this and a bit of that,' I say, realising how lame it sounds.

'What Grace hasn't told you is that she makes a lot of her own clothes,' Jack intervenes. 'Just the other day, she made herself a lovely dress.'

'Really?' Esther looks at me with interest.

Used to thinking on my feet, I don't bat an eyelid. 'It was just a dress to wear around the house,' I explain. 'Nothing fancy. I don't make clothes to wear out in the evening or anything too complicated.'

'I didn't know you were good with a needle.' Diane's eyes gleam. 'I'd love to be able to sew.'

'Me too,' says Esther. 'Perhaps you could teach me, Grace.'

'Maybe we could start a sewing circle with you as our teacher,' Diane suggests.

'I'm really not that good,' I protest, 'which is why I've never mentioned it before. I'm too worried people will ask to see something I've made.'

'Well, if you sew anything like you cook, I'm sure the dress you made is beautiful!'

'You'll have to show it to us sometime,' Esther says.

'I will,' I promise. 'But only if you don't ask me to make you one.'

The constant need to field her remarks makes me feel so tense that I consider skipping dessert, something I wouldn't normally do. But if I don't have one, Diane won't, and because Esther has just professed herself too full to eat another thing, it means that the meal can be rounded up quickly. I weigh the pros and cons but in the end the lure of chocolate fudge cake is too strong. I take another sip of wine, hoping to stave off more of Esther's questioning, wishing she would turn her attention to Diane for a while.

As if reading my mind, she asks Diane about her son. His eating habits is one of Diane's favourite topics of conversation, so I get a few minutes' reprieve while the conversation revolves around how best to get children to eat vegetables they don't like. Jack listens attentively, as if the subject is of real interest to him and my mind turns to Millie, worrying how she will take it if I'm not able to go and see her over the weekend, because it's getting harder and harder to explain my absences to her. Once, it would never have occurred to me to wish her to be any different to how she has always been. Now, I'm constantly wishing that she didn't have Down's, that she wasn't dependent on me, that she could live her own life instead of having to share mine.

Called abruptly back to the present by Diane ordering my dessert for me, I tell Esther, when she asks what I was dreaming about, that I was thinking about Millie. Diane asks if we've seen her recently so I tell her that we saw her the previous Sunday and that Jack took us out for a lovely lunch. I wait for someone to ask if we'll be going to see her again this weekend, but nobody does, so I am none the wiser.

'She must be looking forward to coming to live with you,' Esther says, as the desserts arrive.

'Yes, she is,' I agree.

Jack smiles. 'We're looking forward to it too.'

'What does she think of the house?'

I reach for my glass. 'Actually, she hasn't seen it yet.'

'But didn't you move in a year ago?'

'Yes, but we want everything to be perfect before she sees it,' Jack explains.

'It looked pretty perfect to me when I saw it,' she remarks.

'Her room isn't quite finished yet, but I'm having so much fun doing it up, aren't I, darling?' To my horror, I feel tears welling up inside me and bow my head quickly, conscious of Esther's eyes on me.

'What colour will it be?' asks Diane.

'Red,' says Jack. 'It's her favourite colour.' He nods at my chocolate fudge cake. 'Eat up, darling.'

I pick up my spoon, wondering how I'm going to be able to do as he says.

'It looks delicious,' says Esther. 'I don't suppose you want to share it with me, do you?'

I hesitate, feigning reluctance, wondering why I'm bothering because I won't have fooled Jack. 'Help yourself,' I say, offering her my fork.

'Thank you.' She spears a piece of the cake. 'Did you and Jack come in separate cars?'

'No, we came together.'

'Then I'll drop you back, if you like.'

'It's fine, I intend on taking Grace home before going into the office,' Jack says.

'Isn't that a bit of a detour?' she frowns. 'You can get straight on the motorway to London from here. I'll take her home, Jack, it's really no problem.'

'That's very kind of you, but there are some documents that I need to pick up before seeing one of my clients later this afternoon.' He pauses. 'It's a shame I didn't bring them with me, because I would have let you take Grace home with pleasure.'

'Another time, then.' Esther turns to me. 'Grace, perhaps we can exchange telephone numbers? I'd like to have you all around to dinner, but I need to check with Rufus to see when he's free. He has a trip to Berlin coming up and I'm not sure when it is.'

'Of course.' I give her our home number and she taps it into her mobile.

'And your mobile?'

'I don't have one.'

She does a double take. 'You don't have a mobile?'

'No.'

'Why not?'

'Because I don't see the need for one.'

'But everybody over the age of ten and under the age of eighty has one!'

'Well, not me,' I say, amused—despite myself—at her reaction.

'I know, it's incredible, isn't it?' says Diane. 'I've tried to persuade her to buy one but she isn't interested.'

'But how on earth does anybody get hold of you when you're out and about?' wonders Esther.

I shrug. 'They don't.'

'Which is quite a good thing,' says Diane dryly. 'I can't go shopping without Adam or one of the children phoning to ask me to get them something, or to find out when I'll be back. The number of times I've been standing at the checkout in

Tesco trying to load all my shopping into bags while trying to sort out something at home doesn't bear thinking about.'

'But what if you have a problem?' asks Esther, still trying to get her head round it.

'People managed perfectly well before without mobiles,' I point out.

'Yes, back in the Dark Ages.' She turns to Jack. 'Jack, buy your wife a mobile, for God's sake!'

Jack opens his hands in a gesture of defeat. 'I'd be only too happy to. But I know that if I did, she wouldn't use it.'

'I can't believe that—not once she realises how practical they are.'

'Jack's right, I wouldn't,' I confirm.

'Please tell me you have a computer.'

'Yes, of course I do.'

'Then could I have your email address?'

'Sure. It's *jackangel@court.com*.'

'Isn't that Jack's address?'

'It's mine too.'

She raises her head and looks at me quizzically from across the table. 'Don't you have your own address?'

'What for? Jack and I don't have any secrets from each other. And if people email me, it's usually to invite us for dinner, or something else that concerns Jack too, so it's easier if he sees the messages as well.'

'Especially as Grace often forgets to tell me things,' Jack says, smiling indulgently at me.

Esther looks thoughtfully at the two of us. 'You really are a joined-at-the-hip couple, aren't you? Well, as you haven't got a mobile, I suppose you'll have to resort to pen and paper to take my numbers down. Have you got a pen?'

I know that I don't. 'I'm not sure,' I say, intending to make a show of looking for one. I reach for my bag, which I had slung over the back of my chair, but she gets there first and hands it to me.

'Goodness, it feels empty!'

'I travel light,' I tell her, opening my bag and peering inside. 'No, sorry, I don't have one.'

'It's all right, I'll get them.' Jack takes out his mobile. 'I already have your home number, Esther, from Rufus, so if you just give me your mobile?'

As she reels it off, I try desperately to commit it to memory, but I get lost somewhere near the end. I close my eyes and try to retrieve the last few numbers but it's impossible.

'Thanks, Esther,' says Jack. I open my eyes and find Esther looking at me curiously from across the table. 'I'll write it down for Grace when we get home.'

'Wait a minute—is it 721 or 712 in the middle?' Esther furrows her brow. 'I can never remember which it is. The end is easy enough—9146—it's the bit before I have a problem with. Could you just check, Diane?'

Diane gets out her phone and locates Esther's number. 'It's 712,' she says.

'Oh yes—07517129146. Did you get that, Jack?'

'Yes, it's fine. Right, anyone for coffee?'

But we don't bother, because Diane has to get back to work and Esther doesn't want any. Jack asks for the bill and Diane and Esther disappear off to the toilet. I would like to go too, but I don't bother following them. The bill paid, Jack and I take leave of the others and walk towards the car park.

'Well, did you enjoy that, my perfect little wife?' Jack asks, opening the car door for me.

I recognise one of his million-dollar questions. 'Not really.'

'Not even the dessert you were so looking forward to?'

I swallow hard. 'Not as much as I thought I would.'

'It's lucky Esther was able to help you out then, wasn't it?'

'I would have eaten it anyway,' I tell him.

'And deprived me of so much pleasure?'

A tremor goes through my body. 'Absolutely.'

He raises his eyebrows. 'Do I detect a renewal of your fighting spirit? I'm so glad. To tell the truth, I've been getting quite bored.' He gives me an amused glance. 'Bring it on, Grace—I'm waiting for you.'

PAST

That evening, the evening of my wedding day, when I stepped into the bedroom after my bath, I was dismayed to find it empty. Presuming that Jack had gone off to make a phone call, I felt irritated that something could be more important to him on our wedding day than me. But my irritation quickly turned to anxiety when I remembered that Millie was in hospital and in the space of a couple of seconds I managed to convince myself that something terrible had happened to her, that Mum had phoned Jack to tell him, and that he had left the room because he didn't want me to hear their conversation.

I ran to the bedroom door and flung it open, expecting to see Jack pacing up and down the corridor, trying to work out how to break some tragic news to me. But it was empty. Guessing he had gone down to the lobby and not wanting to waste time going to find him, I searched through my luggage, which had been dropped off at the hotel by the chauffeur, dug out my phone and rang Mum's mobile. As I waited to be connected, it occurred to me that if she was talking to Jack, I wouldn't be able to get through to her anyway. I was about to hang up and call Dad's mobile instead when I heard her phone ringing and, soon after, her voice.

'Mum, what's happened?' I cried before she'd even finished saying hello. 'Has there been a complication or something?'

'No, everything's fine.' Mum sounded surprised.

'So Millie's all right?'

'Yes, she's sound asleep.' She paused. 'Are you all right? You sound agitated.'

I sat down on the bed, weak with relief. 'Jack's disappeared so I thought that maybe you'd phoned with bad news and that he'd gone to talk to you in private,' I explained.

'What do you mean, "disappeared"?'

'Well, he's not in the room. I went into the bathroom to have a bath and when I came out he was gone.'

'He's probably gone down to the reception for something. I'm sure he'll be back in a minute. How did the wedding go?'

'Fine, really well, considering that I couldn't stop thinking about Millie. I hated that she wasn't there. She's going to be so disappointed when she realises that we went ahead and got married without her.'

'I'm sure she'll understand,' Mum soothed, and I felt furious at how little she knew Millie, because of course she wouldn't understand. I was appalled to find I was near to tears, but after all that had happened, Jack's disappearing act was the last straw. Telling Mum that I would see her at the hospital the next morning, I asked her to give Millie a kiss for me and hung up.

As I dialled Jack's mobile, I told myself to calm down. We had never rowed before and shouting at him down the phone like a fishwife wouldn't achieve anything. Something had obviously come up with one of his clients, a last-minute problem that he needed to sort out before we left for Thailand. He would be just as annoyed at being disturbed on his wedding day as I was.

I was relieved when I heard his phone ringing, relieved that he wasn't on the phone to someone, hoping it meant that the problem—whatever it was—had been sorted. When he didn't pick up I stifled a cry of frustration and left a message on his voicemail.

'Jack, where on earth are you? Could you phone me back, please?'

I hung up and began to pace the room restlessly, wondering where he had gone. My eyes fell on the clock on the bedside table and I saw that it was nine o'clock. I tried to imagine why Jack hadn't answered his phone, why he hadn't been able to take my call and wondered if one of the other partners had come to the hotel to talk to him. When another ten minutes had gone by, I dialled his number again. This time it went straight through to his voicemail.

'Jack, please phone me back,' I said sharply, knowing he must have turned his mobile off after my last call. 'I need to know where you are.'

I heaved my suitcase onto the bed, opened it and took out the beige trousers and shirt I planned to wear for travelling the following day. Pulling them on over my camisole and knickers, I dressed quickly, put the key card into my pocket and left the room, taking my telephone with me. Too agitated to wait for the lift, I took the stairs down to the lobby and headed for the reception desk.

'Mrs Angel, isn't it?' The young man behind the desk smiled at me. 'How can I help you?'

'Actually, I'm looking for my husband. Have you seen him anywhere?'

'Yes, he came down about an hour ago, not long after you checked in.'

'Do you know where he went? Did he go to the bar, by any chance?'

He shook his head. 'He went out through the front doors. I presumed he was going to fetch something from the car.'

'Did you see him come back in?'

'Now that you mention it, no, I didn't. But I was busy checking in another client at one point, so it could be that I didn't see him.' He eyed the phone in my hand. 'Have you tried phoning him?'

'Yes, but his mobile's switched off. He's probably in the bar, drowning his sorrows that he's now a married man.' I smiled, trying to make light of it. 'I'll go and have a look.'

I made my way to the bar but there was no sign of Jack. I checked the various lounges, the fitness room and the swimming pool. On the way to check the two restaurants, I left another message on his voicemail, my voice breaking with anxiety.

'No luck?' The receptionist gave me a sympathetic look as I arrived back in the lobby on my own.

I shook my head. 'I'm afraid I can't find him anywhere.'

'Have you looked if your car is still in the car park? At least you'd know whether or not he'd left the hotel.'

I went out through the front doors and followed the path round to the car park at the back of the hotel. The car wasn't where Jack had left it nor was it anywhere else. Not wanting to go back through the lobby and face the receptionist again, I went in through the back door and ran up the stairs to the bedroom, praying that I would find Jack already there, that he would have arrived back while I'd been out looking for him. When I found the bedroom empty, I burst into tears of frustration. I told myself that the fact the car was missing went someway to explaining why he hadn't answered his phone, because he never answered his phone while he was driving. But if he'd had to go back to the office on urgent business, why hadn't he knocked on the bathroom door and told me? And if he hadn't wanted to disturb me in my bath, why hadn't he at least left me a note?

Increasingly worried, I dialled his number and left a tearful message saying that if I didn't hear from him within the next ten minutes I was going to phone the police. I knew that the police would be my last port of call, that before phoning them I would phone Adam, but I hoped that in mentioning the police Jack would realise just how worried I was.

They were the longest ten minutes of my life. Then, just as I was about to call Adam, my phone beeped, telling me I'd received a text message. Letting out a shaky sigh of relief, I opened it and when I saw that it was from Jack, tears of relief fell from my eyes, making it impossible to read what he had written. But it didn't matter because I knew what it would say, I knew it would say that he'd been called away unexpectedly, that he was sorry I'd been worried but that he hadn't been able to answer his phone because he'd been in a meeting, that he'd be back soon and that he loved me.

I reached for a tissue from the box on the desk, wiped my eyes, blew my nose and looked at the message again.

'Don't be so hysterical, it doesn't suit you. Something's come up, I'll see you in the morning.'

Stunned, I sat down on the bed, reading the message over and over again, convinced I had misunderstood it in some way. I couldn't believe that Jack would have written something so cruel or been so cutting. He had never spoken to me in such a way before, he had never even raised his voice to me. I felt as if I'd been slapped in the face. And why wouldn't he be back until the following morning? Surely I deserved some explanation and, at the very least, an apology? Suddenly furious, I called him back, trembling with anger, daring him to answer his phone and, when he didn't, I had to force myself not to leave a voicemail that I would later regret.

I needed to talk to someone, badly, so it was sobering to realise there was no one I could call. My parents and I didn't have the sort of relationship that would allow me to sob down the phone that Jack had left me by myself on our wedding night and for some reason I felt too ashamed to tell any of my friends. I would normally have confided in Kate or Emily, but at the wedding I realised how much I'd neglected them since I met Jack, so I didn't feel able to call them either. I thought about phoning Adam to see if he knew why Jack had been called away so suddenly but as they didn't work in the same field, I doubted he would know. And again, there was the feeling of shame that something could be more important to Jack on our wedding night than me.

Stemming the tears that fell from my eyes with a tissue, I made an effort to understand. If he was with one of the other lawyers, I reasoned, locked in some delicate meeting, it was normal that he had turned his phone off after my first attempt to contact him so that he wouldn't be further disturbed. He had probably intended to phone me back as soon as he had a chance, but the meeting must have gone on longer than expected. Maybe during a quick break he had listened to my messages and, angry at my tone of voice, had retaliated by sending me a sharp text message instead of phoning me. And maybe he had guessed that if he did speak to me, I'd be so overwrought that he wouldn't have been able to get back to his meeting until he'd calmed me down.

It all sounded so plausible that I regretted acting as hysterically as I had. Jack had been right to be angry with me. I had already seen how his work could impinge on our relationship—God knew how many times he had been too tired or too stressed for sex—and he had already apologised for it, and had begged me to understand that the very nature of his work meant that he couldn't always be there, both mentally and physically, for me. I had been proud of the fact that we had never rowed but now, I had fallen at the first hurdle.

I wanted nothing more but to see Jack, to tell him how sorry I was, to feel his arms around me, to hear him say that he forgave me. Reading his message again, I realised that when he said he'd see me in the morning, he probably meant the small hours. Feeling much calmer, and suddenly very tired, I got undressed and climbed into bed, relishing the thought of being woken before too long by Jack making love to me. I just had time to hope that Millie was still sleeping soundly before I fell into a deep sleep.

It hadn't occurred to me that Jack might be spending the night with another woman, but it was the first thought that entered my mind when I woke sometime after eight the next morning and realised that he hadn't come back after all. Fighting down panic, I reached for my mobile, expecting to find a message from him, if only to say at what time he would be at the hotel. But there was nothing, and because there was the possibility that he'd decided to snatch a couple of hours' sleep in the office rather than disturb me, I was reluctant to phone him in case I woke him up. But I was desperate to speak to him, so I called him anyway. When I got his voice-mail, I took a deep breath and left a message in as normal a tone as I could muster, asking him to let me know what time I could expect him at the hotel and telling him that we needed to call by the hospital to see Millie on the way to the airport. Then I showered, dressed and sat down to wait.

As I waited, I realised that I didn't even know what time our flight was due to leave. I vaguely remembered Jack saying something about an afternoon flight so I guessed that we would have to be at the airport at least a couple of hours before. When I eventually received a text message from Jack, almost an hour later, I was again bewildered by its tone. There was no apology, no mention of anything except an order to meet him in the hotel car park at eleven. By the time I struggled into the lift with our two suitcases and my hand luggage, my stomach was churning with anxiety. As I handed the room key in at the reception, I was glad that the man I had spoken to the night before had been replaced by a young woman who, I hoped, knew nothing of my missing husband.

A porter helped me take the luggage out to the car park. I told him that my husband had gone to fill the car with petrol and headed for a nearby bench, ignoring his suggestion that I'd be better off waiting in the warmth of the hotel. I hadn't wanted to take a heavy coat with me to Thailand and because I'd expected to go from the hotel to the car to the airport, barely venturing out into the open, I was only wearing a jacket which was no match for the vicious wind that whipped across the car park. By the time Jack showed up twenty-five minutes later, I was blue with cold and on the verge of tears. Stopping the car only feet away from me, he got out and walked over to where I was sitting.

'Get in,' he said, picking up the cases and loading them into the boot.

Too cold to argue, I stumbled into the car and huddled against the door, wanting only to feel warm again. I waited for him to speak, to say something—anything—which would go some way to explaining why I felt as if I was sitting next to someone I didn't know. When the silence had gone on for too long, I summoned up the courage to look at him. The lack of emotion on his face shocked me. I had expected to see anger, stress or irritation. But there was nothing.

'What's going on, Jack?' I asked unsteadily. It was as if I hadn't spoken. 'For God's sake, Jack!' I cried. 'What the hell is going on?'

'Please don't swear,' he said distastefully.

I looked at him in amazement. 'What do you expect? You disappear without a word, leaving me to spend our wedding night alone and then you turn up half an hour late to fetch me, leaving me waiting in the freezing cold! Surely I have a right to be angry!'

'No,' he said. 'You don't. You have no rights at all.'

'Don't be ridiculous! Is there someone else, Jack? Is that what all this is about? Are you in love with somebody else? Is that where you were last night?'

'Now it's you who's being ridiculous. You're my wife, Grace. Why would I need anybody else?'

Defeated, I shook my head miserably. 'I don't understand. Is there some problem at work, something you can't tell me about?'

'I'll explain everything when we're in Thailand.'

'Why can't you tell me now? Please, Jack, tell me what's wrong.'

'In Thailand.'

I wanted to tell him that I didn't particularly feel like going to Thailand with him in the mood he was in, but I took comfort in the fact that, once there, I would at least have an explanation as to why our marriage had got off to such a bad start. Because his mood seemed to be related to some sort of problem at work, I couldn't help feeling apprehensive that it might be something I'd be seeing a lot more of in the future. I was so busy working out how I would adjust to being married to a man I hadn't known existed that it was a while before I realised we were heading straight out to the airport.

'What about Millie?' I cried. 'We're meant to be going to see her!'

'I'm afraid it's too late,' he said. 'We should have turned off miles back.'

'But I told you in my message that we had to stop by the hospital!'

'Well, as you didn't mention anything about it when you got into the car, I thought you'd changed your mind. Besides, we don't really have time.'

'But our flight isn't until this afternoon!'

'It leaves at three, which means we have to check in at twelve.'

'But I promised her! I told Millie I'd go and see her this morning!'

'When? When did you tell her that? I don't remember.'

'When she was in the ambulance!'

'She was unconscious, so she'll hardly remember.'

'That's not the point! Anyway, I told Mum that we'd call in and she'll have told Millie.'

'If you had checked with me first I would have told you that it wouldn't be possible.'

'How could I check with you when you weren't there! Jack, please turn back, we have plenty of time. The check-in may open at twelve but it won't close until much later. I won't stay long, I promise, I just want to see her.'

'It's out of the question, I'm afraid.'

'Why are you being like this?' I cried. 'You know what Millie's like, you know she won't understand if I don't turn up.'

'Then phone her and explain. Phone her and tell her you got it wrong.'

Frustrated, I burst into tears. 'I didn't get it wrong,' I sobbed. 'We have plenty of time, you know we do!'

He had never seen me cry before and, although I felt ashamed at resorting to tears, I hoped he would realise how unreasonable he was being. So when he swung the car off the road, taking an exit to a service station at the last minute, I wiped my eyes and blew my nose, thinking he was going to turn back.

'Thank you,' I said as he brought the car to a standstill.

Switching off the ignition, he turned towards me. 'Listen to me, Grace, and listen carefully. If you want to go and see Millie, you can. You can get out of the car now and take a taxi to the hospital. But I'm going on to the airport and if you choose to go to the hospital, you won't be coming to Thailand with me. It's as simple as that.'

I shook my head, making fresh tears cascade down my cheeks. 'I don't believe you,' I wept. 'You wouldn't make me choose between you and Millie, not if you loved me.'

'But that is exactly what I'm doing.'

'How can I choose?' I looked at him in anguish. 'I love both of you!'

He gave a sigh of irritation. 'It saddens me that you're making such a song and dance about it. Surely it should be simple. Are you really going to throw away our marriage simply because I refuse to turn back to see Millie when we're already well on the way to the airport? Is that how little I mean to you?'

'No, of course not,' I gulped, swallowing down my tears.

'And don't you think I've been very generous in the past, never complaining about the amount of time we have to spend with Millie each weekend?'

'Yes,' I said miserably.

He nodded, satisfied. 'So what's it to be, Grace? The airport or the hospital? Your husband or your sister?' He paused a moment. 'Me, or Millie?'

'You, Jack,' I said quietly. 'You, of course.'

'Good. Now, where's your passport?'

'In my bag,' I mumbled.

'Can I have it?'

I picked up my bag, took out my passport and handed it to him.

'Thank you,' he said, slipping it into the inside pocket of his jacket. Without another word, he put the car into gear, drove out of the service station and back onto the motorway.

Despite what had happened, I couldn't really believe that he wouldn't take me to see Millie and I wondered if what had just happened had been some kind of test, and that because I had chosen him over her, he was now going to take me to the hospital. When I saw that we were once again heading for the airport, I felt desperate, not just because of Millie but also because, in the six months since I had met Jack, I had never even glimpsed this side of his character. I had never guessed that he could be anything but the kindest, most reasonable man in the universe. All my instincts told me to ask him to stop the car and let me out, but I was scared of what would happen if I did. In the mood he was in, there was no way of knowing if he would do as he had threatened and go on to Thailand without me. And, if he did, where would that leave me, us, our marriage? By the time we got to the airport I felt sick with stress.

As we stood in the queue waiting to check in, Jack suggested that I phone Mum to tell her that we'd been unable to call in at the hospital, telling me that the sooner I did, the better it would be for all concerned. Still bewildered by his attitude, I did as he asked and when my call went straight through to Mum's voicemail I didn't know whether to be upset or relieved. On balance, I decided it was probably just as well that I couldn't speak to Millie, and left a message explaining that because I had made a mistake with the time of our flight, I wouldn't be able to call in after all. I asked Mum to give Millie a kiss from me and to tell her that I would call once we got to Thailand. As I hung up, Jack smiled and took my hand in his, and, for the first time ever, I wanted to snatch it away again.

When it was time for us to approach the desk, Jack was so utterly charming to the hostess, explaining we were newly-weds and that we had had a disastrous wedding day because our bridesmaid, who had Down's syndrome, had fallen down the stairs and broken her leg, that we were upgraded to first class. But it didn't make me feel any better—if anything, the fact that he had used Millie's condition to gain sympathy disgusted me. The old Jack would never have done such a thing and the thought of spending the next two weeks with someone who had become a virtual stranger was terrifying. Yet the alternative—telling Jack I didn't want to go to Thailand with him—was equally so. As we went through passport control, I couldn't shake the feeling that I was making the biggest mistake of my life.

I felt even more confused in the departure lounge when Jack sat and read the paper with his arm draped around my shoulders as if he didn't have a care in the world. I refused champagne when it was offered to us, hoping Jack would understand that I wasn't in the mood for a celebration. But he accepted a glass readily, seemingly unaffected by the chasm that now existed between us. I tried to tell myself that what had happened between us was nothing more than a lovers' tiff, a momentary blip on the path to a long and happy marriage, but I knew it was more serious than that. Desperate to understand where we had gone wrong, I went over everything that had happened since I'd stepped out of the bathroom less than twenty-four hours earlier, and when I remembered the panicked messages I'd left on his phone, I began to wonder if I was the one in the wrong. But I knew I wasn't, I knew it was Jack's fault, it was just that I was so tired I couldn't work out why. Suddenly, I couldn't wait to be on the plane, hoping that after being pampered for fourteen hours I would arrive in Thailand in a better frame of mind.

Because I had also refused to eat anything in the departure lounge, I was desperately hungry by the time we boarded, as I'd been too upset to eat breakfast. Jack was solicitous as we settled into our seats, making sure I had everything I needed, and my mood began to lift slightly. As I began to relax, I could feel my eyes closing.

'Tired?' Jack asked.

'Yes.' I nodded. 'And very hungry. If I fall asleep could you wake me for dinner?'

'Of course.'

I was gone before the plane had even taken off. When I eventually opened my eyes again, the cabin was in darkness and everyone seemed to be sleeping. Only Jack was awake, reading the newspaper.

I looked at him in dismay. 'I thought I asked you to wake me for dinner?'

'I thought it better not to disturb you. But don't worry, they'll be serving breakfast in a couple of hours.'

'I can't wait a couple of hours; I haven't eaten since yesterday!'

'Then ask one of hostesses to bring you something.'

I stared at him over the divide between us. In our other life, before we'd got married, he would have rung for the hostess himself. Where had the perfect gentleman I'd thought him to be gone? Had it all been a facade, had he covered his true self with a cloak of geniality and good humour to impress me? Aware of my eyes on him, he put down his paper.

'Who are you, Jack?' I asked quietly.

'Your husband,' he said. 'I am your husband.' Taking my hand in his, he raised it to his lips and kissed it. 'For better or for worse. In sickness and in health. Till death do us part.' Letting go of my hand, he pushed the button, summoning the hostess. She came immediately.

'Could you bring my wife something to eat, please? She missed dinner, I'm afraid.'

'Certainly, sir,' she smiled.

'There,' said Jack, once she'd left. 'Happy?' He turned back towards his newspaper and I was glad he couldn't see the tears of pathetic gratitude that had pricked my eyes. When my food was brought, I ate it quickly and, not particularly wanting to talk to Jack, I slept until we began our descent into Bangkok.

Jack had insisted on making all the arrangements for our honeymoon because he wanted it to be a surprise for me. He had already been to Thailand several times and knew the best places to stay, so, even though I had hinted heavily about Koh Samui, I had little idea of where we were actually going. I couldn't help feeling disappointed when, rather than head for domestic departures, Jack led me towards the taxi rank. Soon, we were on our way into the centre of Bangkok and I couldn't help feeling excited by the hustle and bustle of the city, although a little appalled at the noise. When the taxi slowed down in front of a hotel called The Golden Temple, my spirits lifted even more as it was one of the most beautiful hotels I had ever seen. But, instead of coming to a stop, the taxi continued on its way until we arrived in front of a good but less luxurious hotel three hundred metres farther down the road. The lobby was better than its facade, but when we arrived in our room and found the bathroom to be so small that Jack would have trouble using the shower, I fully expected him to turn around and leave at once.

'Perfect,' he said, taking off his jacket and hanging it in the wardrobe. 'This will do nicely.'

'Jack, you can't be serious.' I looked around the room. 'Surely we can do better than this?'

'It's time to wake up, Grace.'

He looked so solemn I wondered why it hadn't occurred to me that he might have lost his job, and the more I thought about it the more I realised that I had found the perfect explanation for his sudden change of character. If he had been told sometime on Friday evening, I reasoned, my mind darting back and forth as I tried to work it out, he had probably gone back to the office on Saturday, while I was having my bath, to try to sort things out with the other partners before we left on honeymoon. Of course he wouldn't have wanted to tell me during our wedding, of course my visit to Millie must have seemed paltry compared to what he was going through! No wonder he had wanted to wait until we were in Thailand to tell me what had happened and, as he had obviously changed our hotel reservation for something cheaper, I prepared myself to hear that he hadn't managed to negotiate his job back.

'What's happened?' I asked.

'The dream is over, I'm afraid.'

'It doesn't matter,' I said reassuringly, telling myself that it could be the best thing to happen to us. 'We'll manage.'

'What do you mean?'

'Well, I'm sure you'll be able to find another job easily—or you could even set up on your own if you wanted. And, if things are really tight, I could always go back to work. I wouldn't be able to have my old job back, but I'm sure they'd take me on in some capacity or other.'

He gave me an amused look. 'I haven't lost my job, Grace.'

I stared at him. 'Then what is this all about?'

He shook his head sorrowfully. 'You should have chosen Millie, you really should have.'

I felt a prickle of fear run down my spine. 'What's going on?' I asked, trying to keep my voice calm. 'Why are you being like this?'

'Do you realise what you've done, do you realise that you've sold your soul to me? And Millie's, for that matter.' He paused. 'Especially Millie's.'

'Stop it!' I said sharply. 'Stop playing games with me!'

'It's not a game.' The calmness of his voice sent panic shooting through me. I felt my eyes dart around the room, subconsciously looking for a way out. 'It's too late,' he said, noticing. 'Far too late.'

'I don't understand,' I said, choking back a sob. 'What is it that you want?'

'Exactly what I've got—you, and Millie.'

'You haven't got Millie and you certainly haven't got me.' Snatching up my handbag, I looked angrily at him. 'I'm going back to London.'

He let me get as far as the door. 'Grace?'

I took my time turning round because I wasn't sure how I was going to react when he told me what I knew he was going to tell me, that it had all been some kind of stupid joke. Neither did I want him to see how relieved I was, because I couldn't bear to think what would have happened if he had let me step over the threshold.

'What?' I asked coolly.

He put his hand in his pocket and drew out my passport. 'Aren't you forgetting something?' Holding it between his finger and thumb, he dangled it in front of me. 'You can't go to England without it, you know. In fact, you can't go anywhere without it.'

I held out my hand. 'Give it to me, please.'

'No.'

'Give me my passport, Jack! I mean it!'

'Even if I were to give it to you, how would you get to the airport without money?'

'I have money,' I said haughtily, glad that I had bought some baht before we'd left. 'I also have a credit card.'

'No,' he said, shaking his head regretfully, 'you don't. Not anymore.'

Unzipping my handbag quickly, I saw that my purse was missing, as was my mobile phone.

'Where's my purse, and my phone? What have you done with them?' I lunged for his travel bag and scrabbled through it, looking for them.

'You won't find them in there,' he said, amused. 'You're wasting your time.'

'Do you really think you can keep me a prisoner here? That I won't be able to get away if I want to?'

'That,' he said solemnly, 'is where Millie comes in.'

I felt myself go cold. 'What do you mean?'

'Put it this way—what do you think will happen to her if I stop paying her school fees? An asylum, perhaps?'

'I'll pay her fees—I have enough money from the sale of my house.'

'You paid that money over to me, remember, to buy furniture for our new house, which I did. As for what was left over—well, it's mine now. You don't have any money, Grace, none at all.'

'Then I'll go back to work. And I'll sue you for the rest of my money,' I added savagely.

'No, you won't. For a start, you won't be going back to work.'

'You can't stop me.'

'Of course I can.'

'How? This is the twenty-first century, Jack. If all of this is really happening, if it isn't some kind of sick joke, do you really think I'm going to stay married to you?'

'Yes, because you'll have no choice. Why don't you sit down and I'll tell you why.'

'I'm not interested. Give me my passport and enough money to get back to England and we'll put this down to some terrible mistake. You can stay here if you like and when you get back we can tell everybody that we realised it wasn't meant to be and have decided to separate.'

'That's very generous of you.' He took a moment to consider it and I found I was holding my breath. 'The only trouble is, I don't make mistakes. I never have and I never will.'

'Please, Jack,' I said desperately. 'Please let me go.'

'I'll tell you what I'll do. If you sit down, I'll explain everything to you, just as I said I would. And after, when you've heard what I've got to say, if you still want to leave, I'll let you.'

'Do you promise?'

'You have my word.'

I quickly weighed up my options and, when I realised that I didn't have any, I sat down on the edge of the bed, as far away from him as I could. 'Go on, then.'

He nodded. 'But, before I begin, just so you understand how serious I am, I'm going to let you into a secret.'

I looked at him warily. 'What?'

He leant towards me, a small smile playing at the corner of his mouth. 'There is no housekeeper,' he whispered.

PRESENT

When we arrive back at the house after lunch with Diane and Esther, I go up to my room, as I always do. I hear the click of the key turning in the lock and a few minutes later, the whir of the shutters coming down; a further precaution against the unlikelihood that I should find a way through the locked door and down the stairs into the hall. My ears, finely attuned to the slightest sounds—because there is nothing else, no music, no television, to stimulate them—pick up the whir of the black gates opening and, soon after, the sound of the car scrunching down the gravel drive. I don't feel as anxious by his departure as I normally do, because today I have eaten. Once, he didn't come back for three days, by which time I was ready to eat the bathroom soap.

I look around the room that has been my home for the last six months. There isn't much, just a bed, a barred window and another door. It leads to a small bathroom, my only portal to a different world, where a shower, basin and toilet stand, a tiny cake of soap and towel its only ornaments.

Although I know every inch of these two rooms, my eyes continually search them, because there is always the thought that I might have missed something that would make my life more bearable, a nail that I could use to etch my distress on the edge of the bed, or to at least leave some trace of me should I suddenly disappear. But there is nothing. Anyway, it isn't death that Jack has in mind for me. What he has planned is more subtle than that and, as always when I think about what is coming, I pray frantically that he'll be killed in a car accident on the way home from work, if not tonight then before the end of June, when Millie will come to live with us. Because, after that, it will be too late.

There are no books, no paper or pen that I could use to distract myself. I spend my days suspended in time, a passive lump of humanity. At least, that is what Jack sees. In reality, I am biding my time, waiting for a tiny window of opportunity to open, as it surely will—because if I don't believe that it will, how could I carry on? How could I continue with the charade my life has become?

I almost thought my chance had come today, which in retrospect was pretty stupid of me. How could I have really thought that Jack would let me attend a lunch on my own, where I could have used the opportunity to escape from him?

It was simply that he had never gone as far as taking me all the way before, but had been content to toy with my delusions. Once, the time I pretended to Diane that I'd forgotten I was supposed to be meeting her for lunch, he had driven me halfway to the restaurant before turning back, laughing at the way my face had crumpled in desperate disappointment when I realised that my chance to escape had gone.

I often think about killing him, but I can't. For a start, I don't have the means. I have no access to medicine, knives or any other instrument of destruction, because he has me covered in every way. If I ask for an aspirin for a headache, and he deigns to bring me one, he waits until I have swallowed it so that I can't hide it somewhere and, little by little, headache after headache, stockpile enough to poison him with. Any meal he brings me is served on a plastic plate and accompanied by plastic cutlery and a plastic glass. When I prepare food for a dinner party, he is present at all times and watches carefully as I store the knives back in their boxes, in case I should decide to hide one about my person and use it on him at an opportune moment. Or he cuts and slices what I need. Anyway, what would be the point of killing him? If I were sent to prison, or awaiting trial, what would become of Millie? I haven't always been so passive, though. Before I fully understood the hopelessness of my situation, I was ingenious in my attempts to get away from him. But, in the end, it just wasn't worth it; the price I paid each time became too high.

I get up from where I've been sitting on the bed and look through the window at the garden below. The bars are set so close together it would be futile to break the glass in the hope of squeezing through them, and my chances of finding a convenient object with which to file through them are nil. Even if I were to find something, by some miracle, on one of the rare occasions that I'm allowed out of the house, I wouldn't be able to pick it up because Jack is always with me. He is my keeper, my guardian, my jailer. I am not allowed to go anywhere without him by my side, not even to the toilet in a restaurant.

Jack thinks that if he were to let me out of his sight for even two seconds, I would use the opportunity to tell someone of my plight, to ask for help, to flee. But I wouldn't, not any more, not unless I was a hundred per cent sure that I would be believed, because I have Millie to think about. She is the reason I don't call out for help in the street, or in a restaurant—that, and the fact that Jack is far more credible than I am. I tried it once and was thought of as a madwoman, while Jack got sympathy for having to put up with my incoherent ravings.

There is no clock in my bedroom and I have no watch, but I've become quite adept at judging the time. It's easier in wintertime when night falls early but in the summer I have no real idea of the exact time Jack comes back from work—it could be anything from seven to ten for all I know. Bizarre as it seems, I'm always comforted by the sound of his return. Since the time he didn't come back for three days, I have a fear of starving to death. He did it to teach me a lesson. If I have learnt anything about Jack, it is that everything he does and everything he says is calculated down to the last full stop. He prides himself on uttering only the truth, and enjoys that I am the only one who understands the meaning behind his words.

The comment he made at our dinner party, when he said that Millie coming to live with us would add another dimension to our lives, is just one example of his *double entendres*. His other comment, that it was the knowledge I would do anything for Millie which made him realise I was the woman he'd been looking for all his life, another.

Tonight, he comes home, by my estimation, at about eight o'clock. I hear the front door opening, then closing behind him, his footsteps in the hall, the sound of his keys being thrown down on the hall table. I imagine him taking his phone from his pocket and, seconds later, I hear the rattle as he puts it down next to the keys. There is a pause, then the sound of the door to the cloakroom opening as he hangs up his jacket. I know enough about him to know he'll go straight to the kitchen and pour himself a whisky, but I only know this because my room lies above the kitchen and I've learnt to distinguish the different sounds as his evening begins.

Sure enough, a minute or so later—after he has looked through the post maybe—I hear him walk into the kitchen, open the cupboard door, take a glass out, close the cupboard door, walk across to the freezer, open the door, open the drawer, remove the ice-cube tray, crack it to release the ice cubes, drop two into the glass, one after the other. I hear him turn on the tap, refill the tray, put it back in the drawer, close the drawer, close the door, pick up the bottle of whisky from where it stands on the side, unscrew the cap, pour a shot of whisky into his glass, put the cap back on, replace the bottle on the side, pick up the glass, swirl the whisky around with the ice. I don't actually hear the sound of him taking his first sip but I imagine he does because a few seconds always pass before I hear him walking back across the kitchen floor, out into the hall and into his study. It could be that he'll bring me up some food during the evening but after all I ate at lunch-time, I'm not worried if he doesn't.

There is no regularity to the meals he brings me. I may get one in the morning or one in the evening, or none at all. If he brings me breakfast, there may be cereals and a glass of juice, or a piece of fruit and water. In the evenings, it may be a three-course meal and a glass of wine, or a sandwich and some milk. Jack knows there is nothing more comforting than routine so he denies me any semblance of it. Although he doesn't know it, he is doing me a favour. Without routine, there is no risk of me becoming institutionalised and unable to think for myself. And I must think for myself.

It's horrendous to be dependent on somebody for the mere basics of life, although thanks to the tap in my tiny bathroom I'll never die of thirst. I could die of boredom though, be-cause there's nothing to relieve the empty days that stretch before me into infinity. The dinner parties I used to dread so much are now a welcome diversion. I even enjoy the chal-lenge of Jack's increasingly exacting demands about what we will serve our guests to eat because when I triumph, as I did last Saturday, the taste of success makes my existence bear-able. Such is my life.

Maybe half an hour or so after he arrived home, I hear his footsteps on the stairs, then on the landing. The key turns in the lock. The door opens and he stands in the doorway, my handsome, psychopathic husband. I look hopefully at his hands but he isn't carrying a tray.

'We've received an email from Millie's school, saying they'd like to speak to us.' He watches me for a moment. 'What could they possibly want to talk to us about, I wonder?'

I feel myself go cold. 'I have no idea,' I say, glad he can't see the way my heart has started beating faster.

'Well, we'll just have to go and find out, won't we? Janice apparently told Mrs Goodrich that we planned to visit again this Sunday and she suggested we go down a little earlier so we can have a chat.' He pauses. 'I do hope everything is all right.'

'I'm sure it is,' I say with more calm than I feel.

'It had better be.'

He leaves, locking the door behind him. Although I'm glad that Mrs Goodrich sent the email, because it means I'll get to see Millie again, uneasiness settles in. We've never been summoned to the school before. Millie knows she mustn't say a word, but sometimes I wonder if she really understands. She has no idea of how much is at stake, because how could I ever tell her?

The need to find a solution to the nightmare we are caught up in—the nightmare that I let us be caught up in—presses down on me and I force myself to take deep breaths, not to panic. I have almost four months, I remind myself, four months to find that window of opportunity and to somehow get me and Millie through it by myself, because there is no one to help us. The only people who might have been able to—because some primal maternal or paternal instinct may have told them I was in trouble—are now on the other side of the world, encouraged to move there even more rapidly than they'd intended by Jack.

He is so clever, so very clever. Everything I have ever told him, he has used against me. I wish I'd never told him of my parents' horror when Millie was born. Or how they were counting the days until I fulfilled my promise of having

Millie to live with me so that they could finally move to New Zealand. It allowed him to play on their dread that I would somehow renege on the promise I'd made and that they would end up having to look after Millie themselves. The weekend he asked me to take him to see my parents, it wasn't to ask my father for my hand in marriage but rather to tell him that I'd been talking about Millie going to New Zealand with them, as I wanted to get married and start a family of my own. When my father had almost died of shock, Jack suggested it might be an idea for them to emigrate sooner rather than later, effectively erasing the only people who might have been able to help me.

I sit down on the bed, wondering how I'm going to get through the rest of the evening and then the night. Sleep won't come, not when there's the meeting with Mrs Goodrich hanging over me. Looking at it objectively, it would be the perfect opportunity to blurt out the truth, that Jack is keeping me prisoner, that he means untold harm to Millie, and beg her to help me, to call the police. But I have already been there, I have already done that, and I know to my cost that at this very minute Jack will be planning my downfall should I so much as breathe differently during the meeting. Not only will I end up humiliated and more desperate than I already am, Jack will make sure to exact his revenge. I hold my hands out in front of me and the shaking that I can't control tells me what I've only just begun to realise but what Jack has known all along—that fear is the best deterrent of all.

PAST

'What do you mean?' I asked as I sat on the edge of the bed in our hotel room, wondering why, when he had given me the choice of going to the hospital to see Millie or carrying on to Thailand with him, I had believed, despite everything that had happened since our wedding, that he was still a good man.

'Exactly what I said—there is no housekeeper.'

I sighed, too tired for his rigmaroles. 'What is it you want to tell me?'

'A story. A story about a young boy. Would you like to hear it?'

'If it means that you'll let me leave, yes, I'd love to hear it.'

'Good.' He drew up the one chair in the room and sat down in front of me.

'There was once a young boy who lived in a country far, far away from here with his mother and father. When he was very young, the boy feared the strong and powerful father, and loved the mother. But when he saw that the mother was weak and useless and unable to protect him from the father, the boy began to despise her, and rejoiced in the look of terror in her eyes as the father dragged her down to the cellar to be locked in with the rats.

'The knowledge that the father could instil such terror into another human being turned the boy's fear of him into admiration and he began to emulate him. Soon, the sound of his mother's screams coming up through the floorboards became music to his ears, and the smell of her fear the richest perfume. Such was the effect it had on him that he began to crave it, so that when the father left him in charge the boy would take the mother down to the cellar, her pleas for mercy as she begged him not to leave her there only serving to excite him. And afterwards, as he drank in the sound of her fear and breathed in the smell of it, he wished he could keep her there for eternity.

'One night, when the boy was about thirteen years old, the mother managed to escape from the basement while the father was working outside in the allotment. But the boy knew that if she left, he would never hear the sound of her fear again so he hit her, to stop her from leaving. And when she screamed, he hit her again. And again. And the more she screamed, the more he hit her and he found he couldn't stop, even when she fell to the ground. And, as he looked down at her smashed and bloodied face, he thought she had never looked more beautiful.

'The father, brought by the mother's screams, arrived and pulled the boy off her. But it was too late, because she was already dead. The father was angry and hit the boy and the boy hit him back. When the police came, the boy told them that his father had killed the mother and that he had tried to protect her. So the father went to prison and the boy was glad.

'As the boy grew older, he began to crave someone of his own, someone in whom he could instil fear whenever he wanted, however he wanted, someone he could keep hidden away, someone nobody would ever miss. He knew it wouldn't be easy to find such a person, but he was convinced that if he looked hard enough, he eventually would. And, while he looked, he searched for a way to satisfy his cravings. So do you know what he did?' I shook my head numbly. 'He became a lawyer, specialising in cases of domestic violence. And then do you know what he did?' He leant forward and put his mouth close to my ear. 'He married you, Grace.'

I found I could hardly breathe. All the time he'd been speaking, I hadn't wanted to believe he was the boy in the story, but, now, a terrible shaking took hold of me. As the room swam before my eyes, he sat back and stretched his legs out in front of him, a satisfied look on his face. 'Now, tell me, did you enjoy that story?'

'No,' I said, my voice trembling. 'But I listened to it, so can I go now?' I made to stand up, but he pushed me back down.

'I'm afraid not.'

Tears of fright spilled from my eyes. 'You promised.'

'Did I?'

'Please. Please let me go. I won't tell anyone what you just told me, I promise.'

'Of course you would.'

I shook my head. 'No, no, I wouldn't.'

He was silent for a moment, as if he was considering what I'd said. 'The thing is, Grace, I can't let you go because I need you.' Seeing the fear in my eyes, he crouched down next to me and drew air in through his nose. 'Perfect,' he breathed.

There was something about the way he said it that terrified me and I shrank away from him.

'Don't worry, I'm not going to hurt you,' he said, reaching out and stroking my cheek. 'That isn't why you're here. But let's get back to the story—so, while I was waiting to find someone all of my own, I cloaked myself in respectability. First, I looked for a perfect name and came up with Angel. I actually considered calling myself Gabriel Angel but I thought it might be going a step too far so I had a little think, did a little investigating, discovered that the good men in films are often called Jack and hey presto! Jack Angel was born. Then I found myself the perfect job.' He shook his head in amusement. 'The irony of it never ceases to amaze me—Jack Angel, defender of battered women. But I also needed a perfect life—when a man gets to forty with no sign of a wife in sight people begin to ask questions—so you can imagine how I felt when I saw you and Millie together in the park, my perfect wife and my . . .'

'Never!' I spat. 'I will never be your perfect wife. If you think I'm going to stay married to you after what you've told me, have your children—'

He burst out laughing, cutting me off. 'Children! Do you know what the hardest thing I've ever done is? It wasn't killing my mother or seeing my father go off to prison—both those things were easy, a pleasure even. No, the hardest thing I've ever done is have sex with you. How could you not have guessed, how could you not have seen through my excuses? How could you not have realised when I did finally have sex with you that I found it an effort, disgusting, unnatural? That's why I disappeared last night. I knew you'd be expecting me to make love to you—after all, it was our wedding night—and the thought of having to go through with it just to keep up appearances was more than I could bear. So you see, I am not expecting you to have my children. When people begin asking, we will tell them that we are experiencing problems, and after that they will ask no more out of politeness. I need you to be my wife, but in name only. You are not my reward, Grace, Millie is.'

I stared at him. 'Millie?'

'Yes, Millie. She fits all my requirements perfectly. In another sixteen months, she'll be mine and I'll finally be able to have what I've had to deny myself for so long. Nobody, only you, will ever miss her. Not that I intend to kill her—I made that mistake once before.'

I leapt to my feet. 'Do you honestly think I'll let you harm a hair on Millie's head?'

'If I really wanted to, do you honestly think you'd be able to stop me?' I ran towards the door. 'It's locked,' he said, sounding bored.

'Help!' I yelled, hammering on the door with my fist. 'Help!'

'Do that one more time and you'll never see Millie again!' he barked. 'Come back and sit down.'

Beside myself with fear, I carried on hammering on the door, screaming for help.

'I'm warning you, Grace. Remember what I told you about putting Millie in an asylum? Do you know how easily I can arrange it?' He snapped his fingers together. 'This fast.'

I spun round to face him. 'My parents would never let that happen!'

'Do you really see them rushing over from their cosy lives in New Zealand to rescue her and take her back to live with them? I think not. There is no one, Grace, no one to save Millie, not even you.'

'I'm her legal guardian!' I cried.

'So am I, and I have the paper to prove it.'

'I would never agree for her to be put away!'

'But what if you were also proved to be of unsound mind? As your husband, I would then be responsible for both you and Millie and could do as I wished.' He indicated the door. 'Be my guest—carry on banging on the door and screaming for help. It lays the foundation for your madness.'

'You're the one who's mad,' I hissed.

'Obviously.' He stood up, walked over to the bedside table, yanked the phone from its socket, took a penknife from his pocket and cut through the cord. 'I'm going to give you a little time by yourself to mull over what I've said and, when I come back, we'll talk again. Come and sit on the bed.'

'No.'

'Don't be tiresome.'

'You're not keeping me locked up in here!'

He walked over to where I was standing. 'I don't want to have to hurt you, for the simple reason that I might not be able to stop. But I will if I have to.' He raised his arms and, thinking he was going to hit me, I flinched. 'And if you were to die, where would that leave Millie?'

I felt his hands on my shoulders and went rigid with fear, expecting them to move to my neck. Instead, he manoeuvred me roughly to the bed and pushed me onto it. As relief washed over me that he hadn't strangled me, that I was still alive, the sound of the door opening spurred me from the bed. But, before I could get there, he slipped through it and, as it closed behind him, I beat my fists against it, calling for him to let me out. Hearing his footsteps disappearing down the corridor, I yelled for help over and over again. But nobody came and, distraught, I sank to the floor and wept.

It took me a while to pull myself together. I got to my feet and went over to the sliding doors that led onto the balcony, but no matter how hard I tugged on them I couldn't get them to open. Craning my neck, I looked out over the balcony, but all I could see was blue sky and the roofs of some buildings. Our room was on the sixth floor at the end of a long corridor, which meant there was no neighbouring room on one side. Going over to the other wall, I knocked on it hard several times, but, when there was no corresponding knock back, I guessed that most people were out sightseeing, because it was mid-afternoon.

Needing to do something, I turned my attention to our cases on the bed and began to rummage through them, looking for anything that would help me get out of the room. But there was nothing. Both my tweezers and nail scissors had disappeared. I had no idea how Jack had managed to get them out of my wash bag without me seeing but as it had been in the hold, in my case, I could only presume he had removed them before we left England, probably at the hotel while I'd been in the bathroom. Fresh tears sprang to my eyes at the thought that less than twenty-four hours earlier, I'd been looking forward to starting married life with no inkling of the horror ahead.

Fighting down the panic that threatened to overwhelm me, I forced myself to think rationally about what I could do. Until I heard someone coming back to the room next door, there was little point trying to attract their attention by knocking on the wall. I thought about pushing a note under the door and out into the hall in the hope that someone coming back to a room further down the corridor would see it and be curious enough to come and read it. But my pen had gone from my bag, as had my eye pencils and lipsticks. Jack had pre-empted my every move.

I began to search the room frantically, looking for something—anything—that could help. But there was nothing. Defeated, I sat down on the bed. If I hadn't been able to hear the sounds of doors opening and closing elsewhere in the hotel, I would have thought it deserted, yet comforting though those sounds were, the sense of disorientation I felt was frightening. I found it hard to believe that what was happening to me was real and it crossed my mind that maybe I was caught up in some warped television show where people were put into terrible situations while the world watched to see how they coped.

For some reason, imagining that I was watching myself on screen, and that millions of people were also watching me, allowed me to take a step back and look at my options

objectively. I knew that if I thought about the terrible story
Jack had told me I wouldn't be able to hang on to the relative
calm I had managed to achieve. So, instead, I lay down on the
bed and channelled my thoughts towards what I would do
when Jack came back, what I would say to him, how I would
act. I could feel myself falling asleep and, although I tried to
fight it, the next time I opened my eyes it was already dark
and I realised I had slept for some time. The noise of the busy
nightlife from the streets below told me it was the evening
and I got up from the bed and went over to the door.

I don't know why—maybe because I was still drowsy—but
I found myself instinctively turning the handle. When I realised that it turned easily, and that the door wasn't locked, I
was so shocked it took me a while to react. As I stood there,
trying to work it out, it dawned on me that I hadn't actually
heard him lock the door. I had simply presumed that he had
so I hadn't tried to open it. Nor, I realised, had he said that
he was going to lock me in; I had come to that conclusion all
on my own. When I remembered how I had panicked, how
I had hammered on the door and knocked on the wall, I felt
both stupid and ashamed, imagining Jack laughing as he
walked away.

Tears of fury pricked my eyelids. Blinking them back an-
grily, I reminded myself that as he had my passport and purse,
I was still, to all intents and purposes, a prisoner. But at least
I could get out of the room.

Opening the door quietly, terrified that I might find Jack
standing outside waiting to pounce, I forced myself to look
out into the corridor. Finding it empty, I turned back into
the room, found my shoes, retrieved my handbag from the
floor and left. As I ran towards the lift, the thought that I

might find Jack standing there when the lift doors opened made me decide to take the stairs. I ran down them two at a time, hardly able to believe that I had wasted precious hours thinking I was locked in. When I got to the lobby and found it busy with people, the sense of relief was incredible. Taking a deep breath to steady myself, I walked quickly over to the reception desk, where Jack and I had checked in only hours before, glad that my nightmare was over.

'Good evening, can I help you?' The young girl behind the desk smiled at me.

'Yes, please, I would like you to telephone the British Embassy,' I said, forcing myself to speak calmly. 'I need to get back to England and I've lost my passport and money.'

'Oh, I'm so sorry.' The young woman looked contrite. 'Could I ask you for your room number please?'

'I'm afraid I don't know it, but it's on the sixth floor, my name is Grace Angel and I checked in earlier this afternoon with my husband.'

'Room 601,' she confirmed, checking her screen. 'May I ask where you lost your passport? Was it at the airport?'

'No, I had it here in the hotel.' I gave a shaky laugh. 'I haven't actually lost it, my husband has it, and my purse, he took them and now I can't get back to England.' I looked at her pleadingly. 'I really need you to help me.'

'Where is your husband, Mrs Angel?'

'I have no idea.' I wanted to tell her that he had locked me in the room, but I stopped myself just in time, reminding myself that I'd only thought he had. 'He left a couple of hours ago, taking my passport and money with him. Look, could you phone the British Embassy for me, please?'

'If you would just hold on a moment while I speak to my

manager.' Giving me an encouraging smile, she went over to speak to a man standing a little further away. As she explained my problem to him, he looked over at me and I gave him a watery smile, aware for the first time of how unkempt I must look, wishing I had thought to change out of my crumpled travelling clothes. Nodding his head as he listened, he smiled reassuringly at me, and picking up the phone, began dialling.

'Perhaps you would like to sit down while we sort things out,' the young woman suggested, coming back towards me.

'No, it's fine—anyway, I'll probably need to speak to the Embassy myself.' Realising that the man had hung up, I went over to him. 'What did they say?' I asked.

'It's all being sorted out, Mrs Angel. Why don't you take a seat while you're waiting?'

'Is somebody coming from the Embassy, then?'

'If you would just like to take a seat, perhaps?'

'Grace?' Spinning round, I saw Jack hurrying towards me. 'It's all right, Grace, I'm here.'

Fear coursed through me. 'Get away from me!' I cried. I turned to the young woman who was looking at me in alarm. 'Help me, please, this man is dangerous!'

'It's all right, Grace,' Jack said soothingly. He gave the manager a rueful smile. 'Thank you for letting me know she was here. Now, Grace,' he continued, as if he was speaking to a child, 'why don't we go back up to our room so that you can have a sleep? You'll feel much better once you've rested.'

'I don't need a sleep, all I need is to get back to England!' Aware of people watching us curiously, I made an effort to lower my voice. 'Give me my passport, Jack, and my purse and mobile.' I held out my hand. 'Now.'

He groaned. 'Why do you always have to do this?'

'I want my passport, Jack.'

He shook his head. 'I gave your passport back to you at the airport, as I always do, and you put it in your bag, as you always do.'

'You know very well it isn't there.' I put my bag on the counter and opened it. 'Look,' I said to the woman, my voice trembling with emotion. I shook the contents out onto the counter. 'It isn't in there and neither is my purse. He took them and . . .' I stopped and stared as my passport and purse spilled from my bag, followed by my make-up bag, hairbrush, a packet of wet wipes, a bottle of pills I had never seen before and my mobile.

'You put them back!' I cried accusingly to Jack. 'You came back while I was asleep and replaced them!' I turned to the manager. 'They weren't there before, I swear. He took them, and then he went out, making me believe I was locked in the room.'

The manager looked puzzled. 'But you can open the door from the inside.'

'Yes, but he made me think I'd been locked in!' Even as I said it I could hear how hysterical I sounded.

'I think I know what happened.' Jack picked up the bottle of pills and shook it. 'You forgot to take your medication, didn't you?'

'I'm not on medication, they're not mine, you must have put them there!' I cried.

'That's enough, Grace.' Jack's voice was firm. 'You're being ridiculous!'

'Is there anything we can do to help?' the manager offered. 'A glass of water, perhaps?'

'Yes, you can call the police! This man is a dangerous criminal!' There was a shocked silence. 'It's true!' I added desperately, hearing people murmuring behind me. 'He killed his own mother. Call the police, please!'

'This is exactly what I warned you about,' sighed Jack, exchanging a look with the manager. 'It's not the first time this has happened, unfortunately.' He put his hand under my elbow. 'Come on, Grace, let's go.'

I shrugged him off. 'Will you please just call the police!' The young woman who I had spoken to first looked uneasily at me. 'Please!' I begged. 'I'm telling the truth!'

'Look, Grace.' This time Jack sounded exasperated. 'If you really want to call the police, go ahead. But do you remember what happened last time? We couldn't leave the country until they had investigated your claims and, when they realised they were on a wild goose chase, they threatened to sue you for wasting police time. And that was in America. I don't think the police here will be quite so understanding.'

I stared at him. 'What last time?'

'I really do not advise you to involve the police,' the manager said worriedly. 'Unless, of course, there is good reason to.'

'There's a very good reason to! This man is dangerous!'

'If Mrs Angel really wants to leave, perhaps we could call a taxi to take her to the airport now that she has found her passport,' the young woman suggested nervously.

I looked at her in relief. 'Yes, yes, please do that!' I began stuffing my things back into my bag. 'Please call one immediately.'

'Are you really going to go through with this?' Jack asked resignedly.

'Definitely!'

'Then there's nothing more I can do.' He turned to the manager. 'I really must apologise for all this fuss. Perhaps one of your staff would escort my wife up to our room so that she can collect her case.'

'Of course. Kiko, would you please take Mrs Angel up to her room while I call for a taxi.'

'Thank you,' I said gratefully, as I followed Kiko to the lift, my legs trembling so much I had difficulty walking. 'Thank you so much.'

'You're welcome, Mrs Angel,' she said politely.

'I know you probably think that I'm mad but I can assure you I'm not,' I went on, feeling I owed her some kind of explanation.

'It's fine, Mrs Angel, you don't have to explain.' She smiled, pressing the button for the lift.

'You must call the police,' I told her. 'Once I'm gone you must call the police and tell them that my husband, Mr Angel, is a dangerous criminal.'

'I'm sure our manager will sort everything out.'

The lift arrived and I followed her into it, knowing that she didn't believe for one minute that Jack was dangerous, or a criminal. But it didn't matter, because as soon as I was in the taxi I intended phoning the police myself.

We arrived on the sixth floor and I followed her down the corridor to our room. I took the key from my bag, opened the door and stood back, suddenly apprehensive about going in. But I needn't have worried; everything was just as I'd left it. I went over to my case and rummaged through it for some clean clothes.

'I won't be a moment,' I said, disappearing into the bathroom. 'I'm just going to change.'

I undressed hurriedly, gave myself a quick wash and got dressed again. As I rolled my dirty clothes into a ball, I felt physically refreshed and mentally stronger. Not wanting to delay a moment longer, I opened the door. But, before I could step out of the bathroom, a hand shot out and pushed me back inside while another clapped over my mouth, stifling the scream that tore through me.

'Did you enjoy that little scenario I set up for you?' Jack asked, his face inches from mine. 'I did, immensely. And, even better, I've managed to kill two birds with one stone. First and foremost, you've just proved in front of dozens of people that you're unstable—the manager is, at this very moment, writing an account of your behaviour earlier on so there is a record of it—and, secondly, you have hopefully learnt that I will always be one step ahead of you.' He paused a moment to let his words sink in. 'Now, this is what we're going to do. I'm going to take my hand off your mouth and if you so much as whimper I'll force-feed you enough pills to kill you and make your death look like the suicide of an unbalanced young woman. If that were to happen, as Millie's only surviving guardian, I would, of course, keep the promise we made her and bring her to live in our lovely new house—except that you won't be there and who would protect her? Have I made myself clear?' I nodded mutely. 'Good.'

He removed his hand from my mouth and, dragging me out of the bathroom, threw me onto the bed. 'Now, I need you to listen and listen well. Each time you try to escape, whether by hammering on the door, or speaking to someone, or trying to make a run for it, it is Millie who will pay. For example, because of your attempt to escape today, we won't be going to see her the weekend after we get back, as she is expecting us to do. If you do anything stupid again tomorrow, we won't be going the following week either. And so on. We'll invent a particularly nasty stomach bug that you picked up here in Thailand to excuse our absence, a stomach bug that will go on for as many weeks as necessary. So, if you want to see Millie again within a reasonable amount of time, I suggest you do exactly as I say.'

I began to shake uncontrollably, not only at the menace in his voice but also because of the terrible realisation that in coming back to the room to fetch my case, I'd lost my chance to escape from him. I hadn't needed my case, I could easily have left without it, yet when Jack had mentioned it, it had seemed perfectly reasonable to come up and fetch it. If he hadn't asked somebody to accompany me I might have questioned his motives in making me come back to the room. And if I had realised sooner that the door wasn't locked, if I hadn't fallen asleep, he wouldn't have been able to replace my passport, mobile and purse.

'You're wondering if the outcome would have been different if you had acted differently, aren't you?' he said, amused. 'Let me put you out of your misery—the answer is no, the outcome would have been exactly the same. Had you gone down to the lobby before I'd had the chance to replace your passport, purse and phone, I would have simply put them in your case once you'd left the room—you'll have realised by now that I was watching you the whole time—and suggested, in front of everyone, that you had simply mislaid them. Then I would have had the manager escort you back here to look for them. The thing is, I know you, Grace, I know how you will act, what you will say. I even know that before we leave Thailand, you'll try and escape again, which would be very foolish. But you'll learn, in the end, because you'll have to.'

'Never,' I sobbed. 'I'll never give in to you.'

'Well, we'll see about that. Now, here's what we're going to do. We're going to get some sleep and tomorrow morning we're going to go down to breakfast and, as we pass the reception desk, you'll apologise for the fuss you caused this evening and say that of course you don't want to go back to England. After breakfast, where you'll look lovingly into my eyes, I'll take some nice photographs of you outside the hotel so that we can show all our friends how happy you were here. Then, while I go out to take care of some business, you, my darling, will sunbathe on the balcony so that by the time we go back to England, you'll have a lovely tan.' He began to unlace his shoes. 'After all that excitement, I suddenly feel quite tired.'

'I'm not sleeping in the same bed as you!'

'Then sleep on the floor. And don't bother trying to escape, it really isn't worth it.'

I dragged a cover from the bed and sat down on the floor, wrapping the cover around myself, numb with fear. Although instinct told me to escape as soon as any opportunity came, reason told me that it would be much easier to get away from him and to get him put away forever if I waited until we were back in England. If I tried again here in Thailand, and failed, I hated to think what he might do to me. He thought he knew me, he thought he knew how I would act, he had predicted that I would try to escape again. The only thing I could do was wrong-foot him, make him think that I had given in, that I had given up. Much as I wanted to get away from him, my main priority had to be getting back to England, getting back to Millie.

PRESENT

As we drive to Millie's school on Sunday morning, I'm so stressed about why Mrs Goodrich has asked to see us that it's a relief Jack didn't bring me breakfast before leaving. He didn't bring any food yesterday either, which means I've had nothing to eat since lunch in the restaurant on Friday. I don't know why he chose not to feed me but it was probably because Esther helped me finish my dessert, which he would consider as cheating, knowing all too well that I wouldn't have been able to eat it after the reference he made to Millie's bedroom. In the sick world that Jack has created for me, there are many things I'm not allowed to do and wasting food is one of them.

My heart starts hammering as soon as we're ushered into Mrs Goodrich's office, especially when Janice sits down with us, her face grave. We haven't seen Millie yet, so I presume that she doesn't know Jack and I are already here. But I needn't have worried; all they want to tell us is that because she's been having trouble sleeping, which makes her irritable during the day, the school doctor has prescribed something to calm her before bedtime.

'Do you mean sleeping pills?' I ask.

'Yes,' Mrs Goodrich says. 'To be administered—with your permission, of course—as and when she needs them.'

'I don't have a problem with that, do you, darling?' Jack asks, turning to me. 'If it's in Millie's interest.'

'No, not if the doctor thinks she needs them,' I say slowly. 'It's just that I don't particularly want her to become dependent on drugs to help her sleep.'

'He hasn't prescribed anything too strong, I hope?' Jack enquires.

'No, not at all, they can be bought over the counter.' Mrs Goodrich opens a folder on the desk in front of her, takes out a piece of paper and hands it to him.

'Thank you. I'll just make a note of the name, if you don't mind.'

'I actually gave her one last night because she seemed particularly disturbed,' Janice says as he types the name of the pills into his phone. 'I hope that was all right.'

'Of course,' I say, reassuringly. 'You already have my written permission to take any action you see fit in my absence.'

'What we are wondering,' Mrs Goodrich goes on, 'is if

there is any reason why Millie should suddenly have trouble sleeping.' She pauses delicately. 'Did she seem anxious, or un-happy, when you visited last weekend, for example?'

Jack shakes his head. 'She just seemed her usual self to me.'

'To me too—although she was a little put out that we didn't go to the hotel for lunch,' I say. 'For some reason, it's her fa-vourite place, although Jack and I prefer the restaurant by the lake. But she soon rallied round.'

Mrs Goodrich exchanges a glance with Janice. 'We rather wondered if it's because she hasn't seen the house yet,' she says.

'I doubt it,' I say quickly. 'I mean, she understands that we prefer her to see it once it's completely finished rather than with half of it covered in dust sheets and ladders—unless she mentioned something to you, darling?'

'Nothing at all,' Jack confirms. 'But if it's bothering her, I'm perfectly happy for her to come and see it as soon as her bed-room's finished. The only danger is that she'll probably fall in love with it and won't want to leave,' he adds with a laugh.

'I think it's probably the thought of leaving here that is weighing heavily on her mind,' I suggest, ignoring the way my heart has suddenly plummeted. 'After all, it has been her home for the last seven years and she's been very, very happy here.'

'You're right, of course.' Janice nods. 'I should have thought of that.'

'And she's particularly attached to you. Perhaps you could reassure her that you'll always keep in touch, that you'll con-tinue to see her once she's left,' I go on. 'If you want to, that is.'

'Of course I do! Millie has become like a little sister to me.'

'Well, if you can tell her that you'll come and see her regularly once she's moved in with us, I'm sure that will be enough to allay any fears she may have.'

Jack smiles, understanding only too well what I've just done. 'And if Millie says anything, anything at all, no matter how insignificant it may seem, that gives you cause for concern, please let us know,' he says. 'All we want is for Millie to be happy.'

'Well, may I say once again how fortunate Millie is to have you both,' says Mrs Goodrich.

'It is we who are fortunate,' Jack corrects modestly. 'In fact, with both Grace and Millie in my life, I count myself as the most fortunate man in the world.' He gets to his feet. 'Now, perhaps we can take Millie to lunch. Although she'll probably be disappointed that we won't be going to the hotel—I've reserved a table at a new restaurant. It's meant to have the most wonderful food.'

I don't bother getting my hopes up. If Jack is taking us somewhere new, it means he's already checked it out.

'We go hotel today?' Millie asks hopefully, when we go to fetch her.

'Actually, there's a new restaurant I'd like to take you to,' Jack says.

'I like hotel best,' she scowls.

'Another day. Come on, let's go.'

Millie's face is glum as we make our way to the car, the frustration of not being able to go to the hotel evident. I manage to give her hand a squeeze as we get into the car and, understanding that I'm telling her to be careful, she makes an effort to perk up a bit.

During lunch, Jack asks Millie why she can't sleep at night

and she tells him that she can hear flies buzzing around in her head. He asks if the pill that Janice had given her the night before had helped and she says that it did, that she slept very well, 'like baby', so he tells her that we've given our permission for her to carry on taking them whenever she needs them. She asks if Molly has come back yet and, because my throat has suddenly tightened, as it always does when I think of Molly, it is Jack who tells her gently that it is unlikely she will, that she was probably found by a little girl who doesn't know that she's a runaway and loves her very much. He promises that as soon as she moves in with us, he'll take her to choose a puppy of her own and, when Millie's face lights up with happiness, the urge to grab a knife off the table and stick it deep into his heart is overwhelming. Sensing this perhaps, Jack reaches out and covers my hand with his, making the waitress who has come to take away our plates smile at this display of affection between us.

When we've finished our desserts, Millie says she needs to go to the toilet.

'Go on, then,' says Jack.

Millie looks at me. 'You come, Grace?'

I stand up. 'Yes, I need to go too.'

'We'll all go,' says Jack.

We follow him along to the toilets, which are exactly as I thought they'd be, a single one for women and a single one for men, the two doors side by side. The Ladies' is engaged, so we wait on either side of Jack for it to become vacant. A lady comes out and Jack's hand grips my elbow tightly as a reminder that I'm not to tell her my husband is a psychopath.

As Millie disappears into the cubicle, the lady turns and smiles at us, and I know that all she sees is a charming young couple standing so close to each other that they must be very much in love, which makes me realise, once again, how hopeless my situation is. I'm beginning to despair of anyone ever questioning the absolute perfectness of our lives and, whenever we are with friends, I marvel at their stupidity in believing that Jack and I never argue, that we agree about absolutely everything, that I, an intelligent thirty-two-year-old woman with no children, could be content to sit at home all day and play house.

I long for somebody to ask questions, to be suspicious. My thoughts turn immediately to Esther and I wonder if I should be more careful what I wish for. If Jack becomes suspicious of her constant questioning, he may decide that I've encouraged her in some way and my life will be even less worth living. Were it not for Millie, I would gladly exchange death for this new life that I lead. But were it not for Millie, I wouldn't be here. As Jack has already told me, it is Millie he wants, not me.

PAST

That morning in Thailand, the morning after the night I dis-covered I'd married a monster, I was in no hurry for Jack to wake up because I knew that once he did I was going to have to start playing the role of my life. I had spent most of the long night preparing myself mentally, accepting that if I was to get back to England quickly and safely, I was going to have to pretend to be a broken and frightened woman. I wasn't worried about pretending to be frightened, because I was. Pretending to be broken would be much harder, simply because it was in my nature to fight back. But, as Jack had predicted that I would try to escape again before we left Thailand, I was determined not to. It was important that he thought I had already given up.

Hearing him stir, I huddled further into my blanket and pretended to be asleep, hoping to gain a little more respite. I heard him get out of bed and walk over to where I was sitting slumped against the wall. I could feel him looking down at me. My skin started to crawl and my heart was beating so fast I was sure he could smell my fear. After a moment or two, he moved away, but it was only when I heard the bathroom door opening and the sound of the shower running that I opened my eyes.

'I knew you were pretending to be asleep,' he said, making me cry out in alarm, because he was standing right next to me. 'Come on, get up, you've got a lot of apologising to do this morning, remember.'

As I showered and dressed with him looking on, I took comfort from what he had said the previous evening, that he wasn't interested in me sexually.

'Good,' he said, nodding approvingly at the dress I'd chosen to wear. 'Now, put a smile on your face.'

'When we're downstairs,' I muttered, playing for time.

'Now!' His voice was firm. 'I want you to look at me as if you love me.'

Swallowing hard, I turned slowly towards him, thinking I wouldn't be able to do it, but when I saw the tenderness on his face as he looked back at me, I felt a bewildering sense of displacement, as if everything that had happened in the last forty-eight hours had been a dream. I couldn't hide the longing I felt and, when he smiled lovingly at me, I couldn't help but smile back.

'That's better,' he said. 'Make sure you keep it there during breakfast.'

Appalled at myself for having forgotten even for a minute what he was, my skin burnt with embarrassment.

Noticing, he laughed. 'Think of it this way, Grace—as you obviously still find me attractive, it'll be easier for you to play the loving wife.'

Tears of shame pricked my eyes and I turned away, hating that his physical appearance was so at odds with the evil inside him. If he was able to fool me, if he was able, even for a few seconds, to make me forget what I knew about him, how would I ever be able to convince people that he was a wolf in sheep's clothing?

We took the lift down to the lobby and, as we passed the reception desk, Jack steered me towards the manager and stood with his arm around me while I apologised for my behaviour the previous evening, explaining that because of the time change I had forgotten to take my medication at the prescribed time. I was aware of Kiko watching me silently from behind the counter and I couldn't help hoping that something in her—some kind of female empathy perhaps—would recognise that my distress the night before had been genuine. Maybe she'd had misgivings when Jack had suddenly appeared in the room when I'd been changing in the bathroom and told her he would take it from there. As I finished my apology, I glanced at her, willing her to understand that I was playing a role and to call the Embassy after all. But, as before, she wouldn't meet my eyes.

The manager brushed aside my apologies and escorted us out to the terrace himself, giving us a table in the sunshine. Although I wasn't hungry, I made myself eat, aware that I needed to keep my strength up, and while we ate Jack kept up a steady stream of conversation, telling me—for the benefit of the people sitting at nearby tables—all the things we would be doing that day. In reality, we did none of them. Once breakfast was over, Jack took me along the road to the five-star hotel I had seen from the taxi the previous day and, after taking several photos of me standing in front of the entrance, where I used happy memories of Millie to put the smile that he demanded on my face, he walked me back to our hotel room.

'I'd like to phone Millie,' I said, as he closed the door behind us. 'Could I have my phone, please?'

He shook his head regretfully. 'I'm afraid not.'

'I promised Mum I would phone,' I insisted, 'and I want to know how Millie is.'

'And I want your parents to think that you're having such a wonderful time with me on our honeymoon that all thoughts of Millie have gone right out of your head.'

'Please, Jack.' I hated the pleading tone in my voice, but I was desperate to know that Millie was all right and surprisingly desperate to hear Mum's voice, to know that the world I once knew still existed.

'No.'

'I hate you,' I said, through gritted teeth.

'Of course you do,' he said. 'Now, I'm going out for a while and you're going to wait here on the balcony so that you have a lovely tan to go home with. So make sure you have everything you need because you won't be able to get back into the room once I've gone.'

It took me a moment to understand. 'You're not seriously intending to lock me on the balcony!'

'That's right.'

'Why can't I stay in the room?'

'Because I can't lock you in.'

I looked at him in dismay. 'What if I need to go to the toilet?'

'You won't be able to, so I suggest you go now.'

'But how long will you be gone?'

'Two or three hours. Four, maybe. And just in case you're thinking of calling for help from the balcony, I advise you not to. I'll be around, watching and listening. So don't do anything stupid, Grace, I'm warning you.'

The way he said it made a chill run down my spine, yet once he'd left, it was hard not to give in to the temptation to stand on the balcony and scream for help at the top of my voice. I tried to imagine what would happen if I did and came to the conclusion that even if people did come running, Jack would too, armed with a convincing story about my mental state. And although someone might decide to look further into my claims that I was being held a prisoner and that Jack was a murderer, it could be weeks before anything could be proved.

I could repeat the story he'd told me and eventually the authorities might find a case of a father beating his wife to death which matched the version I had told them and track down Jack's father. But, even if he said that it was his son who had committed the crime, it was doubtful he would be believed some thirty years after the event and the chances were that he was already dead anyway. Also, I had no way of knowing if the story was true. It had sounded horribly plausible but Jack could have made the whole thing up just to frighten me.

The balcony I was to spend the next few hours on gave onto a terrace at the back of the hotel and, looking down, I could see people milling around the swimming pool, preparing for a swim or a spot of sunbathing. Realising that Jack could be anywhere down there watching me, and would be able to see me more easily than I could see him, I moved away from the edge of the balcony. The balcony itself was furnished with two wooden slatted chairs, the uncomfortable kind that left marks on the back of your legs if you sat on them for too long. There was also a small table but no cushioned sunbed, which would have made my time there more comfortable. Luckily, I had thought to bring my towel with me so I made a cushion of it and put it on one of the chairs. Jack had given me just enough time to gather together a bikini, suntan lotion and sunglasses, but I hadn't thought to take one of the many books I had brought with me. Not that it mattered—I knew I wouldn't be able to concentrate, no matter how exciting the story was. After only a few minutes on the balcony, I already felt like a caged lion, which made my desire to escape even stronger and I was glad the room next door was empty because the temptation to call over the balcony for help would have been too strong to resist.

The next week was torture.

Sometimes Jack took me down to breakfast in the morning, sometimes he didn't and it became obvious, from the way that he was treated by the manager, that he was a regular visitor to the hotel. If we did go down for breakfast, Jack would take me straight back to the room once we had finished and I would be locked on the balcony until he came back from wherever he'd been and let me into the room so that I could use the toilet and eat whatever he had brought for me for lunch. An hour or so later, he would force me back onto the balcony and disappear until the evening.

Terrible though it was, there were a few things I was grateful for: there was always a part of the balcony where I could find shade and, because I insisted, Jack gave me bottles of water, although I had to be careful how much I drank. He never left me for more than four hours at a time, but the time passed excruciatingly slowly. When everything—the loneliness, the boredom, the fear, the despair—got too much to bear, I closed my eyes and thought of Millie.

Although I longed to get off the balcony, when Jack did decide to take me out, not because he felt sorry for me but because he wanted to take photographs, they were such stressful occasions that I was often glad to get back to the hotel room. One evening he took me to dinner in a wonderful restaurant where he took photo after photo of me at various stages of the meal. One afternoon, he booked a taxi and we crammed four days' sightseeing into four hours, during which he took more photos of me as proof of the lovely time I was having.

Another afternoon he took me to what must have been one of the best hotels in Bangkok, where he miraculously had access to its private beach and, as I changed into bikini after bikini so it would look as if the photos he took had been taken on different days, I wondered if it was there that Jack spent his days while I was stuck on the balcony. I hoped that the staff back at the hotel where I stayed might wonder why they rarely saw me around, but when Jack took me down to breakfast one morning and they asked me solicitously if I was feeling better, I understood that he had told them I was confined to our room with a stomach bug.

The worst thing about these small forays into normality

was the hope they gave me, because in public Jack reverted to the man I had fallen in love with. Sometimes—over the course of a meal, for example—as he played the attentive and loving husband, I forgot what he was. Maybe if he hadn't been such good company it would have been easier to remember, but even when I did remember, it was so hard to equate the man who looked adoringly at me from the other side of the table with the man who held me prisoner that I almost believed I had imagined everything.

The crashing back down to reality was doubly hard, for along with the disappointment, there was the shame of having succumbed to his charm, and I would look around wildly, searching for a way out, somewhere to run to, someone to tell. Seeing this, he would look at me in amusement and tell me to go ahead. 'Run,' he would say. 'Go on, go and tell that person over there, or perhaps that one over there, that I am holding you prisoner, that I am a monster, a murderer. But first, look around you. Look around this beautiful restaurant I have brought you to, and think, think about the delicious food you are eating and the wonderful wine in your glass. Do you look as if you are a prisoner? Do I look as if I am a monster, a murderer? I think not. But if you want to go ahead, I won't stop you. I'm in the mood for some fun.' And I would swallow my tears and remind myself that once we were back in England, everything would be easier.

At the beginning of the second week in Thailand, I hit such a low that it became hard to resist the temptation to try to escape. Not only was the thought of spending most of the remaining six days stuck on the balcony depressing, I had also begun to recognise the hopelessness of my situation. I was no longer sure that once we were back in England it would be as easy as I thought to escape from Jack, not least because his reputation as a successful lawyer was bound to protect him. When I thought about alerting someone to who he really was, I began to feel that the British Embassy in Thailand might be a safer bct than the local police back home.

There was something else too. For the previous three days, once Jack had unlocked the balcony and let me back into the room for the evening, he had left the room again, telling me he'd be back shortly and warning me that if I tried to escape, he would know about it immediately. Knowing that I could open the door and leave was excruciating and it required all my willpower to ignore the instinct to flee. It was just as well. The first evening, he came back after twenty minutes, the second evening after an hour. But the third evening, he hadn't come back until almost eleven, and I realised he was gradually building up the amount of time he was leaving me by myself. The thought that he might actually stay out long enough for me to get to the British Embassy made me wonder if I should attempt it.

I knew I couldn't count on the hotel management to help me, and that without help I wouldn't get very far, but the fact that the room next door had been occupied since the weekend made me wonder if I could ask my neighbours for help. I couldn't tell what nationality they were, because the voices that came through the wall were muffled, but I guessed they were a young couple, simply because of the type of music they listened to. Although they weren't around a lot during the day—nobody would come to Thailand and spend their time in a hotel room unless they were a prisoner like me—when they were in their room sometimes one or other of them would come out onto their balcony to smoke a cigarette. I guessed it was the man because the silhouette I could vaguely make out through the partition seemed to be male, and sometimes I would hear him call something to the woman in what I thought was either Spanish or Portuguese. They also seemed to spend most evenings in their room, so I guessed them to be honeymooners, content to stay in and make love. On those evenings, with the sound of soft music coming through the walls, my eyes would fill with tears, as, once again, I was reminded of what could have been.

When, on the fourth evening, Jack didn't come back until midnight, I knew I'd been right in my theory that he was gradually building up the amount of time he left me by myself, counting on the fact that I wouldn't try to run. I had no idea where he went on these evenings, but, as he was always in a good mood when he came back, I guessed he visited some kind of brothel. I had decided, during my long hours on the balcony where I had nothing but my thoughts to keep me company, that because of what he had said about making love to me, he must be homosexual, and I concluded that he came to Thailand to indulge in what he didn't dare indulge in at home for fear of being blackmailed. I knew there was something missing in my theory, because being found to be gay was hardly the end of the world but I didn't yet know what.

On the fifth night, when he didn't come back until two in the morning, I seriously began to weigh up my options. There were another five days until we were due to fly back to England and, as well as it seeming an interminably long time to wait, there was also the added fear that we wouldn't leave when we were meant to. That morning, increasingly upset that I still hadn't phoned Millie, I'd asked Jack if we could go and see her as soon as we got back. His reply—that he was enjoying our honeymoon so much he was thinking of extending it—had made silent tears of anguish fall from my eyes. I told myself that it was another of his games, that he was trying to destabilise me, but I'd felt so helpless I spent most of the day crying.

By the time evening came, I was determined to get away from him. Maybe if I hadn't been sure that the couple next door were Spanish rather than Portuguese I would have stayed where I was, but, because I had picked up enough of the language during my travels to Argentina, I was confident I could make them understand that I was seriously in need of help. The fact that they were a couple—that there would be a woman I could talk to—also decided me. Anyway, I was certain they already knew I was in trouble because that afternoon, when the man had come onto the balcony to smoke, he had called worriedly to the woman, telling her that he could hear someone crying. Scared that Jack might see them trying to look over the balcony from wherever he was watching from, I'd stifled my sobs and remained as still as possible so that they would think I had gone back into the room. But I hoped the fact that they had heard me crying would stand me in good stead.

I waited until Jack had been gone for three hours before making my move. It was gone eleven, but I knew the couple were still up because I could hear them moving around in their room. Mindful of what had happened the time before, I checked my bag, my case and the room to make sure my passport and purse weren't there. When I couldn't find them, I went over to the door and opened it slowly, praying I wouldn't find Jack coming down the corridor, on his way back. I didn't, but the thought that he might suddenly appear had me pounding on the Spanish couple's door more loudly than I intended. I could hear the man muttering something, annoyed perhaps at being disturbed so late at night.

'¿Quién es?' he called through the closed door.

'I'm your neighbour, could you help me, please!'

'¿Qué pasa?'

'Can you open the door, please?' The unmistakable sound of the lift coming to a stop further down the corridor had me pounding on the door again. 'Hurry!' I cried, my heart in my mouth. 'Please hurry!' As the bolt was shot back, the noise of the lift doors opening propelled me into the room. 'Thank you, thank you!' I gabbled. 'I . . .' The words died on my lips and I found myself staring in horror at Jack.

'I actually expected you before tonight,' he said, laughing at the shock on my face. 'I was beginning to think I'd got you wrong, I had almost begun to believe that you had heeded my warning after all and wouldn't attempt to escape. Of course, it would have been better for you if you had, but much less fun for me. I must admit I would have been disappointed if all my hard work had gone to waste.'

My body went limp and, as I sank to the floor, shivering with shock, he crouched down next to me. 'Let me guess,' he said softly. 'You thought a Spanish couple had moved into this room, didn't you? Yet there was only me. If you think about it, you never heard the woman reply because the voice came from a radio. You never saw her on the balcony either, yet you still believed that she existed. Of course, you didn't know that I smoked—I don't usually make a habit of it—nor did you know that I spoke Spanish.'

He paused a moment. 'I also told you it would be very foolish to try and escape again before we left Thailand,' he went on, lowering his voice to a whisper. 'So now that you have, what do you think I'm going to do?'

'Do whatever you like,' I sobbed. 'I don't care any more.'

'Brave words, but I'm sure you don't mean them. For example, I'm sure you would be distraught if I decided to kill you, because it would mean you'd never see Millie again.'

'You're not going to kill me,' I said, with more assurance than I felt.

'You're right, I'm not, not yet, anyway. First and foremost, I need you to do for Millie what she can't do for herself.' He stood up and looked down at me dispassionately. 'Unfortunately, I can't punish you here, because there is nothing I can really deprive you of. But because you have now tried to escape twice, we won't be going to see Millie either the first weekend or the second weekend after we get back to England.'

'You can't do that!' I cried.

'Of course I can—what's more, I warned you that I would.' He reached down and hauled me to my feet. 'Come on, let's go.' He opened the door and pushed me out into the corridor. 'It was well worth paying for the extra room,' he said, closing the door behind him. 'Mr Ho—the manager—quite understood why I might need a separate room for myself, given your mental state. How does it feel to know that I was watching you the whole time?'

'Not as good as it'll feel the day I see you go to prison,' I snarled.

'That, Grace, is never going to happen,' he said, bundling me back into our room. 'And do you know why? Because I'm squeaky clean.'

It was the lowest point of my two weeks in Thailand. It

wasn't so much that I'd failed to escape, it was more that, once again, I'd fallen into the trap Jack had so carefully laid for me. I tried to work out why he had gone to such lengths to set me up when I wouldn't otherwise have tried to escape. Maybe it was simply that my acquiescence bored him or maybe it was something more sinister, in that by denying himself the pleasure of breaking me physically, he wanted the pleasure of breaking me mentally. The thought that he was going to turn my imprisonment into some sort of psychological game made my blood run cold. Even if another opportunity to escape presented itself, there would always be the fear that he was orchestrating the whole thing, and I realised that if I didn't get away from him as soon as we arrived in England, before we had even left the airport, it would be much, much harder once we were installed in a house.

Battling despair, I forced myself to think about what I could do, both on the plane and when we arrived at Heathrow. If I told one of the air hostesses, once we had taken off, that Jack was keeping me prisoner, would I be able to remain calm when he maintained that I was delusional? What if he brought out the report from the hotel manager to back up his claim? What would I do then? And, if I managed to remain calm and told them that he meant great harm to me and my sister, would I be able to persuade them to run checks on him while we were still in the air? And, if they did, would they find that he was an imposter or would they find that Jack Angel was a successful lawyer who championed battered women? I didn't know, but I was determined to make myself heard and equally determined that if nobody listened, I would kick up such a fuss once we arrived at Heathrow that I would be taken to a hospital or a police station.

I didn't think too much about it when I began to feel sleepy shortly after our evening flight had taken off. But, by the time we landed the next morning, I was so groggy that a wheelchair had to be brought so that I could get off the plane, and my words were so slurred I could barely speak. Although I couldn't hear what Jack was saying to the doctor who came to check on me, because of the fog that had permeated my brain, I could see that he was holding a bottle of pills in his hand. Aware that my chances of getting away from him were slipping through my fingers, I made a valiant effort to call for help as we were escorted through passport control, but all that came out of my mouth were unintelligible sounds.

In the car, Jack strapped me into my seat and I slumped against the door, unable to fight the drowsiness that rendered me helpless. The next time I came to, it was to find Jack force-feeding me strong black coffee he had bought from a machine at a service station. It cleared my head a little, but I still felt confused and disorientated.

'Where are we?' I slurred, making an effort to sit upright.

'Nearly home,' he replied, and there was such excitement in his voice that I felt afraid.

He got back in the car and as we drove along, I tried to work out where we were, but I didn't recognise the names of any of the villages we passed. After about half an hour, he turned into a lane.

'Well, here it is, my darling wife,' he said, slowing the car down. 'I hope you're going to like it.'

We stopped beside a pair of huge black gates. A little further along there was a smaller single black gate with a bell set into the wall beside it. He took a remote control from his pocket, pressed a button and the double gates swung open.

'The house that I promised you as your wedding present. Now, what do you think of it?'

At first I thought that whatever he had drugged me with was making me hallucinate. But then I realised that I really was looking at the house we had drawn together on a piece of paper in the bar of the Connaught Hotel, the house he promised he would find for me, right down to the little round window in the roof.

'I see that you're lost for words,' he laughed, as he drove in through the gates.

After drawing to a stop near the front door, he got out of the car and came round to open my door for me. When I just sat there, he put his hands under my arms, hauled me unceremoniously from the car and dragged me onto the porch. He unlocked the front door and pushed me into the hall, slamming the door behind him.

'Welcome home,' he said mockingly. 'I hope you'll be very happy here.'

The hall was beautiful, with its high ceiling and magnificent staircase. The doors to the right were closed, as were the huge double doors to the left.

'I'm sure you'd like me to show you around,' he went on. 'But first, wouldn't you like to see Molly?'

I stared at him. 'Molly?'

'Yes, Molly. Don't tell me you'd forgotten all about her?'

'Where is she?' I asked urgently, shocked that I hadn't thought about her once while we'd been in Thailand. 'Where's Molly?'

'In the utility room.' He opened a door to the right of the staircase and switched on a light. 'Down here.'

As I followed him down to the basement, I recognised the

tiles from the photo he had shown me of Molly in her basket. He came to a stop in front of a door. 'She's in there. But before you go and see her, you'd better take one of these.' He took a roll of bin bags from where they were lying on a shelf, tore one off and handed it to me. 'I think you might be needing it.'

PRESENT

Even though the days pass slowly for me, I'm always amazed at how quickly Sundays come round. Today though, I can't help feeling depressed because there is no visit to Millie to look forward to. I don't know this for sure, but it's unlikely that Jack will take me to see her when we've been for the last two Sundays. Still, it could be that he'll surprise me, so I've had my shower just in case, drying both myself and my hair on the small hand towel that he allows me. Bath sheets and hairdryers are luxuries of a past long gone, as are visits to the hairdresser's. Although drying myself is a misery in the winter, it is not all bad. My hair, denied both heat and scissors, is long and shiny and, with a bit of ingenuity, I can manage to tie it in a knot so that it doesn't annoy me.

It wasn't always so bad. When we first arrived in the house, I had a much nicer bedroom, with all sorts of things to keep me amused, which Jack deprived me of with each attempt to escape. First the kettle went, then the radio, then the books. With nothing to distract me, I resorted to relieving the stultifying boredom of the days by playing around with the clothes in my wardrobe, mixing and matching different outfits just for the hell of it. But after another failed attempt to escape, Jack took me from that room and installed me in the box room next door, which he'd stripped of every comfort except for the bed. He even went to the trouble of adding bars to the window. Deprived of my wardrobe, it meant that I had to rely on him to bring me my clothes each morning. I soon forfeited that right too and now, unless we're going out, I'm made to wear pyjamas day and night. Although he brings me clean ones three times a week, there is nothing to relieve the monotony of wearing the same thing day in, day out, especially when each pair is exactly the same as the last. They are all the same style and all the same colour— black—with nothing to distinguish one pair from another. Once, not very long ago, when I asked him if I could have a dress to wear during the day for a change, he brought me a curtain I'd had in my flat and told me to make one for myself. He thought himself funny, because he knew I had no scissors, or needle and thread, but when he found me wearing it the next day, wrapped around me like a sarong and a welcome change from pyjamas, he took it away again, annoyed by my ingenuity. Hence his little joke to Esther and the others about me being something of a seamstress and making my own clothes.

He loves to put me on the spot, to see how I'll cope with something he's thrown nonchalantly into the conversation, hoping I'll mess up so he can punish me. But I'm getting quite good at making it up as I go along. Personally, I'm hoping Esther and the others will ask me again about starting a sewing circle because it'll be Jack who'll have to get me out of that one. Perhaps he'll start by breaking my arm or mangling my fingers in a door. So far, he has never harmed me physically, although there are times when I think that he'd like to.

Sometime in the afternoon, I hear a ring at the gate so I jump off the bed and press my ear to the door. It's the first bit of excitement I've had in a long time, as people never drop in uninvited. I wait to hear if Jack is going to let whoever it is in, or at least enquire what they want, but when the house remains silent I know he's pretending that we're not at home—fortunately for him, it's impossible to see the car parked in the driveway through the black gates. When whoever it is rings again, this time more impatiently, my thoughts turn immediately to Esther.

I've been thinking about her a lot lately, mainly because of the way she repeated her mobile number in the restaurant last week. The more I think about it, the more I'm convinced she understood that I needed to hear it again and I know that if there ever comes a time when I need to ask for help, it will be Esther I'll turn to rather than Diane, who I've known for longer. I've lost all my own friends, even Kate and Emily, who I thought would always stand by me. But my irregular and very short emails to them—dictated by Jack—where I trilled about how wonderful married life was and said I was too busy to see them, ensured that theirs dried up quickly. I didn't even get a birthday card from them this year.

Now that he's got rid of my friends, Jack allows me to reply to other emails addressed specifically to me—from my parents or Diane, for example—rather than reply to them himself, but only to give them a more genuine flavour, although I'm not sure how genuine I manage to make them sound with him breathing down my neck as I write. On these occasions I am brought down to his study, and I welcome these moments where, with both a computer and a telephone within reach, the potential of alerting someone is greater than anywhere else.

My heart always starts beating faster as Jack sits me down, with the computer and telephone only inches away, because there is always the hope that he might be distracted long enough for me to be able to snatch up the phone, dial a quick 999 and scream my despair to the police. Or pound a quick plea for help on the keyboard to whoever I am writing to and press the send button before he can stop me. The temptation to do so is great, but Jack is always vigilant. He stands over me as I write and checks each message before he allows me to send it.

Once, I thought my chance had come when somebody rang at the gate as I was writing, but instead of going to the intercom to see who was there, Jack simply ignored it, as he does the telephone when it rings while I'm seated at the computer. Yet along with the frustration I feel when he escorts me back to my room, at another chance gone, there is also a feeling of near-contentment, especially after I've written to my parents. It's almost as if I believe the lies I have told them, about weekends away that Jack and I have been on, or visits to beautiful gardens, to country houses, to places I have never been and where I will never go, yet am able to describe in such detail. But, as with all highs, the coming down is hard, and once the euphoria has gone I feel more depressed than ever.

There's no third ring at the gate so I go back to the bed and lie down. I feel so restless that I decide to try a bit of meditation to relax me. I taught myself to meditate not long after Jack moved me into this room for fear I would go mad with nothing to do all day. I've become so good at it that sometimes I manage to drift off for what often seems like several hours but is probably a lot less. I usually start by picturing Millie and me sitting in a beautiful garden with a little dog at our feet. Not Molly though—to be able to lose myself, I need to think happy thoughts. Today, however, I'm unable to relax because the only picture I can bring to mind is that of Esther driving away from the house. In my isolation, I've become superstitious and I take it as a sign that I've got it all wrong, that Esther isn't going to be the one to help me.

When I hear Jack coming up the stairs maybe an hour or so after the ring at the gate, I try to guess if he's come to play some sort of game with me or if he's simply bringing me a late lunch. He unlocks the door; there's no tray in his hand so I prepare myself for one of his sadistic games, especially when I see that he is holding a book. The urge to pounce on it and snatch it out of his hand is powerful, but I keep my face impassive and do my best not to look at it, wondering what torment he has devised this time. He knows how I crave to have something to read—I've lost count of the number of times I've pleaded with him to let me have a newspaper, just once a week even, to help me keep up-to-date with what is happening in the world so that I don't appear a complete idiot when we go out to dinner. So I'm fully expecting him to offer me the book, only to withdraw his hand the moment I reach out to take it.

'I have something for you,' he begins.

'What?' I ask, as unenthusiastically as I can.

'A book.' He pauses. 'Would you like it?'

Coming from Jack, it's the question I hate most in the world as I'm damned if I say yes and damned if I say no. 'It depends,' I say, hating that I'm prolonging my agony by trying to keep him there as long as possible because at least he's someone to talk to.

'On what?'

'Its title. If it's called *My Life with a Psychopath*, I'm not interested.'

He smiles. 'Actually, it's the one that Esther recommended.'

'And you decided to buy it for me?'

'No, she dropped it off.' He pauses again. 'Under normal circumstances, I would have put it straight in the bin, but it came with a very charming invitation to dinner a week next Saturday, with a little post scriptum saying that she can't wait to hear what you think of the book. So I suggest you make sure you've read it by then.'

'I'm not sure I'll have time, but I'll do my best,' I tell him.

'Don't get too smart,' he warns. 'You've become so adept at avoiding punishment that I only need the slightest excuse.'

He leaves, and unable to wait any longer, I open the book and read the first page to get an idea of what it's about. I know instantly that I'm going to love it and I hate the thought that it'll only take me a day or so to read it. I wonder if I should wait a while before starting it properly, and limit myself to a chapter a day, but because there's always the possibility that Jack will take it back again before I've had a chance to finish it, I settle down on my bed, ready to spend the best few hours I've had for a long time. I've been reading for about an hour when I notice that one of the words I've just read, the word 'alright', stands out more than the others and, when I look closely, I see that it's been lightly shaded in pencil.

Something about it jogs my memory and, going back a few pages, I find the word 'thing' highlighted in the same manner, but so lightly I'm not convinced I would have noticed had I not been looking for it. I flip back a few more pages and come across the word 'every', which I recognise as the word that had caught my attention earlier, although I had put its darker background down to a printing problem. Intrigued, I carry on turning back the pages and eventually find a tiny 'is' nearer the beginning of the book.

I run it together—'Is everything alright'.

My heart starts beating faster as I consider the possibility that Esther has sent me a message. If she has, there has to be more. With a mounting sense of excitement, I scan the rest of the book for evidence of shading and find 'do', 'you', 'need' and, on the second to last page of the book, 'help'.

The elation I feel, that she has recognised my predicament and wants to help, is short-lived, because how can I reply to Esther when I don't have access to something as mundane as a pencil? Even if I had one, I'd be at a loss as to what to reply. A mere 'yes' wouldn't be enough, a 'yes, get the police' would be futile, because, as I know to my cost, Jack has them in his pocket. Like the staff at the hotel in Thailand, they know me as a manic-depressive, given to accusing my devoted and brilliant lawyer husband of keeping me prisoner. Even if they arrived at the house without warning, Jack would have no trouble explaining away this room, or any other room in the house for that matter. Anyway, he would never let me return the book to Esther without checking it first, just as he always checks my bag before we go out to make sure it's empty.

It suddenly occurs to me that he wouldn't have let me have the book in the first place if he hadn't gone through it thoroughly, which means he's almost certainly seen the shading. It's an appalling thought, not least because Esther could be in danger from him. It also means I'll have to be careful what I say to her when we next meet as, knowing that I can't get a message back to her in kind, Jack will be listening to every word I say. He'll probably be expecting me to say something along the lines of 'I thought the message the author was trying to get across was quite pertinent.' But he's going to be disappointed. I might have been that stupid once, but not anymore. It might be difficult to get a message back to Esther, but I refuse to feel downhearted. I'm so grateful that she has understood so quickly what nobody else ever has—not my parents or Diane or Janice or the police—that Jack controls everything I do.

I find myself frowning, because if she suspects that he controls me, surely she must guess that he also controls everything I come into contact with? If she's realised that Jack is not someone to be trifled with, why would she risk discovery when she has nothing concrete to back up her suspicions?

I go back to reading, hoping to find something that will tell me how I can communicate with Esther without Jack finding out, because how can I let her down when she has reached out to me so amazingly?

Sometime in the evening, when I'm still trying to work

out a way of getting a message back to her, I hear Jack coming up the stairs, so I close the book quickly and place it a little away from me on the bed.

'Finished already?' he remarks, nodding at the book.

'Actually, I'm finding it hard to get into,' I lie. 'It's not the sort of thing I'd normally read.'

'How far have you got with it?'

'Not very far.'

'Well, make sure you finish it before we see her next week.'

He leaves, and I find myself frowning again. It's the second time he's insisted that I read it before we go to Esther's for dinner, which tells me that he knows about the shading and is hoping I'm going to dig a grave for myself. After all, he as good as admitted, when he said earlier that I was getting too clever for my own good, that he misses punishing me, so I can imagine how happy he must have been to see Esther's message—and how he must have laughed at her attempt to help me. But then, the more I think about it, the more I feel that I've missed something. It's only when I remember the amount of time that passed between the ring on the doorbell and Jack bringing the book up to me that it dawns on me that the shading in the book is not Esther's work, but Jack's.

PAST

Molly could only have been dead a few days at the most, because her body hadn't started to decompose. Jack had been very clever in that respect; he had left her some water, but not quite enough to last her the two weeks until we got home. The shock of finding her dead was terrible. The look of malevolent anticipation on Jack's face as he opened the door to the utility room had prepared me for something—that he had left her tied up for the two weeks we were away, or that she wouldn't be there—but not that he had left her to die.

At first, as I looked down at her little body lying on the

floor, I thought the drugs he had given me were playing with my mind, because I was still feeling woozy. But when I knelt down beside her and found her body cold and rigid, I thought about the terrible death she must have endured. It was then that I didn't only vow to kill Jack, but to make him suffer as he had made Molly suffer.

He feigned surprise at my distress, reminding me that he had told me in Thailand there was no housekeeper, and I was grateful I hadn't paid any attention to what he'd said back then. If I'd understood what he was alluding to, I don't know how I would have got through those two weeks.

'I'm so glad to see that you loved her,' he said, as I knelt beside Molly and wept. 'I hoped you would. It's important, you see, that you realise just how much harder it would be if it was Millie lying there rather than Molly. And if Millie were dead, you'd have to take her place. When you think about it, nobody would really miss you and, if anybody asked where you were, I'd say that following the death of your beloved sister you had decided to join your parents in New Zealand.'

'Why can't I replace Millie, anyway?' I sobbed. 'Why do you need her?'

'Because she will be so much easier to terrify than you. Besides, if I have Millie, I'll have everything I need right here and I won't have to go to Thailand anymore.'

'I don't understand.' I dashed tears from my cheeks with the back of my hand. 'Don't you go to Thailand to have sex with men?'

'Sex with men?' He seemed amused by the idea. 'I could do that here if I chose to. Not that I would choose to. You see, I'm not interested in sex. The reason I go to Thailand is so that I can indulge my greatest passion—not that I actually get my hands dirty, you understand. No, my role is more that of observer, and listener.' I stared up at him uncomprehendingly and he bent his head towards mine. 'Fear,' he whispered. 'There is nothing quite like it. I love how it looks, I love how it feels, I love how it smells. And I especially love the sound of it.' I felt his tongue on my cheek. 'I even love the taste of it.'

'You disgust me,' I hissed. 'You must be one of the most evil people that has ever lived. And I'll get you, Jack, I promise. In the end, I'll get you.'

'Not if I get Millie first, which I intend to do.'

'So you're going to kill her,' I said, my voice breaking.

'Kill her? What use would she be to me dead? I'm not going to kill Millie, Grace, I'm just going to scare her a little. Now, do you want to bury that dog or shall I dump it in the bin?'

He didn't lift a finger to help, but stood and watched as I wrapped Mollie's body in the black bin bag and, sobbing with distress, carried her up the stairs, through the kitchen and out onto the terrace that I had told him I wanted. I looked around the vast garden, shivering with cold and shock, wondering where I could put her.

Following me out, he pointed to a hedge at the bottom of the garden and told me to bury her behind it. As I rounded it, I saw a shovel standing ready in the ground and the knowledge that before leaving Molly to die he had prepared a shovel for me to bury her with made me break into fresh sobs. It had rained while we were in Thailand so the ground was soft, but digging her grave was only made bearable by imagining it was his I was preparing. When I had finished, I took Mollie's body out of the bin bag and held her to me for a moment, thinking of Millie, wondering how I was going to be able to tell her that Molly was dead.

'She's not going to come back to life, no matter how long you hold her for,' he drawled. 'Just get on with it.'

Afraid that he would snatch her from me and throw her unceremoniously into the hole I had dug, I placed her gently in it and shovelled the earth back on top. It was then that the full horror of what had just happened hit me and, throwing the shovel down, I dashed behind a tree and was violently sick.

'You're going to have to learn to have a stronger stomach than that,' he remarked, as I wiped my mouth on the back of my hand. His words sent waves of panic shooting through me. Running back to where I'd dropped the shovel, I snatched it up and rushed towards him with it raised high above my head, ready to bring it down on him and beat him to a pulp. But I was no match for him; raising his arm, he caught hold of the shovel and wrestled it from me, causing me to stumble. Righting myself, I broke into a run, screaming for help at the top of my voice. When I saw that the windows of the nearest property were only just visible through the trees, I ran towards it, hoping that someone would have heard my screams, and, as I ran, I looked for a way out of the garden. Realising that the walls that bordered it were too high for me to climb, I drew in air, about to scream again for all I was worth, knowing it might be my only chance. A blow to my back expelled the air I had drawn in with little more than a grunt and, as I fell forward, Jack's hand came around my mouth, silencing me completely. Jerking me upright, he used his other hand to bend my arm behind my back, rendering me helpless.

'I take it you're not in a hurry to see Millie again,' he breathed, as he frogmarched me back towards the house.

'Because of your attempts to escape in Thailand, you had already forfeited your right to see her for the next two weekends; now you won't see her for a third weekend running. And, if you try anything again, you won't see her for a whole month.'

I struggled against him, twisting my head away from him in a frantic effort to free my mouth from his hand, but he simply tightened his grip on me.

'Poor Millie,' he sighed in mock sorrow, as he propelled me along the terrace and into the kitchen, 'she's going to think you've abandoned her, that now you're married you have no time for her.' Releasing me, he pushed me away from him. 'Listen to me, Grace. Provided you don't do anything stupid, I am prepared to treat you well—after all, it is not in my interest to do otherwise. Nevertheless, I shan't hesitate to withdraw any of the privileges I have chosen to accord you should you displease me. Do you understand?'

Slumped against the wall, trembling with fatigue, or from the after-effects of the drugs, or from shock, I could only nod mutely.

'Good. Now, before I show you the rest of the house, I'm sure you'd like a shower.' Pathetic tears of gratitude sprang to my eyes. 'I'm not a monster,' he said with a frown, noticing. 'Well, at least not in that sense. Come on, I'll show you where your bathroom is and once you feel more refreshed I'll give you a tour of the house.'

I followed him into the hall and up the stairs, barely noticing my surroundings. Opening a door, he showed me into a bright and airy bedroom decorated in pale greens and cream. On the double bed I recognised some of the coverings and cushions I had chosen the day we had gone shopping together to buy furniture for the house he had promised to find me. In the hostile world I found myself in, they seemed like old familiar friends and my spirits lifted a little.

'Do you like it?' he asked.

'Yes,' I said reluctantly.

'Good.' He seemed pleased. 'The bathroom's through there and you'll find your clothes in the wardrobe.' He looked at his watch. 'I'll give you fifteen minutes.'

The door closed behind him. Curious, I walked over to the huge wardrobe that ran the length of the left-hand wall. Sliding the doors open, I found the clothes that I had sent to the house ahead of me, the ones I hadn't needed to take to Thailand, hanging there. My T-shirts and jumpers were neatly folded on the shelves and my underwear had been put in specially made drawers. In another part of the wardrobe, my many pairs of shoes had been placed in clear plastic boxes. Everything seemed so normal that once again I experienced a feeling of disconnect. It was impossible to equate the beautiful room Jack had prepared for me and the promise of a shower with what had gone before, and I couldn't rid myself of the feeling that if I were to lie down on the bed and sleep for a while, I would wake up to find it had all been a terrible nightmare.

I went over to the window and looked out. It gave onto the side of the house, where a rose garden had been planted. Just as I was appreciating the beauty of the flowers and the stillness of the afternoon, a black bin bag, caught in a sudden gust of wind, came scudding around from the back of the house and became snagged in one of the rose bushes. Recognising it as the one I had carried Molly out to the garden in, I gave a cry of distress, turned from the window and hurried over to the door, realising I had wasted precious minutes when I should have been trying to escape. Yanking it open, I was about to run out into the hall when Jack's arm came shooting out, blocking my way.

'Going somewhere?' he asked pleasantly. I stared at him, my heart thumping painfully in my chest. 'You wouldn't have been thinking of trying to leave, would you?'

I thought of Millie, about how upset she would be by my non-appearance over the next three weeks and knew I couldn't risk another punishment. 'Towels,' I mumbled. 'I was wondering where the towels were.'

'If you'd looked in the bathroom, you would have found them. Hurry up, you only have ten minutes left.'

As he closed the door on me, imprisoning me again, I went over to the bathroom. It had a walk-in shower and separate bath, as well as a sink and a toilet. There was a large pile of fluffy towels on top of a low cupboard and, on opening it, I saw it was generously stacked with bottles of shampoo, conditioner and shower gel. Suddenly desperate to wash away the filth that seemed to permeate from every pore of my body, I stripped off, turned on the shower and, arming myself with everything I would need, stepped under the water. I adjusted the temperature to the hottest I could bear, shampooed my hair and scrubbed away at my body, wondering if I would ever feel clean again. I would have stayed longer under the water, but I didn't trust Jack not to come in and pull me out of the shower as soon as my ten minutes were up so I turned off the tap and dried myself quickly.

In the cupboard under the sink, I found a pack of toothbrushes and some toothpaste and used a precious two minutes of the time I had left brushing my teeth until my gums bled. I hurried through to the bedroom, opened the wardrobe, pulled a dress off one of the hangers, took a bra and pair of knickers from a drawer and dressed quickly. The bedroom door opened as I was zipping up my dress.

'Good,' he said. 'I didn't particularly want to have to come and drag you out of the shower, but I would have.' He nodded towards the wardrobe. 'Put something on your feet.' After a slight hesitation, I chose a pair of shoes with a small heel rather than the slippers my feet ached for, hoping they would make me feel more in control. 'Now for the tour of the house. I hope you're going to like it.'

I followed him down the stairs, wondering why he should care whether I liked it or not. Although I was determined not to be impressed, reason told me that giving him the positive reaction he obviously craved might be in my interest.

'It's taken me two years to get the house exactly as I wanted it,' he remarked, as we reached the hall, 'especially as I had to make last-minute changes that I hadn't accounted for. For example, the kitchen originally didn't lead onto a terrace, but I had one built because I thought it was an excellent idea. Fortunately, I managed to steer the rest of your desires towards what was already here,' he went on, confirming what I had already worked out, that the day he had asked me to describe the sort of house I would like, he had cleverly manoeuvred me into describing one he had already bought.

'If you remember, you said you wanted a toilet on the ground floor for guests to use, but when I suggested a whole cloakroom, you readily agreed.' Opening a door on the right, he revealed a cloakroom that housed a wardrobe, large mirror and a separate washroom.

'Very clever,' I said, referring to the way he had manipulated me.

'Yes, it was rather,' he agreed. Moving on down the hall, he opened the next door along. 'My study and library.'

I caught a quick glimpse of a room covered from floor to ceiling with book-lined shelves and, in an alcove to the right, a mahogany desk.

'It's not a room you'll have to come into very often.' Crossing over to the other side of the hall, he threw open the huge double doors that I had noticed earlier. 'The sitting room and dining room.'

He held the doors open, inviting me to go in, and I stepped into one of the most beautiful rooms I had ever seen. But I barely noticed the four sets of French windows that gave onto the rose garden at the side of the house, or the high ceilings, or the elegant archway that led through to the dining room, because my eyes were immediately drawn to the fireplace where *Fireflies*, the painting I had done for Jack, was hanging.

'It looks quite perfect there, don't you think?' he said. Remembering the love and effort I had put into it, and the fact that it was composed of hundreds of kisses, I felt sick to my stomach. Turning abruptly on my heels, I went back out into the hall. 'I hope that doesn't mean you don't like the room,' he frowned, following me out.

'Why should you care whether or not I like it?' I snarled.

'I have nothing against you personally, Grace,' he said patiently, as he continued down the hall. 'As I explained in Thailand, you are the means to the end I have always dreamed of having, so it's normal that I feel some sort of gratitude towards you. Therefore, I would like your experience here to be as pleasant as possible, at least until Millie arrives. Once she does, I'm afraid it will be extremely unpleasant for you. And for her, of course. Now, you didn't get a chance to see the kitchen properly yesterday, did you?' He opened the kitchen door and I saw the breakfast bar that we had decided we'd have, complete with four high, shiny stools.

'Oh, Millie will love those!' I cried, imagining her turning herself around on them.

In the silence that followed, everything that had happened caught up with me and the room began to spin so fast that I felt myself falling. Aware of Jack's arms reaching out to catch me, I made a feeble attempt to fight him off before passing out.

When I next opened my eyes, I felt so wonderfully rested my first thought was that I was on holiday somewhere. Looking around, still drowsy with sleep, I saw all the equipment necessary to make tea and coffee on a table near the bed and decided I was in a hotel, but where I didn't know. As I took in the pale-green walls that were both familiar and unfamiliar, I suddenly remembered where I was. Leaping from the bed, I ran to the door and tried to open it. When I found that I was locked in, I began hammering on it, screaming at Jack to let me out.

The key turned in the lock and the door opened.

'For goodness' sake, Grace,' he said, clearly annoyed. 'You only had to call me.'

'How dare you lock me in!' I cried, my voice trembling with rage.

'I locked you in for your own good. If I hadn't, you might have been foolish enough to try and escape again, and I would have had to deprive you of yet another visit to Millie.' He turned and reached for a tray, which lay on a small table out-side my door. 'Now, if you move back a little, I'll give you something to eat.'

The thought of food was tempting; I couldn't remember the last time I had eaten but it must have been well before leaving Thailand. But the open door was even more tempt-ing. Moving aside, but not back as he had asked, I waited un-til he had come right into the room, then lunged towards him, knocking the tray from his hands. Amid the sound of breaking crockery and his roar of rage, I ran towards the stairs and went down them two at a time, registering too late that the hall below was in complete darkness. Arriving at the bottom of the stairs, I searched for a light switch and, finding none, felt along the wall until I arrived at the kitchen door. Throwing it open, I found that it too was in darkness. Remembering the four sets of French windows I had seen in the sitting room the day before, I crossed the hall and groped along the wall until I found the double doors. The total dark-ness inside the room, without even a glimmer of light coming in from the windows, as well as the silence—because the house was eerily quiet—became suddenly terrifying. The knowl-edge that Jack could be anywhere, that he could have crept down the stairs behind me and be standing within feet of me made my heart race with fear.

Stepping into the room, I slid to the floor behind one of the doors, drew my knees up around my chest and curled my-self into a ball, expecting his hands to reach down and grab me at any moment. The suspense was terrible and the thought that he might decide not to find me until it suited him made me regret ever having left the relative safety of the bedroom.

'Where are you, Grace?' His voice came from somewhere

out in the hall and his soft sing-song tone only added to my terror. In the silence, I heard him sniffing the air. 'Hmm, I do so love the smell of fear,' he breathed. His feet padded across the hall and, when they got nearer, I shrank back against the wall. They stopped and, as I strained my ears, trying to work out where he was, I felt his breath on my cheek.

'Boo!' he whispered.

As I burst into tears of relief that my ordeal was over, he roared with laughter. A whirring sound heralded the beginnings of daylight filtering into the room and, raising my head, I saw Jack holding a remote control in his hand.

'Steel shutters,' he explained. 'Every window on the ground floor has been fitted with them. Even if you happen, by some miracle, to find a way out of your room while I'm at work, you certainly won't find a way out of the house.'

'Let me go, Jack,' I begged. 'Please, just let me go.'

'Why would I do that? In fact, I think I'm going to enjoy having you here, especially if you continue trying to escape. At least you'll keep me amused until Millie comes to live with us.' He paused. 'You know, I was almost beginning to regret not arranging for her to move in as soon as we came back from our honeymoon. Just think—she could have been arriving at any moment.'

I drew in my breath sharply.

'Do you really think I'm going to let Millie come anywhere near this house?' I cried. 'Or you anywhere near her?'

'I seem to remember having this conversation with you in Thailand,' he said, sounding bored. 'The sooner you accept that the wheels are already in motion and that there is nothing you can do to stop them the better it will be for you. There is no escape—you're mine now.'

'I can't believe you think you're going to get away with it! You can't keep me hidden away forever, you know. What about my friends, our friends? Aren't we meant to be having dinner with Moira and Giles when we return the car to them?'

'I shall tell them exactly what I intend to tell Millie's school—it will now be four weeks until you see her, by the way—which is that you picked up a nasty bug in Thailand and are indisposed. And, when I do eventually allow you to see Millie again, I will watch your every move and listen to every word. Should you try to inform anyone of what is going on, you and Millie will both pay. As for your friends, well, you're not really going to have time for them now that you're so happily married and, when you no longer reply to their emails, they'll forget all about you. It will be a gradual thing, of course. I'll let you maintain contact for a while, but I'll vet your emails before you send them just in case you try to alert anyone to your situation.' He paused. 'But I can't imagine you would be so foolish.'

Until that point, I had never doubted that I would be able to escape from him, or at least tell someone that I was being held prisoner, but there was something about the matter-of-fact way he spoke that was chilling. His absolute certainty that everything would pan out exactly as he had planned made me, for the first time, doubt my ability to outwit him. As he escorted me back to my bedroom, telling me that I would get no food until the following day, all I could think about was what he had done to Molly and what he would do to me if I tried to get away from him again. I couldn't afford to risk not seeing Millie for yet another week and the thought of her disappointment when I didn't turn up for the next few Sundays made me feel even more wretched than I already felt.

It was the hunger pains I was experiencing that gave me the idea of pretending I had appendicitis so that Jack would have no choice but to take me to hospital, where I felt I'd be able to get someone to listen to me. When he eventually brought me food the next day, as he had promised he would, it was already late evening, so I hadn't had anything to eat for over forty-eight hours. It was hard not to eat much of what he'd brought me and, as I clutched my stomach and moaned that it hurt, I was grateful for the cramps that made my pain more genuine.

Unfortunately, Jack remained unmoved, but when he found me doubled up the next morning, he agreed to bring me the aspirin that I asked for, although he made me swallow it in front of him. By the evening, I'd progressed to writhing around on the bed, and during the night, I hammered on the door until he came to see what all the noise was about. Telling him that I was in agony, I asked him to call an ambulance. He refused, saying that if I was still in pain the next day he would call a doctor. It wasn't the result I had wanted but it was better than nothing and I planned carefully what I would say to the doctor when he came, knowing—after my experience in Thailand—that I couldn't afford to sound hysterical.

I hadn't foreseen that Jack would stay with me while the doctor examined me and, as I acted out being in pain every time he probed my stomach, my mind raced frantically ahead, aware that if I didn't seize the moment, all my play-acting and depriving myself of food would have been for nothing. When I asked the doctor if I could speak to him alone, insinuating that the pain I was experiencing might be due to a gynaecological problem, I felt victorious when he asked Jack if he would mind stepping out of the room.

After, I wondered why it hadn't occurred to me that Jack's willingness to leave the room meant that he wasn't worried about the outcome of my tête-à-tête with the doctor. Neither did the doctor's sympathetic smile, as I told him urgently that I was being held prisoner, make me suspicious. It was only when he began questioning me about what he called my suicide attempt and a supposed history of depression that I understood Jack had covered all angles before the doctor had even set foot in my bedroom. Appalled, I begged him to believe that Jack wasn't who he said he was and repeated what he had told me, that he had beaten his mother to death when he was little more than a child and had let his father take the blame. But, even while I was speaking, I could hear how unbelievable it sounded and, as he wrote out a prescription for Prozac, I became so hysterical that it gave weight to what Jack had told him, that I was an attention-seeking manic-depressive. He even had the paperwork to prove it—a copy of my medical reports from the time of my overdose and a letter from the manager of the hotel in Thailand detailing my behaviour the night we arrived.

Devastated by my failure to convince the doctor that I was speaking the truth, the enormity of the task before me seemed once again insurmountable. If I couldn't persuade a professional to consider what I had told him, how was I going to be able to get anyone else to understand what was going on? Even more pertinent, how was I ever going to be able to talk to anyone freely when Jack wouldn't allow me any communication with the outside world unless it was controlled by him?

He began to monitor the emails I received and, if he didn't dictate my reply word for word, he stood over me and read every word I wrote. As I was locked in my room day and night, people were forced to leave a message on the answerphone, unless Jack was around to take their calls. If they asked to speak to me personally, he would tell them that I was in the shower or out shopping and would call them back. And, if he did allow me to call them back, he would listen to what I said. But I didn't dare object as my conversation with the doctor had cost me another week's visit to Millie, as well as the right to have tea and coffee in my room. I knew that if I wanted to see her again in the near future I'd have to behave exactly as Jack wanted, at least for a while. So I submitted, without complaint, to the restraints he placed on me. When he came to bring me food—he brought it morning and evening back then—I made sure he found me sitting impassively on my bed, subservient, docile.

My parents, with their move to New Zealand imminent, were suspicious of the mysterious bug I had apparently picked up in Thailand and which prevented me from visiting Millie. To discourage them from visiting, Jack had told them it was potentially contagious, but I could tell from their anxious phone calls that they were worried my interest in Millie had waned now that I was married.

I only saw them once before they left, when they came to say a hurried goodbye, and it was then, during a quick tour of the house, that I finally saw the rest of the rooms on the first floor. I had to hand it to Jack; not only had he made me tidy away all my belongings so that he could pass my bedroom off as one of the guest rooms, he had strewn my clothes around his bedroom to make it look as if I slept there too. I longed to tell my parents the truth, to beg them to help me, but with Jack's arm heavy on my shoulder, the courage to say anything at all never came.

I still might have said something if it hadn't been for Millie's room. As my parents exclaimed over the pale-yellow walls, the beautiful furnishings and the four-poster bed piled high with cushions, I couldn't believe that Jack would have gone to so much trouble if he really had evil intentions towards her. It gave me hope, hope that buried somewhere deep down inside him there remained a small pocket of decency. That he'd control me, but leave Millie free.

The week after my parents left, Jack finally took me to see Millie. It was a long five weeks after our return from Thailand and, by that time, Millie's leg had mended and we were able to take her out for lunch. But the Millie I found waiting for me was vastly different from the happy girl I'd left behind.

My parents had mentioned that Millie had been difficult while we'd been away and I'd put it down to her disappointment at not being our bridesmaid. I knew she also resented that I hadn't gone to see her as soon as we'd got back from our honeymoon, because during my phone calls to her, where Jack had stood breathing down my neck, she'd been practically monosyllabic. Although I quickly won her over with the souvenirs Jack had allowed me to buy for her at the airport, as well as a new Agatha Christie audio book, she all but ignored him and I could tell that he was furious, especially as Janice was present. I tried to pretend that Millie was upset because we hadn't brought Molly with us, but as she hadn't made a fuss when I'd told her we'd left her digging up bulbs in the garden it hadn't rung true. When Jack told her, in an effort to rescue the situation, that he was taking us to a new hotel for lunch, she replied that she didn't want to go anywhere with him and that she didn't want him to live with us either. Janice, in an attempt to defuse the situation, diplomatically took Millie off to fetch a coat, whereupon Jack lost no time in telling me that if she didn't change her attitude, he'd make sure I never saw Millie again.

Searching again for something else to excuse Millie's behaviour, I told him that, in view of what she'd said about him not living with us, she obviously hadn't realised that once we were married he would be with me all the time and resented having to share me with him. I didn't believe for a minute what I was saying—Millie understood very well that being married meant living together—and I knew I would have to get to the bottom of Millie's attitude towards Jack before he lost his patience and carried out his threat of the asylum. But with him always at my side, watching my every move and gesture, I couldn't see how I was going to be able to talk to her in private.

My chance came at the hotel Jack took us to for lunch. At the end of the meal, Millie asked me to go with her to the toilet. Realising it was my chance to talk to her, I got to my feet, only for Millie to be told by Jack that she was perfectly capable of going on her own. But she insisted, her voice getting louder and louder, forcing Jack to give way. So he came with us. When he saw that the Ladies' toilets was down a short corridor where he wouldn't be able to accompany us without it looking suspicious, he dragged me back and reminded me, in a whisper that sent a chill down my spine, that

I wasn't to tell Millie—or anyone else for that matter—anything, adding that he would wait for us at the end of the corridor and warning that we weren't to take long.

'Grace, Grace,' Millie cried, as soon as we were on our own, 'Jack bad man, very bad man. He push me, he push me down stairs!'

I put my finger against her mouth, warning her to be quiet, looking around me fearfully. The fact that the cubicles were empty was the first piece of luck I'd had for a very long time.

'No, Millie,' I whispered, terrified that Jack had come down the corridor anyway and was listening from outside the door. 'Jack wouldn't do that.'

'He push me, Grace! At the wedding house, Jack push me hard, like this!' She bumped me with her shoulder. 'Jack hurt me, broke leg.'

'No, Millie, no!' I hushed. 'Jack is a good man.'

'No, not good.' Millie was adamant. 'Jack bad man, very bad man.'

'You mustn't say that, Millie! You haven't told anybody, have you, Millie? You haven't told anybody what you've just told me?'

She shook her head vigorously. 'You say always tell Grace things first. But now I tell Janice that Jack bad man.'

'No, Millie you mustn't, you mustn't tell anyone!'

'Why? Grace not believe me.'

My mind raced, wondering what I could tell her. By now I knew what Jack was capable of and suddenly it made sense, especially when I remembered that he had never wanted her to be our bridesmaid. 'Look, Millie.' I took her hands in mine, knowing that Jack would be suspicious if we were too long. 'Shall we play a game? A secret game for just you and me? Do you remember Rosie?' I asked, referring to the imaginary friend she invented when she was younger to take the blame for her own wrongdoings.

She nodded vigorously. 'Rosie do bad things, not Millie.'

'Yes, I know,' I said solemnly. 'She was very naughty.' Millie looked so guilty that I couldn't help smiling.

'I not like Rosie, Rosie bad, like Jack.'

'But it wasn't Jack who pushed you down the stairs.'

'Was,' she said stubbornly.

'No, it wasn't. It was somebody else.'

She looked at me suspiciously. 'Who?'

I cast desperately around for a name. 'George Clooney.'

Millie stared at me for a moment. 'Jorj Koony?'

'Yes. You don't like George Clooney, do you?'

'No, don't like Jorj Koony,' she agreed.

'He was the one who pushed you down the stairs, not Jack.'

A frown furrowed her brow. 'Not Jack?'

'No, not Jack. You like Jack, Millie, you like Jack very much.' I gave her a little shake. 'It's very important that you like Jack. He didn't push you down the stairs, George Clooney did. Do you understand? You have to like Jack, Millie, for me.'

She looked at me closely. 'You scared.'

'Yes, Millie, I'm scared. So please, tell me that you like Jack. It's very important.'

'I like Jack,' she said obediently.

'Good, Millie.'

'But don't like Jorj Koony.'

'No, you don't, you don't like George Clooney at all.'

'He bad, he push me down the stairs.'

'Yes, he did. But you don't have to tell people that. You mustn't tell people that George Clooney pushed you down the stairs. That's a secret, like Rosie. But you must tell people that you like Jack. That's not a secret. And you must tell Jack that you like him. Do you understand?'

'I understand.' She nodded. 'Must tell Jack like him.'

'Yes.'

'I tell him I not like Jorj Koony?'

'Yes, you can tell him that too.'

She leant in closer to me. 'But Jack Jorj Koony, Jorj Koony Jack,' she whispered.

'Yes, Millie, Jack is George Clooney but only we know that,' I whispered back. 'Do you see what I mean? It's a secret, our secret, like Rosie.'

'Jack bad man, Grace.'

'Yes, Jack bad man. But that's our secret too. You mustn't tell anyone.'

'I not live with him. I scared.'

'I know.'

'So what you do?'

'I'm not sure yet, but I'll find a solution.'

'Promise?'

'Promise.'

She looked closely at me. 'Grace sad.'

'Yes, Grace sad.'

'Don't worry, Millie here. Millie help Grace.'

'Thank you,' I said, hugging her. 'Remember, Millie, you like Jack.'

'I not forget.'

'And you mustn't say you don't want to live with him.'

'Won't.'

'Good, Millie.'

Outside, we found Jack waiting impatiently for us.

'Why were you so long?' he asked, giving me a long look.

'I have period,' said Millie importantly. 'Need long time for period.'

'Shall we go for a walk before we go back?'

'Yes, I like walk.'

'Maybe we can find an ice cream along the way.'

Remembering what I told her, she beamed at him. 'Thank you, Jack.'

'Well, she seems to have recovered some of her good humour,' Jack remarked, as Millie skipped along in front of us.

'When we were in the toilets, I explained that now that we are married, it is normal that you are always with me, and she's understood that she has to share me with you.'

'As long as that was all you said.'

'Of course it was.'

Janice was waiting when we dropped her off at school an hour later. 'You look as if you've had a nice time, Millie,' she smiled.

'Have,' Millie agreed. She turned to Jack. 'I like you, Jack, you nice.'

'I'm glad you think so,' he nodded, looking over at Janice.

'But don't like Jorj Koony.'

'That's fine by me,' he told her. 'I don't like him either.'

And Millie had howled with laughter.

PRESENT

We're going to Esther and Rufus's tonight, and to see Millie tomorrow. I know for certain that we're going because Janice took the liberty of phoning yesterday to check with Jack that we were. It seems she has a family lunch that she can't miss and there is nobody to look after Millie if we don't go, but, as we haven't been for three weeks, I can't help thinking it's an excuse. Privately, I think she's getting a little fed up with us not turning up to take Millie out, something I'm surprised Jack isn't more careful about. At the expense of punishing me, he's risking Janice questioning our commitment to Millie. But, as that can only be in my favour, I'm hardly going to point it out to him.

Maybe it's because I know I'll be seeing Millie tomorrow that I feel less stressed than usual about going out tonight. Dinners at friends' are the equivalent of walking through a minefield for me as I'm always worried about doing or saying something Jack will use against me. I'm pleased that I didn't fall into the trap he set me by shading the words in Esther's book, although I'll have to be careful that I don't say anything to her that he could misconstrue.

He took the book away with him when he brought me my breakfast this morning and I laughed to think of him scouring the pages in vain for anything untoward, a word or two scored through with my nail perhaps. It obviously annoyed him to find there was nothing because he spent most of the day in the basement, always a bad sign. And very boring for me. I prefer it when he moves around as it amuses me to chart his movements as he goes from one room to the next, trying to work out what he's doing from the sounds that come to me from below.

I know he's in the kitchen at the moment and that he's just made himself a cup of tea because a few minutes ago I heard the sound of the kettle being filled with water, and the click when it switched itself off. I envy him. One of the many things I hate about being kept a prisoner is not being able to make myself a cup of tea whenever I want and I miss my kettle and the regular supply of teabags and milk I used to have. When I think about it now, Jack was a pretty generous jailer in the beginning.

From the way the sun is beginning to dip in the sky, I guess that it's somewhere around six in the evening and, as we have to be at Esther's for seven, Jack should be coming to let me into the bedroom next door, the one that used to be mine, so that I can get ready. Before long, I hear his footsteps on the stairs. A moment later, the key turns in the lock and the door swings open.

When I see him standing there, I feel as dismayed as I always do at how normal he looks, because surely there should be something—pointed ears or a pair of horns—to warn people of his evilness. He stands back to let me pass and I go eagerly into the room next door, glad to have the chance to dress up, to wear something other than black, something other than slippers on my feet. I slide open the wardrobe door and wait for Jack to tell me what to wear. When he doesn't say anything, I know he is out to give me false hope by letting me believe I can wear what I want only to tell me to take it off again as soon as I've put it on. Maybe because I managed to see through his ruse with the book, I decide to gamble and choose a dress that I don't want to wear at all, because it's black. I take my pyjamas off. Uncomfortable though it is to have Jack looking on as I dress and undress, I can't do anything about it as I lost my right to privacy long ago.

'You're beginning to look a bit scrawny,' Jack remarks, as I put on my underwear.

'Maybe you should bring me something to eat a little more often,' I suggest.

'Maybe I should,' he agrees.

By the time I've got into the dress and am doing the zip up, I begin to think I've got it wrong.

'Take it off,' he says, as I smooth it down. 'Wear the red one.'

I feign disappointment and take off the black dress, pleased that I've managed to outwit him, because the red is the one I would have chosen to wear. I slip it on and, maybe because of the colour, I feel more confident. I walk over to the dressing table, sit down in front of the mirror and look at myself for the first time in three weeks. The first thing I notice is that my eyebrows need plucking. Much as I hate having to do such rituals in front of Jack, I take my tweezers from the drawer and start perfecting my eyebrows. I had to negotiate the right to wax my legs, pointing out that I couldn't look perfect if they were covered in hair, and, fortunately, he agreed to add a packet of wax strips to the minimal supply of toiletries he brings me each month.

When I've finished my eyebrows, I put on my make-up and, in honour of my dress, choose a brighter lipstick than usual. I stand up, walk over to the wardrobe and look through the shoeboxes, looking for my red-and-black high-heeled shoes. I slip them on my feet, take the matching bag off the shelf and hand it to him. He opens it and looks inside, checking that sometime over the past three weeks I haven't managed to conjure up pen and paper out of thin air and transport a note through solid walls and into the bag. Passing it back to me, he looks me up and down and nods approvingly, which ironically I know is more than some women get from their husbands.

We go downstairs and in the hall, he takes my coat from the cupboard and holds it open while I slip my arms into it. In the drive outside, he holds the car door for me and waits until I'm in. As he closes it behind me, I can't help thinking it's a shame he's such a sadistic bastard, because he has wonderful manners.

We arrive at Esther and Rufus's house and, along with a huge bouquet of flowers and a bottle of champagne, Jack hands Esther back her book, which I presume he's returned to its original state. She asks me what I thought of it and I tell her what I told Jack, that it took me a while to get through it because it wasn't the sort of book I would normally read. She seems overly disappointed, which makes me wonder if it was her who highlighted the words after all and, hiding my panic, I look at her anxiously. But there's nothing on her face to suggest I might have missed an opportunity, and my heartbeat slows back down.

We go through to where Diane and Adam are waiting, Jack's arm around my waist. I don't know if it's because of all the little courtesies he's accorded me or because I managed to wear the dress that I wanted, but, by the time we've finished our drinks and are heading for the table, I'm beginning to feel as if I'm a normal woman on a normal night out instead of a prisoner out with her jailer. Or maybe it's just that I've had too much champagne to drink. As we wind our way through the delicious dinner that Esther has cooked for us, I'm aware of Jack watching me from across the table as I eat too much and talk a lot more than I usually do.

'You look pensive, Jack,' Esther remarks.

'I was just thinking how much I'm looking forward to Millie coming to live with us,' he says, in what only I recognise as a call to order.

'It can't be long now,' she says.

'Seventy-five days.' Jack sighs happily. 'Did you know that, Grace? Only another seventy-five days until Millie moves into her lovely red bedroom and becomes part of our family.'

I'd been about to take a sip of wine, but my heart plummets so fast that the glass comes to an abrupt stop in mid-air and a little slops over the side.

'No, I didn't know,' I say, wondering how I could have sat there so complacently when time is running out, wondering how I could have forgotten, even for one minute, the desperate situation that I'm in. Seventy-five days—how could there be so little time left? More importantly, how am I ever going to be able to think of a way of escaping from Jack when I haven't been able to in the three hundred and seventy-five days that must have passed since we came back from our honeymoon? Back then, even after the horror I had been through—and the ones that had faced me when we arrived at the house—I had never doubted that I would be able to escape before Millie came to live with us. Even when each attempt I made failed, there had always been a next time. But I hadn't tried for more than six months now.

'Carry on, Grace,' says Jack, nodding at my glass of wine and smiling at me. I stare back at him numbly and he raises his glass. 'Let's drink to Millie coming to live with us.' He looks around the table. 'In fact, why don't we all drink to Millie?'

'Good idea,' Adam says, raising his glass. 'To Millie.'

'To Millie,' everyone chimes, as I try to fight the panic rising inside me. Aware of Esther looking at me curiously I raise my glass quickly, hoping she won't notice my shaking hand.

'While we're in a celebratory mood,' Adam says, 'perhaps you'd all care to raise your glasses again.' Everybody looks at him in interest. 'Diane is expecting a baby! A brother or sister for Emily and Jasper!'

'What wonderful news!' says Esther, as congratulations fly around the table. 'Don't you think so, Grace?'

To my horror, I burst into tears.

In the shocked silence that follows, the thought of the punishment that Jack is going to exact from me for my lack of self-control makes me cry even more. I try frantically to stem the tears but it's impossible and, horribly embarrassed, I get to my feet, aware of Diane at my side, trying to comfort me. But it is Jack who takes me in his arms—because how can he do otherwise?—and holds me close, cradling my head against his shoulder, murmuring soothing words of comfort, and I cry even harder, thinking of how it could have been, of how I had thought it would be. For the first time, I want to give up, to die, because suddenly everything is too much and there is no solution in sight.

'I can't go on like this,' I sob to Jack, not caring that everyone is listening.

'I know,' he soothes. 'I know.' It's as if he's acknowledging that he's gone too far and, for a split second, I actually believe that everything is going to be all right. 'I think we should tell them, don't you?' He raises his head. 'Grace had a miscarriage last week,' he announces. 'And I'm afraid it wasn't the first.'

There's a collective gasp and a few seconds of appalled silence before everyone starts talking at once in subdued voices, commiserating with us. Although I know that their kind words of sympathy and understanding relate to a miscarriage I've never had, I manage to derive enough comfort from them to be able to pull myself together.

'I'm sorry,' I mumble to Jack, hoping to dilute the anger I know I'll have to face later.

'Don't be silly,' says Diane, patting my shoulder. 'But I wish you'd told us. I feel awful about Adam announcing my pregnancy like that.'

'I can't go on any longer,' I say, still speaking to Jack.

'You'd find it much simpler if you just accept everything,' he says.

'Can we just leave Millie out of it?' I ask desperately.

'I'm afraid not,' he says solemnly.

'Millie doesn't have to know, does she?' asks Esther, puzzled.

'There's no point upsetting her,' Diane frowns.

Jack turns to them. 'You're right, of course. It would be foolish to tell Millie about Grace's miscarriage. Now, I think I should take Grace home. I hope you'll forgive me for breaking up the party, Esther.'

'I'm fine,' I say quickly, not wanting to leave the safety of Esther and Rufus's house, because I know what will be waiting for me once I get home. I move out of Jack's arms, appalled that I could have taken comfort there for so long. 'Really, I'm fine now and I'd like to stay.'

'Good, I'm glad. Please, Grace, sit back down.' The shame in Esther's eyes tells me that her remark, the one that had prompted my tears, had been barbed and that she feels guilty for having laboured the point that Diane was pregnant. 'I'm sorry,' she says quietly, as I take up my place again. 'And about your miscarriage.'

'It's all right,' I say. 'Please, let's just forget it.'

As I drink the coffee that Esther has served, I work harder than I've ever worked before, horribly conscious of how stupid I was to let my guard down. Aware that I need to redeem myself if I want to see Millie tomorrow, I look lovingly at Jack and explain to everyone around the table that the reason I broke down was because I feel dreadful that, for the moment, I seem unable to give Jack the thing he wants most in the world, a baby. When we finally stand up to leave I know that everyone admires my speedy and charming recovery and I sense that Esther likes me a lot more than she did before, which can only be a good thing, even if it's only because of my imperfect womb.

Reality hits me once I'm sitting in the car on the way home. Jack's grim silence tells me that however much ground I've made up in relation to the others, he's still going to make me pay for my stupidity. The thought of not going to see Millie is more than I can bear and, as silent tears spring from my eyes, I'm shocked at how weak I've become.

We arrive at the house. Jack unlocks the front door and we go into the hall.

'You know, I have never questioned who I am,' he says thoughtfully as he helps me off with my coat. 'But tonight, for a split second, when I was holding you in my arms, when everybody was commiserating with us about your miscarriage, I had a taste of what it was like to be normal.'

'You could be!' I tell him. 'You could be, if you really wanted to be! You could get help, Jack, I know you could!'

He grins at my outburst. 'The trouble is, I don't want help. I like who I am, I like it very much indeed. And I'll like it even better in seventy-five days' time, when Millie comes to live with us. It's a shame we won't be going to see her tomorrow—I'm almost beginning to miss her.'

'Please, Jack,' I beg.

'Well, I certainly can't let you off for your appalling lack of restraint tonight so if you want to see Millie tomorrow, you know what you have to do.'

'You couldn't stand that I didn't fall into your pathetic trap, could you?' I say, realising that he had set out to upset me during the dinner by mentioning Millie coming to live with us.

'Pathetic trap?'

'Yes, that's right, pathetic. Couldn't you come up with anything better than shading words in a book?'

'You really are becoming too clever for your own good,' he snaps. 'Whichever way I look at it, you need to be punished.'

I shake my head pitifully. 'No, I can't. I've had enough. I mean it, Jack, I've had enough.'

'But I haven't,' he says. 'I haven't had nearly enough. In fact, it hasn't even begun for me. That's the trouble, you see. The nearer I get to having what I've been waiting for for so long, the more I crave it. It's got to the point where I'm tired of waiting. I'm tired of waiting for Millie to move in with us.'

'Why don't we go back to Thailand?' I say desperately, terrified he'll suggest Millie moves in with us sooner than planned. 'It will do you good—we haven't been since January.'

'I can't—I have the Tomasin case coming up.'

'But you won't be able to go once Millie comes to live with us,' I point out, eager to consolidate my position, needing to keep Millie safely at school for as long as possible.

He gives me an amused glance. 'Trust me, once Millie comes to live with us, I won't want to. Now, get moving.'

I start shaking so much that I have difficulty walking. I make my way to the stairs and put my foot on the bottom step.

'You're going the wrong way,' he says. 'Unless you don't want to see Millie tomorrow, of course.' He pauses a moment to make it sound as if he's giving me a choice. 'So what's it to be, Grace?' His voice is high with excitement. 'A disappointed Millie—or the basement?'

PAST

After what Millie had told me about Jack pushing her down the stairs, the pressure to get away from him intensified. Even though I'd made her promise not to tell anyone, I couldn't be sure that she wouldn't suddenly blurt it out to Janice, or even accuse Jack to his face. I don't think it had occurred to him that she might have realised her fall was more than an accident. It was easy to underestimate Millie, and presume that the way she spoke was a reflection of the way her mind worked, but she was a lot cleverer than people gave her credit for. I had no idea what Jack would do if he discovered that she knew very well what had happened that day. I supposed he would dismiss her accusations as quickly as he had dismissed mine and suggest that she was jealous because he and I were now together, and was trying to break us up by making false accusations against him.

The only thing that kept me going through that bleak time was Millie. She seemed so at ease with Jack that I thought she'd forgotten he had pushed her down the stairs, or at least had come to terms with it. But whenever I told myself it was for the best, she would trot out what was fast becoming her mantra, 'I like you Jack, but don't like Jorj Koony,' as if she knew what I was thinking and wanted to let me know that she was keeping her side of the bargain. As such, the pressure to keep my side of it grew and I began to plan my next move.

After what had happened when I'd tried to get the doctor to help me, I decided that next time, the more people who were around, the better it would be. So when I felt ready to try again, I pleaded with Jack to take me shopping with him, hoping that during the course of the trip I'd be able to get help from a shop assistant or member of the public. As I got out of the car, I thought my prayers had been answered when I saw a policeman standing only yards away from me. Even the way Jack held on to me tightly when I tried to break free lent weight to the fact that I was being kept prisoner and, when the policeman came hurrying over in response to my cries for help, I honestly thought my ordeal was over, until his concerned words—'Is everything all right, Mr Angel?'—told me otherwise.

My behaviour from that point on confirmed what Jack had thought to tell the local constabulary some time before, namely that his wife had a history of mental problems and was prone to causing disturbances in public places, often by accusing him of keeping her prisoner. As Jack held my flailing limbs in a vice-like grip, he suggested to the policeman, in full hearing of the large crowd that had gathered, that he come and see the house that I called a prison. As the crowd looked on, whispering about mental illness and throwing Jack looks of solidarity, a police car arrived and, while I sat in the back with a policewoman who tried to still my tears of despair with soothing words, the policeman asked Jack about the work he did on behalf of battered women.

Afterwards, once it was all over and I was back in the room I had thought never to see again, the fact that he had so readily agreed for me to accompany him on the shopping trip confirmed what I had already worked out in Thailand, which was that he derived enormous pleasure from allowing me to think I had won, then snatching my victory away from me. He enjoyed preparing the ground for my downfall, rejoiced in his role as my loving but harassed husband, delighted in my crushing disappointment and, when it was all over, took pleasure in punishing me. Not only that, his ability to predict what I was going to do meant that I was doomed to failure from the start.

It was another three weeks before I saw Millie again and Jack's explanation—that I had been too busy with friends to visit—hurt and confused her, especially as I couldn't tell her otherwise with Jack constantly at our sides. Determined not to let her down again, I began to toe the line so that I could see her regularly. But, rather than please Jack, my subservience seemed to annoy him. I thought I had got him wrong, however, when he told me that because of my good behaviour he was going to allow me to paint again. Suspicious of his intentions, I hid my delight from him and gave him a list of what I needed half-heartedly, not daring to believe he would actually bring me what I was asking for. The next day, however, he duly arrived with pastels and oils in a variety of colours, as well as my easel and a new canvas.

'There's only one stipulation,' he said, as I rejoiced over them like old friends. 'I get to choose the subject matter.'

'What do you mean?' I frowned.

'You paint what I want you to paint, nothing more, nothing less.'

I looked at him warily, trying to weigh him up, wondering if it was another of his games. 'It depends what you want me to paint,' I said.

'A portrait.'

'A portrait?'

'Yes. You have painted some before, haven't you?'

'A few.'

'Good. So, I'd like you to paint a portrait.'

'Of you?'

'Yes or no, Grace?'

All my instincts told me to refuse. But I was desperate to paint again, desperate to have something to fill my days besides reading. Although the thought of painting Jack revolted me, I told myself he was hardly going to stand and pose for me hour after hour. At least, I hoped not.

'Only if I can work from a photograph,' I said, relieved to have found a solution.

'Done.' He fished in his pocket. 'Would you like to start now?'

'Why not?' I shrugged.

He drew out a photograph and held it in front of my face. 'She was one of my clients. Don't you think she's beautiful?'

With a cry of alarm, I backed away from him, from it, but he followed me relentlessly, grinning inanely. 'Come on, Grace, don't be shy, take a good look. After all, you're going to be seeing a lot of her over the next couple of weeks.'

'Never,' I spat. 'I'll never paint her!'

'Of course you will. You agreed, remember? And you know what happens if you go back on your word?' I stared at him. 'That's right—Millie. You do want to see her, don't you?'

'Not if this is the price I have to pay,' I said, my voice tight.

'I'm sorry—I should have said, "You do want to see her again, don't you?" I'm sure you don't want Millie to be left to rot in some asylum, do you?'

'You'd better not lay a finger on her!' I yelled.

'Then you had better get painting. If you destroy this photograph, or deface it in any way, Millie will pay. If you don't reproduce it on canvas, or pretend that you are unable to, Millie will pay. I will check daily to see how you're progressing and, if I decide you are working too slowly, Millie will pay. And, when you've finished, you will paint another, and another, and another, until I decide I have enough.'

'Enough for what?' I sobbed, knowing I was beaten.

'I'll show you one day. I promise, Grace, I'll show you one day.'

I cried and cried over that first painting. To have to look at a bruised and bloodied face hour after hour, day after day, to have to examine a broken nose, a cut lip, a black eye in minute detail and reproduce it on canvas was more than I could stomach and I was often violently sick. I knew that if

I was to keep hold of my sanity I had to find a way of dealing with the trauma of painting something so grotesque, and I found that by giving the women in subsequent paintings names, and looking beyond the damage that had been done to them, imagining them as they were before, I was able to cope better. It also helped that Jack had never lost a case, as it meant that the women in the photographs—all ex-clients of his—had managed to get away from their abusive partners, and it made me all the more determined to get away from him. If they could do it, so could I.

We must have been about four months into our marriage when Jack decided that we'd spent enough time wrapped up in each other and that if people weren't to become suspicious, we would have to begin socialising as we had before. One of the first dinners we went to was at Moira and Giles's, but as they were primarily Jack's friends, I behaved exactly as he told me I should and played the loving wife. It made me sick to the stomach to do so, but I realised that if he didn't start trusting me, I'd be confined to my room indefinitely, and my chances of escaping would be drastically reduced.

I knew I'd done the right thing when, not long after, he told me that we'd be dining with colleagues of his. The rush of adrenalin I felt on hearing that they were colleagues and not friends was enough to convince me that it would be the perfect opportunity to get away from him, as they were more likely to believe my story than friends who had already had the wool pulled over their eyes by Jack. And, with a bit of luck, Jack's success in the firm might mean there was somebody just waiting for the opportunity to stab him in the back. I knew I would have to be ingenious; Jack had already drummed into me how I was to act when other people were present—no going off on my own, not even to the toilet, no following anybody into another room, even if it was only to carry plates through, no having a private conversation with anybody, no looking anything but wonderfully happy and content.

It took me a while to work out what to do. Rather than try to get help in front of Jack, who was so very good at dismissing my accusations, I decided it would be better to try to get a letter to someone, because there was less chance of me being dismissed as a hysterical madwoman if I put everything in writing. Indeed, in view of Jack's threats, it seemed the safest way forward. But getting my hands on even a small piece of paper proved impossible. I couldn't ask Jack outright because he would have been immediately suspicious and not only would he have refused, he would have watched me like a hawk from then on.

The idea of cutting relevant words out of the books he had thoughtfully supplied me with came to me in the middle of the night. Using a pair of small nail scissors from my toilet bag, I cut out 'please', 'help', 'me', 'I', 'am', 'being', 'held', 'captive', 'get', 'police'. I looked for a way of putting them in some kind of order. In the end, I put one on top of the other, starting with 'please' and finishing with 'police'. They made such a tiny pile that the possibility of them being mistaken for just a screw of paper and being thrown away made me decide to secure them with one of my hairgrips, which I had in my make-up bag. Surely, I reasoned, anyone who found a hairgrip holding a bundle of little pieces of paper together would be curious enough to look at them.

After a lot of thought, because I couldn't afford to have it opened in Jack's presence, I decided to leave my cry for help somewhere on the table once dinner was over so it could be found after we'd left. I had no idea where we were having dinner, but I prayed it would be in someone's house and not in a restaurant where the danger of the clip being scooped up in the tablecloth along with other debris was higher.

In the event, my careful planning came to nothing. I had been so concerned as to where I should leave my precious bundle of words that I forgot I had to get it past Jack first. I wasn't overly worried until he came to fetch me and, after watching me for a moment as I slipped on my shoes and picked up my bag, asked why I was so nervous. Although I pretended it was because I would be meeting his colleagues, he didn't believe me, especially as I had already met most of them at our wedding. He searched my clothes, getting me to turn out my pockets and then demanded that I give him my bag. His anger when he found the hairclip was predictable, his punishment exactly as he had promised. He moved me into the box room, which he had stripped of every comfort and began to starve me.

PRESENT

Waking in the basement, my mind instantly craves sunlight to anchor my internal clock. Or something to make me feel I haven't, finally, lost my mind. I can't hear Jack, but I sense he's near, listening. Suddenly, the door swings open.

'You're going to have to move quicker than that if we're to be in time to take Millie for lunch,' he remarks, as I get slowly to my feet.

I know I should feel pleased that we're going but the truth is, seeing Millie gets harder with each visit we make. Ever since she told me that Jack had pushed her down the stairs, she's been waiting for me to do something about it. I'm beginning to dread the day she'll actually manage to persuade Jack to take us to the hotel because I don't want to have to tell her I still haven't found a solution. Back then, it never occurred to me that I would still be a prisoner a year on. I had known that it would be difficult to get away from him but not that it would be impossible. And now, there is so little time left. Seventy-four days. The thought of Jack counting down the days until Millie comes to live with us like a child waiting impatiently for Christmas makes me feel sick.

As usual, Millie and Janice are waiting on the bench for us. We chat for a while—Janice asks us if we enjoyed the wedding the previous weekend and our visit to friends the weekend before that and Jack leaves it to me to invent that the wedding was in Devon, and very lovely, and that we enjoyed the Peak District, where our friends live, very much. Jack, ever charming, tells Janice that she's a treasure for allowing us to take advantage of the short time we have left together before Millie comes to live with us and Janice replies that she doesn't mind at all, that she adores Millie and is happy to step in for us whenever we need her to. She adds that she's going to miss her when she leaves and reiterates her promise to come and visit us often, which Jack will make sure that she never does. We talk about how Millie has been and Janice tells us that thanks to the sleeping pills the doctor prescribed, she's getting a good night's sleep, which means that she's back to her normal self during the day.

'I'm sorry,' she says apologetically, looking at her watch. 'I'm afraid I'm going to have to leave you. My mother will kill me if I'm late for lunch.'

'We need to get going too,' Jack says.

'Can we go to hotel today, please?' Millie asks eagerly.

Jack opens his mouth, but before he can tell us that he's taking us somewhere else, Janice intervenes.

'Millie has been telling me all about the hotel and how much she likes it there and she's promised to tell us about it in class on Monday, haven't you, Millie?' Millie nods enthusiastically. 'She's already told us about the restaurant by the lake and the one that serves the pancakes so we're looking forward to hearing about this one. And Mrs Goodrich is thinking of taking the staff to the hotel for the end-of-school-year dinner,' she adds, 'so she's commissioned Millie to write a report on it.'

'Need to go to hotel for Mrs Goodrich,' Millie confirms.

'Then the hotel it is,' says Jack, hiding his annoyance by smiling indulgently at her.

Millie chats away happily during lunch and, when we've finished, she says she needs to go to the toilet.

'Go on then,' says Jack.

She stands up. 'Grace come with me.'

'There's no need for Grace to go with you,' Jack tells her firmly. 'You're perfectly able to go by yourself.'

'I have period,' Millie announces loudly. 'Need Grace.'

'Very well,' says Jack, hiding his distaste. He pushes his chair back. 'I'll come too.'

'Jack not allowed in Ladies' toilet,' Millie says belligerently.

'I meant that I'll come as far as the toilets with you.'

He leaves us at the end of the corridor, warning us not to

be long. There are two ladies at the sinks chatting away happily as they wash their hands and Millie hops from foot to foot, impatient for them to leave. I rack my brains for something to tell her, something that will make her think I have a solution in mind and marvel at the way she contrived to get Jack to bring us here by drawing Janice and Mrs Goodrich into the equation.

'That was clever of you, Millie,' I tell her, as soon as the door closes behind the women.

'Need to talk,' she hisses.

'What is it?'

'Millie have something for Grace,' she whispers. She slips her hand into her pocket and draws out a tissue. 'Secret,' she says, handing it to me. Puzzled, I unfold the tissue, expecting to find a bead or a flower and find myself looking at a handful of small white pills.

'What are these?' I frown.

'For sleep. I not take them.'

'Why not?'

'Don't need them,' she says, scowling.

'But they're to help you sleep better,' I explain patiently.

'I sleep fine.'

'Yes, you do now, because of the pills,' I insist. 'Before, you didn't, remember?'

She shakes her head. 'I pretend.'

'Pretend?'

'Yes. I pretend can't sleep.'

I look at her, perplexed. 'Why?'

She closes my hand over the tissue. 'For you, Grace.'

'Well, it's very kind of you, Millie, but I don't need them.'

'Yes, Grace need them. For Jorj Koony.'

'George Clooney?'

'Yes. Jorj Koony bad man, Jorj Koony push me down stairs, Jorj Koony make Grace sad. He bad man, very bad man.'

Now it's my turn to shake my head. 'I'm afraid I don't understand.'

'Yes, you understand.' Millie is adamant. 'It simple, Grace. We kill Jorj Koony.'

PAST

The following month, we went back to Thailand, but I didn't dare try to escape again. I knew that if I did, Jack was capable of arranging for me to die while we were there. We went to the same hotel and had the same room and were greeted by the same manager. Only Kiko was missing. I spent my days as I had spent them before, locked on the balcony or kept in the room, only being allowed out for photographs. My experience the second time round was made even worse by the knowledge that when Jack wasn't with me, he was exhilarating in someone else's fear. I didn't know how he got his kicks, but I presumed it was by doing something he couldn't do in England and, remembering the story he had told me about his mother, I wondered if he came to Thailand to beat up women. It seemed inconceivable that he would be able to get away with it but he once told me that in Thailand, as long as you had money, you could buy anything—even fear.

Maybe that was why, a week after we got back, I smashed him over the head with a bottle of wine in the kitchen, half an hour before Diane and Adam were due to arrive for dinner, hoping to stun him long enough to escape. But I didn't hit him hard enough and, incandescent with rage, he controlled himself long enough to phone and cancel our guests, pleading a sudden migraine on my part. As he put the phone down and turned to me, I was afraid only for Millie, because there was nothing left he could deprive me of. Even when he told me that he was going to show me Millie's room, I still wasn't afraid for myself because all I presumed was that he had stripped it of its beautiful furnishings, as he had done mine. As he pushed me into the hall, my arms twisted painfully behind my back, I felt desperately sad for Millie because it was the room she had always dreamt of having. But, instead of taking me up to the first floor, he opened the door that led down to the basement.

I fought like mad not to go down the stairs but I was no match for Jack, his already powerful strength inflamed by fury. Even then, I had no idea what was waiting for me. It was only when he dragged me past the utility room where he had kept Molly, through what seemed to be a storeroom and came to a stop in front of a steel door cleverly hidden behind a stack of shelves that I began to feel real fear.

It wasn't some sort of torture chamber, as I'd first feared, because there were no instruments of torture as such. Devoid of furniture, the whole of the room, including the floor and ceilings, had been painted blood red. It was terrible, chilling, but it wasn't the only thing that caused me to cry out in distress.

'Take a good look,' he snarled. 'I hope Millie will appreciate it as much as I do because this is the room where she's going to stay, not the pretty yellow bedroom upstairs.' He shook me hard. 'Look at it and tell me how scared you think she's going to be.'

I could feel my eyes rolling in my head as I tried to look anywhere but at the walls, where the portraits he had forced me to paint for him hung.

'Do you think Millie is going to like the paintings you've done specially for her? Which one do you think will be her favourite? This one?' His hand on the back of my head, he pushed my face hard up against one of the portraits. 'Or this one?' He dragged me over to one of the other walls. 'Such beautiful handiwork, don't you think?' Moaning, I screwed my eyes shut tight. 'I hadn't intended to show you this room just yet,' he went on, 'but now you can try it for size. You really shouldn't have hit me with that bottle.'

After giving me a final shove, he went out of the room, leaving the door to slam shut behind him. I scrambled to my feet and ran to the door. When I saw that there was no handle, I began hammering on it with my fists, screaming at him to let me out.

'Scream all you like.' His voice came through the door. 'You don't know how much it excites me.'

Unable to control my fear—that he would never let me out, that he would leave me to die there—I became hysterical.

Within seconds, I found I couldn't breathe and, as I began to hyperventilate, the pain in my chest brought me to my knees. Realising that I was having some sort of panic attack, I fought to regain control of my breathing, but the sound of Jack laughing excitedly from the other side of the door only increased my distress. Tears streamed from my eyes and, unable to catch my breath, I honestly believed I was going to die. The thought that I would be leaving Millie at Jack's mercy was truly terrible and, as a picture of her wearing her yellow hat and scarf came into my mind, I clung on to it, wanting it to be the last thing I remembered.

It was a while before I noticed that the pain in my chest had eased, making it possible for me to draw in deeper breaths. I didn't dare move in case I started everything off again; instead, I stayed as I was, my head on my knees, and concentrated on my breathing. The relief that I was still alive, that I could still save Millie, gave me the strength to lift my head and look for another way out of the room. But there wasn't even a small window. I began searching the walls, running my hands over them and moving the paintings aside, hoping to find some sort of switch that would open the door.

'You're wasting your time,' Jack's voice drawled, making me jump. 'It can't be opened from the inside.' Just knowing he was on the other side of the door made me start shaking again. 'How do you like the room?' he went on. 'I hope you're enjoying yourself in there as much as I am listening to you out here. I can't wait to hear what Millie thinks of it— hopefully she'll be even more vocal than you.'

Suddenly exhausted, I lay down on the floor and curled myself into a ball, wedging my fingers in my ears so that I wouldn't have to listen to him. I prayed for sleep to take me but the room remained brightly lit, making it impossible.

As I lay there, I tried not to consider the possibility that he would never let me out of the hell he had created for Millie, and when I remembered how I had truly believed, on the strength of a beautiful yellow bedroom, that somewhere deep inside him lay a tiny shred of decency, I wept at my stupidity.

PRESENT

I stare at Millie, the pills still in my hand, wondering if I've heard her correctly. 'Millie, we can't.'

'Yes, can. Have to.' She nods her head determinedly. 'Jorj Koony bad man.'

Frightened of where the conversation is going and conscious of Jack waiting, I fold the pills back into the tissue. 'I think we should flush these down the loo, Millie.'

'No!'

'We can't do anything bad, Millie,' I say.

'Jorj Koony do bad thing,' she says darkly. 'Jorj Koony bad man, very bad man.'

'Yes, I know.'

A frown furrows her brow. 'But I come live with Grace soon.'

'Yes, that's right, you are coming to live with me soon.'

'But I not live with bad man, I scared. So we kill bad man, we kill Jorj Koony.'

'I'm sorry Millie, we can't kill anybody.'

'Agata Christie kill people!' she says indignantly. 'In *And Then There None*, lots of people die, and Mrs Rogers, she die from sleeping medicine.'

'Maybe she does,' I say firmly. 'But they're just stories, Millie, you know that.'

Yet even while I'm telling her that we can't, my mind races on ahead, wondering if there are enough pills to at least knock Jack out long enough for me to escape. Common sense tells me that even if there are enough, the chances of being able to get them into him are almost negligible. But despite what I've just told Millie, I know I'll never be able to flush them down the toilet because they represent the first glimmer of hope I've had in a long time. But I also know that whatever I decide to do with them—if anything—Millie can't be involved.

'I'm going to flush the pills away,' I tell her, walking into one of the cubicles. As I flush the chain, I quickly stuff the tissue up my sleeve but immediately panic when I realise that Jack will see the bulge and ask what it is. Fishing it back out, I look up and down my person, wondering where I can hide it. I can't put it in my bag, because Jack always checks it before I put it away, and hiding it down my bra or knickers is out because he always watches me undress. Stooping, I slip the scrunched-up tissue into my shoe, wedging it firmly into the toe. It's difficult to get my shoe back on and I know it's going to be even more uncomfortable once I start walking, but I feel safer with the pills hidden there than on my body. I have no idea how I'm going to be able to get them out of my shoe if a time comes when I feel I can use them but just knowing they are there gives me comfort.

'Grace stupid!' Millie says furiously, as I come back out. 'Can't kill Jorj Koony now!'

'That's right, Millie, we can't,' I agree.

'But he bad man!'

'Yes, but we can't kill bad men,' I point out. 'It's against the law.'

'Then tell police Jorj Koony bad man!'

'That's a good idea, Millie,' I say, seeking to soothe her agitation. 'I'll tell the police.'

'Now!'

'No, not now, but soon.'

'Before I come live with you?'

'Yes, before you come to live with me.'

'You tell police?'

I take her hand in mine. 'Do you trust me, Millie?' She nods reluctantly. 'Then I promise I'll find a solution before you come to live with me.'

'Promise?'

'Yes, I promise,' I tell her, fighting back tears. 'And now you must promise me something. You must promise that you'll continue to keep our secret.'

'I like Jack but I don't like Jorj Koony,' she intones, still upset with me.

'Yes, that's right, Millie. Now, let's go back out and see Jack. Maybe he'll buy us an ice cream.'

But even the thought of an ice cream, one of Millie's favourite things, isn't enough to lift her spirits. When I think about how proud and excited she'd been when she handed me the carefully wrapped pills, how clever she'd been to find a solution to the desperate situation we're in, I hate that I can't tell her how amazing she is. But despite the surge of hope I'd felt when I placed the pills in the toe of my shoe, I don't see how I'll be able to use them.

The walk to the nearby park, and the ice-cream van that is parked there, is so uncomfortable because of my squashed toes that I know I'm not going to be able to spend the next three hours walking around. Millie is so downcast I'm worried Jack will guess that something transpired between us during our time in the toilets and start asking questions that she won't know how to answer. In an effort to distract her, I ask her which flavour ice cream she's going to choose and, when she shrugs unenthusiastically, Jack's appraising look tells me that even if he hadn't noticed before, her change of spirits has now caught his attention. Looking for a way to distract him, and to brighten Millie's mood, I suggest going to the cinema, which will also get me off my feet.

'Would you like that?' Jack asks, turning to Millie.

'Yes,' she says unenthusiastically.

'Then we'll go. But first, Millie, I want to know what happened in the toilet.'

'What you mean?' Caught off guard, Millie is defensive.

'Just that you were happy when you went into the toilet and miserable when you came out,' he says reasonably.

'I have period.'

'You knew that before you went in. Come on, Millie, tell me what happened to upset you.' His voice is encouraging, coaxing and, sensing Millie hesitate, I feel a prickle of fear. It's not that I think she's suddenly going to blurt out to Jack about the pills, but he's so good at manipulating people I'd be stupid not to be afraid and, in the mood she's in, Millie is more likely to let her guard down. As well as that, she's angry with me. I turn my head towards her, hoping to be able to warn her with my eyes to be careful but she refuses to look at me.

'Can't.' Millie shakes her head.

'Why not?'

'Is secret.'

'I'm afraid you're not allowed to have secrets,' Jack says regretfully. 'So why don't you tell me? Did Grace say something that upset you? You can tell me, Millie. In fact, you have to tell me.'

'She say no,' she says, shrugging.

'No?'

'Yes.'

'I see. And what did Grace say no to?'

'I tell her kill Jorj Koony and she say no,' she says darkly.

'Very funny, Millie.'

'Is true.'

'The thing is, Millie, even if it is, I don't believe that's why you're in a bad mood. I know you don't like George Clooney, but you're not stupid, you know very well that Grace can't kill him. So I'll ask you again. What did Grace say that upset you?'

I cast around quickly for something that sounds genuine. 'If you must know, Jack, she asked if she could come and see the house and I said no,' I say, sounding exasperated.

He turns towards me, understanding exactly why I want to keep Millie away from the house.

'Is that so?' he says.

'Want to see my bedroom,' Millie confirms, looking at me to show me she has understood what I want her to say.

'Then so you shall,' Jack says with a flourish, as if he is granting her a wish. 'You're right, Millie, you should be allowed to see your room. In fact, you'll probably love it so much you might ask to move in with us at once rather than go back to school. Don't you think that might be the case, Grace?'

'Is yellow?' Millie asks.

'Of course it is.' Jack smiles. 'Come on, let's go to the cinema—I've got quite a bit of thinking to do.'

At the cinema, I sit in the darkness, glad that nobody can see the tears that spring to my eyes when I realise how reckless I've been. In telling Jack that Millie had asked to see her room, because I couldn't think of anything else to say, I may have brought the danger that is awaiting her even nearer. After what she told me in the toilets, about not wanting to live with Jack, I doubt she would ask to move in with us sooner than later, as Jack had suggested she might. But what if Jack suggests it himself? After the remark he made last night about being tired of waiting, I wouldn't put it past him. And what reason would there be to say no? What excuse could I come up with to keep Millie safely at school? Even if I found one, Jack would never back me up. I steal a glance at him, hoping to find him absorbed in the film, or asleep, but the look of quiet satisfaction on his face tells me he's already realised that inviting Millie to the house might be to his advantage.

The knowledge that I've set something that is potentially dangerous to Millie in motion horrifies me, as does knowing that I have no way to stop it. Just as the hopelessness of my situation threatens to overwhelm me, Millie, seated on the other side of Jack, bursts out laughing at something on screen and I know that I have to save her, at whatever cost to myself, from the horror Jack has in store for her.

The film over, we drive back to the school to drop Millie off. Janice is already there and, as we say goodbye, she asks us if we'll be coming back the following Sunday.

'Actually, we thought we'd bring Millie down to the house instead,' Jack says smoothly. 'It's about time she saw where she's going to be living, don't you think so, darling?'

'I thought you wanted to wait until all the work had been completed,' I point out, trying to keep my voice steady, appalled that he has made his move so quickly.

'It will be by the weekend.'

'You said my bedroom not finished,' Millie says accusingly.

'I was joking,' Jack explains patiently. 'I wanted your visit to us next weekend to be a surprise. So how about we pick you up at eleven o'clock and drive you down. Would you like that?'

Millie hesitates, unsure of what she's meant to say. 'Yes, I like,' she says slowly. 'I like to see house.'

'And your bedroom,' Jack reminds her.

'Is yellow,' Millie says, turning to Janice. 'I have yellow bedroom.'

'Well, you'll be able to tell me all about it when you get back,' Janice tells her.

The fear that Millie might not get back, that Jack will invent a broken-down car to keep her with us, or simply tell Janice and Mrs Goodrich that she has asked to stay on with us, makes it difficult for me to think straight. Aware of how little time I have to act, my mind races, looking for a way— not of stopping the ball from rolling, because it's too late for that—but of diverting it from its path.

'Why don't you come too?' I hear myself say to Janice. 'Then you can see Millie's bedroom for yourself.'

Millie claps her hands in delight. 'Janice come too!'

Jack frowns. 'I'm sure Janice has better things to do with her weekend.'

Janice shakes her head. 'No, its fine, in fact I would love to see whcrc Millie is going to live.'

'Then could I ask you to bring her down?' I ask hurriedly before Jack can dream up a reason for Janice not to come.

'Of course I will! It would be silly for you and Mr Angel to drive all the way here only to go back again. It's the least I can do. If you just give me your address . . .'

'I'll write it down for you,' Jack says. 'Do you have a pen?'

'Not on me, I'm afraid.' Janice looks at my bag. 'Do you have one?'

I don't even pretend to look. 'Sorry,' I say apologetically.

'No problem, I'll just pop and get one.'

She leaves. Painfully aware of Jack's eyes boring into me, I'm unable to answer the questions Millie fires excitedly at me about her forthcoming visit to our house. His fury at the way I've invited Janice along is tangible and I know I'm going to have to come up with an excellent and believable reason as to why I did. But if Janice brings Millie down, there is the unspoken assumption that she'll be going back with her and therefore less chance for Jack to manipulate things so that she ends up staying on with us.

Janice returns with pen and paper and Jack writes down our address and hands it to her. She folds the paper and puts it in her pocket and, maybe because she's used to us cancelling things at the last minute, confirms that the invitation is for the following Sunday, 2 May. When I hear the date, something occurs to me and I find myself grabbing at it with both hands.

'I've just had a thought—why don't we make it the Sunday after instead?' Millie's face falls and I turn to her quickly. 'Then we'll be able to celebrate your eighteenth birthday at the same time. It's on the tenth,' I remind her. 'Would you like that, Millie? Would you like a party in your new house?'

'With cake?' she asks. 'And balloons?'

'With cake, candles, balloons, everything,' I say, hugging her.

'What a lovely idea!' exclaims Janice, as Millie squeals in delight.

'It will also give us time to get the house completely finished,' I add, thrilled at the way I've managed to buy myself more time. 'What do you think, Jack?'

'I think it's an excellent idea,' he says. 'How very clever of you to have thought of it. Now, shall we go? It's getting late and there's something we need to do tonight, isn't there, darling?'

Dread replaces the joy I felt only minutes before at having outsmarted him, as he can only be referring to one thing.

Not wanting him to see how much his words have affected me, I turn and kiss Millie goodbye.

'We'll see you next Sunday,' I tell her, despite knowing that Jack will never allow me to come in view of my invitation to Janice. 'Meanwhile, I'll start getting things ready for your party. Is there anything special you'd like?'

'Big cake,' she laughs. 'Very big cake.'

'I'll make sure Grace makes you the most beautiful cake in the world,' Jack promises.

'I like you, Jack,' she beams.

'But you don't like George Clooney,' he finishes. He turns to Janice. 'In fact, she dislikes him so much that she asked Grace to kill him.'

'Not funny, Millie,' Janice frowns.

'She was joking with you, Jack,' I say calmly, knowing that he understands just how much Millie hates being reprimanded.

'Still, you shouldn't joke about things like that.' Janice is firm. 'Do you understand, Millie? I wouldn't like to have to tell Mrs Goodrich.'

'I sorry,' says Millie, her face crestfallen.

'I think you've been listening to too many Agatha Christie stories,' Janice goes on sternly. 'No more for a week, I'm afraid.'

'I shouldn't have said anything,' Jack says contritely, as tears well up in Millie's eyes. 'I didn't mean to get her into trouble.'

I bite back the angry retort that springs to my lips, surprised that I had even thought of contradicting him. It's something I stopped doing long ago, especially in public.

'Well, we really must be off,' I say to Janice instead. I give

Millie a last hug. 'You can think about what dress you'd like to wear to the party and tell me when I see you next week,' I tell her, hoping to cheer her up.

'What time would you like us to arrive on the ninth?' Janice asks.

'Around one?' I say, looking at Jack for confirmation.

He shakes his head. 'The earlier the better, I think. Besides, I can't wait to show Millie her room. So why don't we say twelve-thirty?'

'Lovely,' Janice smiles.

In the car on the way home, I brace myself for whatever is to come. Jack doesn't say anything for a while, perhaps because he knows that the anticipation of his anger is sometimes, but not always, worse than the event. I tell myself that I can't afford to let fear muddle my thinking and concentrate instead on finding a way of deflecting his fury. The best way, I decide, is to make him think I've given up, that there is no hope left, and I take comfort from the thought that my lethargy over the last few months, which I'd been berating myself for, might actually have served me well, as a slide into total apathy won't seem so contrived.

'I hope you realise that you've made everything much worse for yourself by inviting Janice along,' he says when he feels he's let me sweat enough.

'The reason I invited Janice along is so that she'll be able to report back to Mrs Goodrich that our beautiful house is perfect for Millie,' I say tiredly. 'Do you honestly think that the school where Millie has lived for the last seven years is going to wave goodbye to her without checking up on where she's going?'

He nods approvingly. 'That's very noble of you. But now I have to ask myself why you should choose to be noble, given the circumstances.'

'Because I suppose I've accepted that there's nothing I can do to prevent the inevitable,' I say quietly. 'I think I realised it long ago, actually.' I let a sob choke my voice. 'For a while, I honestly thought that I would be able to find a way out. And I tried; I tried so hard. But you've always been one step ahead of me.'

'I'm glad you've realised it,' he says. 'Although I must admit that I've missed your futile attempts to escape from me. They were amusing, if nothing else.'

The small glow of satisfaction I feel at having out-manoeuvred Jack is precious. It gives me the confidence that I can do it again, that I can turn a bad situation around and turn a negative into a positive. I don't quite know where I'm going to find the positive in Millie coming to the house for lunch, but at least it is only lunch. Her inevitable delight when she sees the house will be hard enough to bear during the few hours she'll spend with us. To have to endure it for any longer when I know what Jack has in store for her, and when I don't know if I'm going to be able to find the solution that I promised her, is unimaginable.

My throbbing toes make me want to ease my shoe off but I don't dare for fear I won't be able to slip it back on easily when we arrive at the house. In the light of her imminent visit, the pills Millie gave me take on a new importance. I had planned to leave them safely tucked into the toe of my shoe, until the time came when I could use them, but I no longer have time for such luxuries. If I am ever to use them, I need to get them into my bedroom, where they will be more easily accessible. But with Jack watching my every move, it's going to be almost impossible.

I use the rest of the journey to consider what I can do. The only way the pills are going to be of any use to me is if I manage to get enough of them into Jack to render him un-conscious. But if getting them into my bedroom seems im-possible, administering them to him seems even more so. I tell myself that I can't afford to look that far ahead, that all I can do is take one step at a time, and concentrate instead on the present.

We arrive at the house and, as we're taking off our coats, the phone starts ringing. Jack answers it, as he always does, while I wait obediently, as I always do. It would be no use me carrying on up the stairs to try to take the pills from my shoe because Jack would simply follow me.

'She's fine today, thank you, Esther,' I hear him say and, after a moment of puzzlement, the events of the previous eve-ning come flooding back and I realise Esther is phoning to see how I am. He pauses a moment. 'Yes, we've just walked in the door, actually. We took Millie out for lunch.' Another pause. 'I'll tell Grace you called. Oh, of course, I'll pass her to you.'

I don't show my surprise when Jack hands me the phone, but the fact is I am surprised, as he normally tells anyone who asks to speak to me that I'm unavailable. But I suppose that as he's told Esther we've just walked in the door he could hardly say that I was in the shower or asleep in bed.

'Hello, Esther,' I say cautiously.

'I know you've just got in so I won't keep you long, but I wanted to see how you are, you know, after last night.'

'I'm fine, thank you,' I tell her. 'Much better.'

'My sister had a miscarriage before having her first child so I know how emotionally draining it can be,' she goes on.

'Even so, I wish I hadn't inflicted my disappointment on all of you,' I say, aware of Jack listening to what I'm saying. 'It's just that it was hard hearing about Diane's pregnancy.'

'Of course it must have been,' Esther sympathises. 'And I hope you know that if you ever need anyone to talk to, I'm here.'

'Thank you,' I say. 'That's kind of you.'

'So how was Millie?' she asks, obviously eager to add a bit of cement to our growing friendship. Ever wary of her inquisitive streak, I'm just about to wind up the conversation with 'She was fine, thank you for calling, I'm afraid I have to go, Jack's waiting for his dinner,' when I decide to keep talking, as I would if I was living a normal life.

'Very excited.' I smile. 'Her carer, Janice, is bringing her down for lunch the Sunday after next so that she can see the house at last. She'll be eighteen on the Monday so we'll be having a little celebration for her.'

'How lovely!' Esther enthuses. 'I hope you'll let me bring around a card for her.'

I'm about to tell her that we would prefer it to be just the four of us this first time but that she'll be welcome to meet Millie once she's moved in, when it dawns on me that she will never get to see Millie. If everything goes as Jack wants, she will have to be kept out of sight, because how could he let anyone see her when he intends to keep her prisoner? And when he can no longer stall the people who ask where Millie is with pretend illnesses, he will say it didn't work out, that Millie was too institutionalised to adapt to living with us and, as a result, has moved into a wonderful new home at the other end of the country. From being out of sight, Millie will quickly pass to being out of mind and I realise that the more people who meet Millie, the harder it will be to keep her hidden away. But I need to be careful.

'That's very kind of you,' I say, making sure to sound hesitant. 'And you're right, Millie really should have a proper party for such an important birthday. I know she'll love to meet your children.'

'Goodness, I certainly didn't mean to suggest that you should be giving Millie a party, or that you should invite Sebastian and Aisling along!' Esther exclaims, sounding embarrassed. 'I just meant I would pop in quickly by myself with a card.'

'Why not? Diane and Adam have always wanted to meet Millie.'

'Honestly, Grace, I don't think any of us would want to intrude.' Esther sounds more confused than ever.

'Not at all. It's a very good idea. Shall we say three o'clock? That'll allow me and Jack to have lunch with Millie and Janice first.'

'Well, if you're sure,' says Esther doubtfully.

'Yes, it will be lovely for Millie,' I say, nodding.

'I'll see you on the ninth, then.'

'I look forward to it. Goodbye, Esther, thank you for phoning.'

I put the phone down, steeling myself.

'What the hell was all that about?' Jack explodes. 'Have you really just invited Esther to some sort of birthday party for Millie?'

'No, Jack,' I say wearily, 'Esther decided that we should

give Millie a proper party and then invited herself and the children along. You know what she's like—she almost ordered me to invite Diane and Adam along as well.'

'Why didn't you refuse?'

'Because that kind of role doesn't come easily to me any more. I'm too used to being perfect, to saying the right thing, just as you've wanted me to do. But, if you want to go ahead and un-invite them, please do. Our friends may as well get used to the fact that they're never going to meet Millie. Didn't Moira and Giles say they couldn't wait to see her? What excuse are you going to give them, Jack?'

'I thought I'd tell them that your parents suddenly realised how much they missed their beautiful daughter and that she's gone to live with them in New Zealand,' he says.

Horrified at exactly how much he intended Millie to be out of sight and mind, I'm determined that the party for Millie will go ahead.

'And what if my parents decide to come over for Christmas?' I ask. 'What will you do if they turn up here, expecting to see Millie?'

'I doubt very much that they will and anyway, maybe she'll have given up and died before then. Although I hope not—it would be most inconvenient if she only managed to last a few months after all the trouble I've gone to.'

I turn away abruptly so he can't see the way the colour has drained from my face and the only thing that stops my legs from giving way beneath me is the murderous rage that has filled my heart. I clench my fists and noticing, he laughs. 'You would just love to kill me, wouldn't you?'

'Eventually, yes. But first, I'd like you to suffer,' I tell him, unable to help myself.

'Not much chance of that, I'm afraid,' he says, seeming amused by the thought.

I know I have to keep focused, that the chances of Millie being a flesh-and-blood person to our friends rather than someone they only know about second hand are slipping away fast. I also know that if Jack suspects I want the party to go ahead, he'll phone Esther back and tell her that we prefer it to be a private gathering.

'Just cancel the party, Jack,' I say, sounding as if I'm close to tears. 'There's no way I could sit through it and pretend that everything is fine.'

'Then it is the perfect punishment for inviting Janice in the first place.'

'Please, Jack, no,' I plead.

'I do so love it when you beg,' he sighs, 'especially as it has the opposite effect that it's meant to. Now, up to your room—I have a party to prepare for. Maybe it's not such a bad idea after all—at least once people have actually met Millie, they'll be even more impressed by my generosity.'

I let my shoulders slump and drag my feet as I walk up the stairs in front of him in what I hope is a perfect picture of dejection. In the dressing room, I take off my clothes slowly while my mind looks for a way to distract him so that I can take the pills from my shoe and hide them somewhere on me.

'So, have you told the neighbours that as well as having a manic-depressive wife, you have a mentally retarded sister-in-law?' I ask, slipping off my shoes and beginning to undress.

'Why would I have? They're never going to meet Millie.'

I hang my dress back up in the wardrobe and take my pyjamas from the shelf. 'But they'll see her in the garden, when she's having her party,' I say, putting them on.

'They can't see into our garden from their house,' he points out.

I reach for the shoebox. 'They can if they're standing at the window on the first floor.'

'Which window?'

'The one that overlooks the garden.' I nod towards the window. 'That one over there.' As he turns his head, I crouch down, place the shoebox on the floor and pick up my shoes.

He cranes his neck. 'They wouldn't be able to see from there,' he says, as I prise the tissue from my shoe. 'It's too far away.'

Still crouching, I tuck the tissue into the waistband of my pyjamas, place the shoes in the box and stand up.

'Then you've got nothing to worry about,' I say, putting the box back in the wardrobe.

I walk towards the door, praying that the tissue won't slip from its hiding place and spill pills all over the floor. Jack follows me out and I open my bedroom door and go in, half expecting Jack to pull me back and demand to know what I have stuffed into my waistband. As he closes the door behind me, I don't dare believe that I've actually managed to pull it off, but when I hear the key turning in the lock, the relief is so great that my legs give way and I sink to the floor, my whole body trembling. But because there's always the possibility that Jack is only letting me think I've got away with it, I get to my feet and slide the tissue under the mattress. Then I sit down on the bed, and try to take in the fact that I've achieved more in the last fifteen minutes than I have in the last fifteen months, acknowledging all the while that, if I have, it's thanks to Millie. I'm not shocked that she expected me to kill Jack because murder is commonplace in the detective stories she listens to and she has no real idea of what it means to actually kill someone. In her mind, where the line between fact and fiction is often blurred, murder is simply a solution to a problem.

PAST

That first time, I was ashamed of the way I clung to Jack when he finally came to let me out of the room in the basement. It had been a long, terrible night, made worse by the knowledge that I had helped make it the nightmare it was. Until then, I'd had no real idea what he intended for Millie. I knew that fear would be a part of it, but I had been confident that I would be able to protect her from the worst of it, that she would be able to run to me, that I would be with her at all times. Even though Jack had told me he wanted someone he could hide away, it had never occurred to me that he meant to keep Millie locked up in a terrifying room in the basement so that he could feed off her fear whenever he wanted. To know the extent of his depravation was bad enough, but the fear that he would leave me there to die of dehydration, like Molly did, that I might not get out in time to save Millie, broke me—which was why, when he eventually unlocked the door the next morning, I was almost incoherent with gratitude, promising that I would do anything, anything, as long as he didn't take me down there again.

He took me at my word and turned it into a game. He began setting me tasks he knew I would fail so that he would have an excuse to take me down to the basement. Before I hit him with the bottle, Jack would let me choose the menu for the dinner parties we gave and I would choose dishes that I'd cooked many times before. From then on, he imposed the menu on me and made sure the dishes he chose were as complicated as possible. If the meal wasn't perfect—if the meat was a little too tough, or the fish a little overcooked—he would take me down to the room once our guests had gone and lock me in overnight. I was a fairly confident cook, but under such pressure I made stupid mistakes, so much so that the dinner where Esther and Rufus had been invited was the first time everything had gone smoothly in five months.

Even when we went to friends' for dinner, if I said or did anything that displeased Jack—once, I couldn't finish my dessert—I would get taken down to the basement as soon as we got home. Aware that my fear had a potent effect on him, I would try to remain calm, but, if I did, he would stand on the other side of the door and, his voice hoarse with excitement, tell me to imagine Millie in there, until I begged him to stop.

PRESENT

It's the day of Millie's party. Just as I'm beginning to think that Jack is never going to come and let me into the bedroom next door so that I can get ready, I hear him coming up the stairs.

'Party time!' he says, throwing open the door. He seems so excited that I wonder what he has up his sleeve. But I can't afford to worry about it. Although I'm happy with the progress I've made over the last two weeks, it's important that to-day, of all days, I keep calm.

I go into my old bedroom and open the wardrobe, hoping

that Jack will choose something pretty for me to wear in honour of Millie's birthday. The dress Jack picks out for me was already a little big for me, so when I put it on it highlights how thin I am now. I see Jack frowning, but, as he doesn't tell me to change out of it, I guess it's my appearance in general that concerns him. My face, when I look in the mirror, looks gaunt, making my eyes seem enormous.

I put on a little make-up and, when I'm ready, I follow Jack downstairs. He has prepared the lunch we are to have with Millie and Janice, and has had caterers prepare the food for the party this afternoon rather than allow me to make it, as I had wanted. It all looks perfect. He checks the time on his watch and we go into the hall. He types a code into the key-pad on the wall and the front gates whir open. Minutes later, we hear the sound of a car approaching. Jack walks to the front door and opens it just as Janice brings her car to a stop.

Janice and Millie get out of the car. Millie rushes towards me wearing a pretty pink dress with a matching ribbon in her hair while Janice follows at a more leisurely pace, looking around her, taking everything in.

'You look lovely, Millie,' I tell her, giving her a hug.

'Love house, Grace!' she cries, her eyes shining. 'Is beautiful!'

'It certainly is, 'Janice says admiringly, coming up behind her. She shakes Jack's hand, then mine.

Millie turns to Jack. 'House beautiful.'

He gives a gracious bow. 'I'm very glad you like it. Why don't we go in and I'll show you around. But perhaps you'd like a drink first. I thought we could have it on the terrace, unless you feel it's too cold.'

'The terrace will be lovely,' says Janice. 'We should make

the most of this gorgeous weather, especially as it's not going to last.'

We go through the hall, into the kitchen and out onto the
terrace, where cans of cold drinks and fruit juices are sitting
in ice. The glasses are already on the table; there will be no
going back inside to fetch them and leaving me alone with
Janice and Millie. With so many people joining us this afternoon, Jack is going to have his work cut out keeping an eye
on me.

We sip our drinks and make polite conversation. Millie
doesn't sit still for long; she's far too excited and goes off to
explore the garden. We catch up with her while we're show-
ing Janice around.

'Would you like to see your bedroom, Millie?' Jack asks.

She nods enthusiastically. 'Yes please, Jack.'

'I hope you're going to like it.'

'I like yellow,' she says happily.

The four of us go upstairs and Jack opens the door to the
master bedroom where he sleeps and where, this time, items
I have never seen before but which are obviously meant to
belong to me—a silk dressing gown, bottles of perfume and
some magazines—give the impression that I sleep there too.
When Millie shakes her head and tells him that it's not her
bedroom, he shows her one of the guest bedrooms, which is
decorated in blue and white.

'What do you think?' he asks.

She hesitates. 'Is pretty, but not yellow.'

He moves on to the room I used to inhabit. 'What about
this one?'

Millie shakes her head. 'Don't like green.'

Jack smiles. 'It's just as well it's not your room then.' Janice joins in the game. 'Maybe it's over there,' she says, pointing to the door further down the landing. Millie runs and opens it and finds a bathroom.

'Why don't you try that door?' suggests Jack, pointing to the door to my box room.

She does as he says. 'Is horrible.' She frowns, peering inside. 'I not like it.'

'It is horrible, isn't it?' I agree.

'Don't worry, Millie, I'm only teasing,' Jack laughs. 'There's still one door that you haven't tried, opposite the master bedroom. Why don't you have a look in there?'

She runs back down the landing, opens the door and lets out a squeal of delight. By the time we've caught up with her, she's bouncing up and down on the bed, the skirt of her pink dress billowing around her, and she looks so happy that tears well up inside me. I swallow them down quickly, reminding myself of all that is at stake.

'I think she likes it,' Jack says, turning to Janice.

'Who wouldn't? It's gorgeous!'

He only gets Millie to leave the room with the promise of lunch. We go downstairs and, on the way to the dining room, where we are to eat, Jack shows Millie and Janice the rest of the house.

'What in here?' Millie asks, trying the door to the basement. 'Why it locked?'

'It leads to the basement,' Jack tells her.

'What the basement?'

'It's where I like to keep things,' he says.

'Can I see?'

'Not now.' He pauses a moment. 'But, when you come and live with us, I'll be more than happy to show you.'

It's hard to carry on, but with his hand hard on my back I don't have much choice. We eat an informal lunch of cold meats and salads and, while we're having coffee, Millie asks if she can explore the garden again, so we carry our cups out onto the terrace.

'I hope you approve of the home we've provided for Millie,' Jack says, pulling out chairs for us to sit on.

'Definitely.' Janice nods. 'I can see why you wanted to wait until the work was finished before Millie saw the house. It really is marvellous. It must have been a huge undertaking.'

'Well, it wasn't exactly easy living with building work going on the whole time, but it was worth it, wasn't it, darling?'

'Yes,' I agree. 'Where are we going to have Millie's party, outside or in?'

'I had intended to set it up in the dining room, but it's such lovely weather perhaps we could have it here on the terrace. That way Millie and the other children can play in the garden.'

'I didn't realise you'd invited anyone else,' Janice exclaims.

'We wanted to make it a real celebration for Millie and we thought it important that she meets our friends,' Jack explains. 'And, although the other children are younger than Millie, I'm hoping they'll treat her as a big sister.' He looks at his watch. 'We invited them for three, so would you mind keeping an eye on Millie while Grace and I get everything ready?'

Janice nods. 'I'll go and get her tidied up a bit.'

'Before you go, I have something for her.' Jack calls Millie up from the bottom of the garden. 'Millie, if you go into the sitting room, you'll find a big box behind one of the chairs. Do you think you could bring it to me?'

She disappears into the house and I try not to worry about what it is he has for her, telling myself that he wouldn't do anything stupid in front of Janice. Still, I can't help feeling relieved when Millie opens the box and takes out a yellow satin dress with a full skirt and a wide belt.

'It's lovely, Jack,' I say, hating my gratitude, and, when Millie throws her arms around his neck, I feel the same pang of regret that I always feel whenever I'm reminded of how it could have been.

'I'm glad you approve.'

Janice looks at me in surprise. 'You didn't help him choose it?'

'No, I'm afraid Jack quite took over the preparations for Millie's party. But, as you can see, he's perfectly capable of managing on his own.'

'Why don't you take Millie up to her room and get her changed there?' Jack suggests. 'Go on, Millie, go with Janice.'

As they leave, he turns to me. 'She may as well enjoy it while she can—somehow, I don't think she's going to like her real bedroom quite as much, do you? Right, time to get the table ready.'

He extends the already large wooden table to its maximum length so that it will seat everybody—nine adults and five children—without too much trouble. As we move between kitchen and terrace, carrying plates and glasses, I try not to let his reference to Millie's bedroom detract from what I have to do this afternoon.

'What do you think?' asks Jack, looking at the table heaving with food.

'It's lovely,' I say, admiring the banner and balloons he has strung around the terrace. 'Millie will love it.'

As if on cue, she and Janice appear, Millie radiant in her new dress and a ribbon in her hair.

'What a beautiful young lady!' Jack exclaims, making Millie blush with pleasure. I look at her anxiously, hoping that she isn't going to start being taken in by Jack.

'Thank you, Jack.' She looks around at everything in awe. 'It beautiful!' she breathes.

'You look lovely, Millie,' I say going over to her.

She throws her arms around my neck. 'I not forget he bad man,' she whispers in my ear.

'You're right, Millie, Jack is a very nice man,' I laugh, knowing that Jack will have seen the whisper.

She nods in agreement. 'Jack nice.' The doorbell peals. 'Party start!' she says delightedly.

Jack takes my hand in a gesture that is anything but affectionate and we go to open the door, leaving Janice and Millie on the terrace. We usher Esther and Rufus and their two children through the kitchen and make the necessary introductions. They've just finished telling Millie how pretty she looks when Moira and Giles arrive, followed soon after by Diane, Adam and their children.

'We heard you out here, so we didn't bother ringing at the door,' Diane explains, kissing me.

There are so many people for Jack to greet, so many introductions to be made that he has no option but to take his eyes off me and it occurs to me that I have ample time to whisper 'Help me, Jack's a maniac' into Diane's ear. But, even with the note of urgency in my voice, she would think I was joking, or referring to the obvious expense Jack has gone to to give Millie a perfect party. He takes me with him into the kitchen to fetch champagne for the adults and colourful drinks for the children and, when I sit down at the table, the pressure of his hand in mine warns me that he is listening to everything I say while making conversation of his own, as only he can.

Millie begins to open her presents. I've no idea what we've bought Millie as I didn't dare ask in case I upset the relative calm I've managed to achieve over the last two weeks. As usual, Jack has come up trumps, buying her a pretty silver locket engraved with an 'M'.

'Pretty!' Millie beams, holding it up so everyone can see it.

'It's actually from me because Grace has her own special present for you,' Jack says. Millie looks at me questioningly and I smile back at her, hoping he has chosen something nice. 'She's done some lovely paintings for your new bedroom, haven't you, darling?'

I feel the colour wash from my face and grip the edge of the table hard.

Millie claps her hands excitedly. 'I can see?'

'Not just yet,' Jack says apologetically. 'But they'll be hanging in your room by the time you move in, I promise.'

'What sort of paintings are they?' Rufus asks.

'Portraits,' Jack tells him. 'And very realistic ones at that— Grace has a wonderful eye for detail.'

'Are you all right, Grace?' Esther looks at me in concern.

'The heat,' I manage. 'I'm not used to it.'

Jack hands me a glass of water. 'Have a drink, darling,' he says solicitously. 'It'll make you feel better.'

Aware of Millie looking at me anxiously, I take a sip of water. 'That's better,' I tell her. 'Open your other presents, then you can play some games.'

There's a silver bangle from Moira and Giles, and a silver

trinket box from Diane and Adam, but I barely see them because it's an effort to keep myself together. I sense Esther looking curiously at me, but for once I don't care that she's seen I'm upset.

'Esther, aren't you going to give Millie our present?' Rufus asks.

'Of course.' Esther rallies herself and hands Millie a beautifully wrapped present. 'I hope you like it,' she says, smiling at her.

Millie opens it and finds a large red velvet box, its lid prettily decorated with sequins and glass beads. It's exactly the sort of thing that Millie loves and, as she gasps in delight, I take a grip on myself and smile gratefully across at Esther.

'It's to keep things in,' Esther tells her. 'I bought it to match your new bedroom.'

Millie beams at her. 'Is yellow,' she says proudly. 'My bedroom is yellow.'

Esther looks puzzled. 'It's red, isn't it?'

Millie shakes her head. 'Yellow. It my favourite colour.'

'I thought your favourite colour was red.'

'Yellow.'

Esther turns to Jack. 'Didn't you say that you were decorating Millie's bedroom red because it was her favourite colour?'

'No, I don't think so.'

'Yes, Jack, you did,' Diane confirms. 'At least, that's what you told us that time you gatecrashed our lunch in town.'

'Well, if I did, I'm very sorry. I must have been thinking of something else at the time.'

'But you said it on more than one occasion,' Esther insists. 'When you came to dinner at ours you said that you couldn't wait for Millie to see her red bedroom.' She looks over at me. 'Isn't that what he said, Grace?'

'I'm afraid I don't remember,' I mumble.

'Does it really matter?' Jack nods at Millie who is busy putting her other presents into the box. 'Look, she loves it.'

'But it's strange to have made the same mistake twice,' Esther says, genuinely puzzled.

'I wasn't aware that I had.'

'Well, I could take it back and change it for a yellow one, I suppose,' she says doubtfully.

'Please don't,' I tell her. 'Jack's right, Millie loves it.'

For the next ten minutes, I watch her watching Jack, and I'm glad that in his efforts to destabilise me, he has overplayed his hand—not that anyone except Esther seems to have noticed. At one moment, she looks from Jack to the red box, a frown on her face. Suddenly, she turns her attention back to me.

'I hope you don't mind me asking, Grace,' she says, 'but are you sure you're all right? You look very pale.'

'I'm fine,' I reassure her.

'I've noticed it too.' Diane nods. 'And you've lost weight—you haven't been dieting, have you?'

'No, it's just that I don't seem to have much appetite at the moment.'

'Maybe you should go and see your doctor.'

'I will,' I promise.

'You really need to take more care of her, Jack.' Esther looks at him appraisingly.

'I intend to.' Smiling, he slips his hand into the inside pocket of his jacket and draws out an envelope. 'I didn't see why Millie should be the only one to have a present today.'

'Adam, please take note,' Diane groans.

'Here we are, darling,' Jack hands me the envelope. 'Open it.'

I do as he says and find myself looking at a pair of plane tickets.

'Come on, Grace, don't keep us in suspense,' Diane implores. 'Where's Jack taking you?'

'Thailand,' I say slowly, horribly aware that everything I've managed to put in place since Millie gave me the pills will all have been for nothing if we go away.

'What a lucky girl,' says Moira, smiling at me.

'I think you're meant to say something, Grace,' Esther prompts.

I raise my head quickly. 'It's just such a shock. I mean, it's a lovely thought, Jack, but do we really have time to go away?'

'You did say that you wanted one last holiday in Thailand before Millie comes to live with us,' he reminds me, making it sound as if I think of Millie as some sort of burden.

'But you said we wouldn't be able to—didn't you say that you had the Tomasin case coming up?'

'Yes, but I'm working hard to make sure it'll be over by then.'

'When are you going?' Giles asks.

'I've booked tickets for the fifth of June.'

Adam looks at him in surprise. 'Will the Tomasin case be finished so soon?'

'I hope so—it's going to court next week.'

'Even so. I mean, it's not so clear-cut this time, is it? From what the papers are saying, her husband is squeaky clean.'

Jack raises his eyebrows. 'Don't tell me you believe what you read in the papers.'

'No, but the theory that it's a set-up and that she's out to frame her husband because she has a lover is an interesting one.'

'It's also total fabrication.'

'So you're confident of winning?'

'Absolutely—I've never lost a case yet and I don't intend to start now.'

Adam turns to me. 'What do you think, Grace? You must have read the papers.'

'Me? I think the husband is as guilty as hell,' I say, wondering what they would say if they knew that I barely know what they're talking about.

'Sorry, but I can't imagine him as a wife-beater,' says Diane. 'He just doesn't look the type.'

'Jack tells me that they're the worst kind,' I say lightly.

Esther's eyes flicker towards me. 'It must be exciting having a husband who deals with such high-profile cases,' she says, holding my gaze.

'Actually, Jack rarely talks about his work when he comes home and especially not the details of his cases, for reasons of client confidentiality—I'm sure it's the same for you, Diane.' I turn to Jack with pretended anxiousness. 'But to get back to our holiday—wouldn't it be better to postpone it until Millie can come with us?'

'Why?'

'Well, if there's a risk that your case might not be over in time.'

'It will be.'

'But what if it isn't?' I insist.

'Then you'll go on ahead and I'll join you.'

I stare at him.

'We're not cancelling the holiday, Grace. As everybody has pointed out, you need a rest.'

'You'd really let me go on ahead without you?' I say, knowing he would never allow such a thing.

'Of course.'

Esther looks at him approvingly. 'That's very generous of you, Jack.'

'Not at all. I mean, why would I deprive my beautiful wife of a holiday just because I can't go?'

'I'd be more than happy to keep her company until you arrive,' Diane offers.

'Sorry to disappoint you, but I have no intention of not being able to make it,' Jack tells her, getting to his feet. 'Grace, I need your help in the kitchen, darling.'

I follow him in, stunned at how wrong everything seems to be going.

'You don't seem very keen to go to Thailand,' he says, handing me candles to stick in the cake. 'Yet you were the one who suggested it.'

'It's just that it doesn't seem such a good idea with your court case coming up.'

'So you think it would be better for me to cancel it?'

Blessed relief floods through me. 'Definitely'.

'Then do you think Millie will be able to move in with us earlier, next week, for example? In fact, she could even stay behind today and I could drive up and collect her things during the week while she settles into her lovely red bedroom. What do you think, Grace? Shall I go out and suggest it? Or shall we go to Thailand next month?'

'We'll go to Thailand next month,' I say stonily.

'I thought that's what you would say. Now, where are the matches?'

It's hard not to give in to the desperation I feel as I sing 'Happy Birthday' along with the others and applaud as Millie blows out her candles. I look around at everybody laughing and joking together and struggle to understand how my life has become a living hell that nobody present could even begin to imagine. If I were to suddenly demand their attention and tell them that Millie is in great danger from Jack, that he intends to keep her locked up in a terrifying room until she goes mad with fear, that he is in reality a murderer who has kept me prisoner for the last fifteen months, nobody would believe it. And what would Jack tell them in return? That he only realised once we were married that I had a history of mental illness, that it only became apparent on our honeymoon when I accused him of keeping me a prisoner in front of a lobby full of people, that the hotel manager, our local doctor and the police would be happy to confirm that I am unbalanced. That the last fifteen months have been a terrible strain on him, especially as he has to accompany me everywhere for fear of what I'll say in public. Even if Millie were to come to my defence and accuse him of pushing her down the stairs, he would look appalled and say that I must have put the idea into her mind. Why would the people gathered here today believe my version over Jack's when his sounds so much more plausible?

We eat the cake, drink more champagne. Millie and the children resume their games and the rest of us sit around chatting. I have trouble concentrating, but when I hear Janice saying that she'll enjoy coming to see Millie in our beautiful house, I seize the chance to make it a reality.

'Why don't we fix a date now?' I turn to the others. 'And maybe we could take Millie and the children to the music festival and have a picnic there—they seem to be getting along well. Doesn't it start at the beginning of July?'

'What a good idea!' Diane exclaims. 'And is anybody interested in a trip to the zoo? I've promised to take mine as soon as school breaks up.'

'Millie would love that,' I say, eager to fill her diary.

'Before you get carried away, Grace,' Jack interrupts, 'I have another surprise for you. Well, for you and Millie actually.'

I feel myself go cold. 'Another surprise?'

'Don't look so worried,' Moira jokes. 'Knowing Jack, I'm sure it'll be something nice.'

'I didn't really want to tell you yet,' Jack says apologetically to me, 'but, as you're making all these arrangements for the summer holidays, I think you should know that I'm taking you and Millie to New Zealand, to see your parents.'

'New Zealand!' breathes Diane. 'Gosh, I've always wanted to go to New Zealand.'

'When?' I stammer.

'Well, I thought we'd give Millie a few days to settle in and leave around the middle of July,' he says.

'But Millie's meant to be starting work at the garden centre in August,' I say, wondering what he's playing at. 'It's a long way to go for a couple of weeks.'

'I'm sure they won't mind if she starts a week or two later, especially if we explain why.'

'Don't you think it'll be too much for Millie, going to New Zealand so soon after moving in? Surely it would be better to wait until Christmas?'

'I think she'll be thrilled,' Janice intervenes. 'She's been dreaming of going since we did a class project on New Zealand, just after your parents moved there.'

'If I went to New Zealand, I'm not sure I'd want to come back,' says Diane. 'It's meant to be quite beautiful.'

'That's one of the dangers, of course,' agrees Jack. 'Millie could end up loving it so much that she might ask to stay there permanently, with her parents.'

The pennies begin to drop and I realise that he's preparing Millie's exit from society. 'She would never do that,' I say fiercely. 'For a start, she would never leave me.'

'But what if you decided to stay there too?' Jack asks. His tone is playful, but I understand only too well that he's preparing the ground for my exit as well.

'I wouldn't,' I say. 'I could never leave you, Jack, surely you know that?'

But I could kill you, I add silently. In fact, I'm going to have to.

PAST

The pile of pills under my mattress gave me a new lease on life. For the first time in six months escaping from Jack became a real possibility and I felt humbly grateful to Millie for stepping in and forcing me to take charge again. After the trouble she had gone to, to get me the pills, I was determined not to let her down. But I needed to plan carefully. Not least of my problems was the fact that the pills were an unknown quantity. Even if I managed to get them into Jack, I had no idea how long it would be before they started to take effect, or what that effect would be. And how many pills would it take to knock him out? There were so many variables, so many ifs and buts.

I began by looking for a way to get them into one of Jack's drinks. The only time we ever took a drink together was when we were at dinner, with other people around, and if my plan was to work I would have to get him to take the pills here, in this house, while we were on our own. I spent the night considering every possibility and, by the time he brought me my dinner the following evening, I already had an idea of how I could do it. But I needed to start laying the foundations at once.

I made sure he found me sitting despondently on the bed, my back to the door. When I didn't turn around and take the tray, as I usually did, he placed it beside me on the bed and left without saying a word. Just knowing that the food was there was difficult, especially as I hadn't eaten since lunch with Millie the previous day, but I was determined not to eat it. The next day he didn't bother bringing me any food at all but, as the tray was still there and I was even hungrier, it was hard not to be tempted. But whenever I considered giving in and eating just a little to stave off the hunger pangs, I conjured up a picture of the room in the basement and placed Millie inside it. Then it was easy.

On the third day, mindful perhaps that he had neglected to feed me the day before, Jack brought me breakfast. When he saw that the tray he had brought me two days previously was untouched, he looked at me curiously.

'Not hungry?'

I shook my head. 'No.'

'In that case, I'll take your breakfast back down to the kitchen.'

He left, taking both meals with him, and without food around it was easier. To help me ignore the hunger pains, I meditated. But when I still hadn't eaten anything by the weekend, nor touched any of the wine he had brought me, Jack got suspicious.

'You're not on some kind of hunger strike, are you?' he hazarded as he picked up another tray of uneaten food and replaced it with a fresh one.

I shook my head lethargically. 'I'm just not hungry, that's all.'

'Why not?'

I took a while in replying. 'I suppose I never really thought it would come to this,' I admitted, picking nervously at the bedcover. 'I always thought that, in the end, I'd find a way of saving Millie from you.'

'Let me guess—you thought that good would triumph over evil or that a knight in shining armour would come along and rescue you and Millie from your fate.'

'Something like that.' I let a sob catch my throat. 'But it's not going to happen, is it? Millie is going to move in with us and there's nothing I can do about it.'

'If it's any consolation, there never was anything you could do about it. But I'm glad you've begun to accept the inevitable. It will make everything easier for you in the long run.'

I nodded at the glass of wine on the tray he'd just brought me, trying to ignore the chicken and potatoes that looked so delicious. 'I don't suppose I could have a whisky instead of the wine, could I?'

'Whisky?'

'Yes.'

'I didn't know you drank whisky.'

'And I didn't know you were a psychopath. Just bring me a whisky, Jack,' I went on, rubbing my eyes tiredly. 'I used to drink it with my father, if you must know.'

I felt him looking at me, but I kept my head bowed in what I hoped was a picture of misery. He left the room, locking the door behind him. I had no way of knowing whether he would bring me the whisky I'd asked for and the smell of the chicken was so tantalising that I began a slow count, promising myself that if he hadn't come back by the time I got to a hundred I would eat the lot. I wasn't even at fifty when I heard his footsteps on the stairs. At sixty, the key turned in the lock and I closed my eyes, knowing that if he hadn't brought me a whisky I would probably burst into tears, because the effort of denying myself food for almost a week would have been for nothing.

'Here.'

I opened my eyes and looked at the plastic cup he was holding out to me. 'What is it?' I asked suspiciously.

'Whisky.' I made to take it, but he pulled his hand back. 'First, eat. You'll be no good to me if you're too weak to look after Millie.'

Although his words chilled me, they also told me that I was on the right track, because he had never given in to any of my demands before, not even when I had asked for a larger towel to dry myself with. But I supposed that with his end goal in sight he couldn't afford to let anything happen to me, which meant he was more likely to give in to any requests I made as long as they were reasonable. It was a major triumph and, although I had planned to hold out a little longer before eating, I reasoned that if I wanted Jack to bring me more whisky I would have to meet him halfway. But I wanted him to bring it to me as soon as he got in from work, I wanted him to get into the habit of pouring my whisky at the same time as he poured his.

'I asked for whisky because I hoped it would give me an appetite,' I said, my arm still outstretched. 'So can I have it, please?'

I expected him to refuse, but after a small hesitation he handed it to me. I raised the cup to my lips with pretend eagerness. The smell made my stomach turn, but at least I knew it was whisky I was about to drink and not something else. Conscious of his eyes on me, I took a sip. I had never drunk whisky before in my life and the bitter taste was a shock.

'Not to your liking?' he mocked, and I knew he didn't really believe that I liked whisky and had only given it to me to find out what my real motive was in asking for it in the first place.

'Have you ever drunk whisky out of a plastic cup?' I demanded, taking another sip. 'Believe me, it doesn't taste quite the same. Maybe you can bring it in a glass next time.' I raised the cup again and knocked the whole lot back.

'Now, eat something,' he said, pushing the tray towards me.

My head spinning from the whisky, I put the tray on my lap. The food looked so good I would have been capable of clearing the plate in fifteen seconds. It was hard not to wolf it down, but I made myself eat slowly, as if I had no pleasure in what I was tasting. I only allowed myself to eat half of it and, when I put my knife and fork down, I'm not sure who was more disappointed, me or Jack.

'Can't you eat a little more?' he frowned.

'No, sorry,' I said unenthusiastically. 'Maybe tomorrow.'

He left, taking the tray with him and, although I was still

hungry, the taste of victory was sweeter than anything I could have eaten.

Jack wasn't stupid. The next day, when I didn't eat anything again, he decided to hit me where he knew it would hurt me most.

'I'm cancelling our visit to Millie tomorrow,' he said, as he picked up the untouched tray. 'There's no point taking her out to lunch if you're not going to eat.'

I'd known there was a risk he wouldn't take me to see Millie, but it was a sacrifice I was willing to make.

'All right,' I shrugged. From the look of surprise he gave me, I knew he'd been expecting me to insist that I was well enough to go and I was glad I had wrong-footed him.

'Millie is going to be so disappointed,' he sighed.

'Well, it won't be the first time.'

He thought for a moment. 'This wouldn't be some little ploy to get me to cancel Millie's birthday party, would it?'

It was a conclusion I hadn't expected him to come to and one that was far from the truth, but I wondered if I could get it to work in my favour.

'Why would I want you to do that?' I asked, playing for time.

'You tell me.'

'Maybe you should try and put yourself in my position for once. If Millie comes here, she's going to fall in love with this house. How do you think that's going to make me feel, knowing what you have in store for her and knowing I can do nothing to prevent it from happening?'

'Let me guess.' He pretended to think for a moment. 'Not good?'

I willed tears of self-pity into my eyes. 'Yes, that's right, Jack, not good. So bad, in fact, that I'd prefer to die.'

'So this is some kind of hunger strike then.'

'No, Jack, of course it isn't. I know that Millie is going to need me, I know I have to keep my strength up. But I can't help it if I've lost my appetite. I'm sure most people would, given the circumstances.' I let my voice rise an octave. 'Have you any idea what it's like for me on a day-to-day basis, not being able to choose what I want to eat or when I want to eat? Have you any idea what it's like to have to rely on you for absolutely everything, to sometimes have to wait two or three days for food because you decide I need punishing, or can't be bothered to bring me anything? You're not exactly the most generous of jailers, Jack!'

'Perhaps you shouldn't have made so many attempts to es-cape,' he snapped. 'If you hadn't, I wouldn't have needed to confine you to this room and you could have led a perfectly decent life with me.'

'Decent! With you controlling my every move? You don't even know the meaning of the word! Go on, Jack, punish me. Deprive me of food, see if I care. If I don't eat again for a week, at least I'll be too weak to attend Millie's birthday party next Sunday.'

'You'd better start eating again,' he threatened, realising the truth of what I'd said.

'Or what, Jack?' I taunted. 'You can't force me to eat, you know.' I paused. 'But, as it isn't in Millie's interest that I die, or in yours, why don't you do us both a favour and pour me a whisky in the evenings when you pour your own and my ap-petite might come back a little.'

'I call the shots around here, remember,' he reminded me.

However, when it came to food, he no longer did. Realising that he needed to keep me healthy, he began to do as I'd asked. I made sure that I never ate much, because it was important he thought I really had lost my appetite, but it was equally important that I ate enough to merit the small amount of whisky he brought me when he got in from work. By the time Millie's party came round, I was confident I'd be able to achieve my aim before Millie came to live with us, two months down the line—as long as nothing happened to interrupt the routine of Jack bringing me whisky every evening.

PRESENT

1

I stand in front of the house, my case at my feet. The double gates are shut but the small gate—the one that I came out of—is ajar. I hear Esther's car approaching and, turning back towards the house, I give a little wave. She pulls up next to me, gets out and opens the boot.

'I could have come all the way to the door, you know,' she reproaches, helping me to lift my suitcase into the car.

'I thought it would save time. Thank you for coming to fetch me at such short notice.'

'No problem,' she smiles. 'But we're going to have to hurry

if you're to make your flight.' As she closes the boot, I wave towards the house again, blow a kiss and pull the gate closed behind me.

'I wish he was coming with me,' I say fretfully. 'I hate leaving him when he's so down.'

'It's the first case he's lost, isn't it?'

'Yes—I think that's why he's taken it so hard. But he did think the husband was guilty or he wouldn't have taken it on in the first place. Unfortunately, Dena Anderson was less than truthful with Jack and hid certain things from him, including the fact that she had a lover.'

'It seems he was the real culprit.'

'I don't know all the ins and outs of it, but I expect he'll tell me when he joins me. It's funny—I used to travel all over the world on my own yet the thought of spending a few days alone in Thailand is disconcerting. I'm so used to having Jack with me. I'm not sure quite what he expects me to do for the next four days.'

'Have a nice rest, I suppose.'

'I would rather have waited for him but he was so insistent,' I go on. 'And I know better than to argue with him when he's made up his mind about something.' I look over at her. 'You see, he can be a little imperfect sometimes.'

'Insisting that you go ahead of him on holiday is not imperfect,' she reminds me.

'No, I suppose not. Once he explained that he wouldn't enjoy the holiday if he had to face all the paperwork when he came back, I understood better. He really needs to be able to relax on this holiday, especially as it's probably the last we'll be able to have on our own. It's normal that he prefers to stay and get everything filed away—although I rather think that if he had won the case, he wouldn't have minded quite so much about being reminded of it when we got back,' I add ruefully.

'He probably wants to lick his wounds in private,' she agrees. 'You know what men are like.'

'The thing is, we're hoping to conceive a baby while we're in Thailand, which is another reason he wants to be completely relaxed. It's about the right time,' I admit, blushing a little.

She takes her hand off the wheel and gives mine a squeeze. 'I really hope it works out for you both.'

'Well, if it does, you'll be the first to know,' I promise. 'I can't wait to have Jack's child. He was so disappointed when I had my last miscarriage. He tried to be strong for me, but it really affected him, especially when I didn't conceive again immediately afterwards. I told him that these things take time, that my body needed to recover first, but he began wondering if it was down to him and the demands of his job, you know, the stress and everything.'

'Do you think he'll want to come round for dinner or something over the weekend?'

'To be honest, I think he'd rather stay and plough through his paperwork. But you can always ask him, although I'm not sure you'll be able to get hold of him as he doesn't intend answering his phone over the next few days. He already had to deal with the media when he came out of court this afternoon and he knows they're going to be on his back over the next few days. But you can always leave a message on his voicemail—that's what he told me to do if I can't get through to him, especially with the time difference and everything.'

'And he's joining you on Tuesday?'

'Yes—well, early Wednesday morning. He's taking the Tuesday evening flight—although he did say that he might be delayed a day or two. But I think he was joking—at least, I hope he was.'

'So you'll only have four days on your own. Gosh, what I wouldn't give for four days of peace! Does he need taking to the airport on Tuesday? Rufus would do it.'

'No, it's fine. Adam offered, but Jack's going to take the car and leave it at the airport. We'll need it for when we get back—the flight gets in around six in the morning and we wouldn't ask anyone to come and pick us up at that ungodly hour.'

I'm surprised how easily we chat on the way to the airport. I was expecting a far more uncomfortable ride, but she seems content to talk about the most ordinary of things. She asks if she and the children can go and see Millie at the weekend, and maybe take her out for tea, and, remembering how well Millie and Aisling got on at the party, I agree gratefully, glad that Millie will have some visitors while I'm away. She asks me to let Janice know that they'll call by on Sunday and I promise that I will.

We arrive at the airport with fifteen minutes to spare. She drops me off at Departures and leaves me with a cheery wave. I go into the terminal building, find the British Airways counter, check in my case and make my way to the departure lounge. Then I take a seat in the corner and wait for my flight to be called.

PAST

Until the day of Millie's party, I never really thought I would kill Jack. I'd dreamt about it often enough, but in the cold light of day I baulked at the thought of killing another human being. It was probably why my attempt to stun him with the bottle failed—I'd been too scared to hit him any harder in case I killed him. There was also the fact that if I did kill him, I would almost certainly be sent to prison and be held in custody while I awaited trial, which would be terrible for Millie. So all I wanted was to knock him out long enough for me to be able to escape from him. But the minute he mentioned taking me and Millie to New Zealand, I knew I was going to have to kill him, whatever the consequences, because getting away from him would never be enough.

'So that's how you're going to do it,' I said bitterly, once we'd waved Millie and Janice off after the party. 'You're going to shut up the house, pretend we've all gone off to New Zealand, then suddenly reappear on your own and tell everyone that Millie and I have decided to stay over there when, in reality, we'll be hidden away in the basement.'

'More or less,' he confirmed. 'Except that it'll be too much trouble to shut up the house and pretend I'm not here so I'll find an excuse to send the two of you on to New Zealand ahead of me, and in the end I'll be so delayed it won't be worth joining you because you'll be practically on your way back. And then, just as I'm about to leave for the airport to pick you up, I'll get a tearful call from you saying that Millie refused to get on the plane and that you, torn between loving husband and lunatic sister, didn't get on the plane either. And loving husband that I am, I'll tell everybody that because I know how difficult it's going to be for you to leave Millie behind, I've given you permission to stay on a little longer—except the little longer will become a lot longer until one sad day, you tell me you're never coming back. And because I'm broken-hearted, people won't dare mention your name to me and, eventually, they'll forget that you and Millie ever existed.'

'And my parents?' I demanded. 'How will you explain our disappearance to them?'

'I'll probably just kill them. Now, get up to your room.'

I turned away from him so that he couldn't see how much his words had shocked me. Finding a way out—killing

Jack—had never seemed more urgent and I knew that if I went back to my room, another opportunity would be lost. It was time to put the next part of my plan into action.

'Can't I stay down here for a while?' I asked.

'No.'

'Why not?'

'You know very well why.'

'When was the last time I tried to escape? Look at me, Jack! Do you really think you're in danger from me? Have I done anything except behave as perfectly as possible for the last six months? Do you honestly think that I want to risk going down to the basement?'

'It's true that your trips down there seem to have had the desired effect, but, nonetheless, you'll be going up to your room.'

'Then could I move into another room?'

'Why?'

'Why do you think? Because I need a change of scene, that's why! I'm fed up looking at the same four walls, day in, day out!'

'All right.'

I looked at him in surprise. 'Really?'

'Yes. Come on, I'll take you down to the basement and you can look at the four walls there instead. Or do you think that maybe your room isn't so bad after all?'

'I think maybe my room isn't so bad after all,' I said dully.

'That's a shame. You see, I think the room in the basement has been empty for far too long. Shall I let you into a secret?' He leant down towards me and lowered his voice to a whisper. 'It was hard, very hard, to let Millie leave just now, much harder than I thought it would be. In fact, it was so hard that I'm going to suggest she moves in as soon as we get back from Thailand. What do you think, Grace? Won't it be lovely to be one happy family?'

I knew then that not only would I have to kill Jack, I would have to kill him before we left for Thailand. Terrible though it was to realise how little time I had left, having a deadline helped me focus. As I went up the stairs in front of him, I was already planning my next move.

'When you bring me up my whisky, will you stay and have one with me?' I asked, as I got undressed.

'Now why would I want to do that?'

'Because I'm tired of being cooped up for twenty-four hours a day with no one to talk to,' I said listlessly. 'Have you any idea what it's like? Sometimes I feel as if I'm going mad. In fact, I wish I would.' I let my voice rise. 'What would you do then, Jack? What will you do if I go mad?'

'Of course you're not going to go mad,' he retorted, pushing me into my bedroom and closing the door.

'I might!' I called after him. 'I just might! And I want my whisky in a glass!'

I don't know whether it was because he'd refused me everything else I'd asked for or if he was worried that I really would go mad, but, whatever the reason, when he came back ten minutes later, he was carrying two glasses.

'Thank you,' I said, taking a sip. 'Can I ask you something?'

'Go ahead.'

'It's about the Tomasin case. He married an actress, didn't he? Dena somebody or other? I seem to remember reading something about it, back in the days when I was allowed to read newspapers.'

'Dena Anderson.'

'So is she accusing him of beating her up?'

'I'm not allowed to discuss my cases.'

'Well, everybody here today seemed to know about it so either you haven't been very discreet or it's common knowledge,' I said reasonably. 'Doesn't he give most of his fortune to good causes?'

'It doesn't mean he's not a wife-beater.'

'What did Adam mean about her having a lover?'

'Adam was just being provocative.'

'So there's no truth in what he said.'

'None at all. One of the tabloids invented the story to discredit her.'

'Why would they do that?'

'Because Antony Tomasin is one of the shareholders. Now, drink up—I'm not leaving here without the glass.'

Once he'd left, I took the screw of tissue out from under my mattress and opened it. I counted out the pills; there were twenty in all. I had no idea if that would be enough to kill Jack, especially as I was going to have to use some on myself, first of all to find out how strong they were and, secondly, to see if they would dissolve in liquid once they'd been crushed. Going into the bathroom I tore two sheets of toilet paper from the roll and, after a lot of deliberation, put four of the pills between them, hoping it would be enough to knock me out without making me ill. I put the paper on the floor and crushed them as best I could with my foot. I had no cup to put the resulting granules in so I used the top from my shampoo bottle as a receptacle and added some water. They dissolved a little, but not quite enough and, as I drank them down, I knew I'd have to find a way of grinding the rest of the pills into a finer powder.

I started to feel drowsy some fifteen minutes later and fell asleep almost immediately. I slept solidly for fourteen hours and, when I woke, I felt slightly groggy and unbelievably thirsty. As Jack was almost twice my weight, I reckoned that eight of the pills would have more or less the same effect on him but that sixteen wouldn't be enough to kill him outright. It was a major blow, as it meant that I'd have to find a way, once he was unconscious, of finishing everything myself. But even though I wanted him dead, I wasn't sure that when it actually came down to it I would be capable of going down to the kitchen, fetching a knife from the drawer, and sticking it into his heart.

I decided not to think that far ahead and concentrated instead on getting Jack to stay a little longer with me when he brought me my whisky in the evenings, reiterating what I'd told him before, that I felt as if I was going mad with no one to talk to all day. I hoped that eventually he would feel comfortable enough to start bringing up a whisky for himself, as he had on the day of Millie's party, because if he didn't, I would have no way of drugging him.

My lucky break came when the Tomasin case didn't turn out to be as straightforward as he expected. A week into the court case, as I sat on the bed sipping the whisky he had brought me and listened to him moaning about the number of character witnesses Antony Tomasin had brought in, I told him he looked as if he could use a drink himself and he went down to fetch one. From then on, every evening he brought up two glasses and, when he began to linger longer than before, I understood that he needed to talk about what had happened in court that day. He never discussed the case with me in depth, but from what he said it was obvious that

Antony Tomasin was putting up a robust defence, with a string of influential people attesting to his good character. The case began to drag on and, because Jack never mentioned our trip to Thailand, I presumed he had cancelled it, or at least postponed it.

On the evening before we'd been due to leave, Jack came up to my room carrying the usual two glasses of whisky.

'Drink up,' he said, handing me a glass. 'You need to pack.'

'Pack?'

'Yes—we're going to Thailand tomorrow, remember.'

I stared at him in horror. 'But how can we go away if the case isn't over yet?' I stammered.

'It will be tomorrow,' he said grimly, swilling his whisky in his glass.

'I didn't realise the jury were out.'

'They've been out for two days. They've promised the verdict before lunch tomorrow.'

Looking at him closely, I noticed how drawn he looked. 'You are going to win, aren't you?'

He knocked back most of his whisky. 'That stupid bitch lied to me.'

'What do you mean?'

'She did have a lover.'

'So it was him?'

'No, it was her husband,' he said stonily, because he couldn't bring himself to say anything else, not even to me.

'Then you've got nothing to worry about, have you?'

He finished his glass. 'You don't know how glad I am that we're going to Thailand. If I've failed to convince the jury, it'll be the first case I've ever lost and the press are going to have a field day. I can see the headlines already—"Fallen

Angel" or something equally trite. Right, have you finished? It's time to pack.'

As I took clothes out of the wardrobe in the bedroom next door with Jack looking on, I hoped he wouldn't notice how shaken I was. I threw them into the case without giving any thought to what I was doing, preoccupied by the knowledge that the following day, when he came back from court, I was going to have to kill him, long before I planned to because I'd foolishly counted on our holiday being cancelled. But he too seemed lost in thought and, realising how much winning meant to him, I felt anxious about the sort of mood he'd be in when he came back the next day. If he lost, he might insist on leaving for the airport straight away to get away from the press, even though our flight was in the evening—which meant that I wouldn't have time to drug him. That night, I prayed as I had never prayed before. I reminded God of all the evil Jack had already done and all the evil he was going to do. I thought about Molly, about how he had locked her up and left her to die of dehydration. I thought about Millie and the fate he planned for her. I thought about the room in the basement. And, suddenly, I had the answer to my problem. I knew exactly how I could make sure that he died. It was perfect, so perfect that if it worked, I would literally get away with murder.

PRESENT

It's only when the flight takes off that I begin to relax a little. But I know that even when I arrive in Bangkok, I'll be looking over my shoulder the whole time. I doubt the feeling of menace will ever leave me; even the fact that Millie is safe at school isn't enough to allay my fears that Jack will somehow get to us. I had thought to bring her with me, I had wanted to tell Janice that Jack had given Millie his place on the plane and ask her to bring her to the airport. But it's better that she isn't involved in what is to come. I'm going to have a hard enough time keeping my nerve; to have to watch over Millie at the same time might prove too much for me. After everything I've been through in the last few hours, the slightest thing could make me lose the control I'm trying so hard to maintain. But I remind myself that there will be time enough to let my mask slip a little when I arrive in Thailand, once I'm behind closed doors.

Going through passport control in Bangkok is a nightmare, the fear of Jack's hand on my shoulder never greater, although it would have been impossible for him to have got here before me. Even so, I find myself checking the face of the taxi driver before I get into his car to make sure it isn't Jack sitting behind the wheel.

At the hotel, I'm warmly greeted by Mr Ho, the manager who wrote the letter about me and, when he expresses surprise that I am alone, I express equal surprise that he hasn't received Mr Angel's email asking him to look after me until he arrives. Mr Ho tells me he will be delighted to do so and commiserates when I tell him that work commitments have kept my husband from joining me until Wednesday.

I sense the manager hesitate—is it possible, he asks, that my husband, Mr Jack Angel, is the Mr Angel mentioned in some of the English newspapers recently in relation to the Antony Tomasin case? I admit, in strictest confidence, that he and my husband are indeed one and the same, and that we hope we can count on him to be discreet as we would rather nobody knows where we are staying. He tells me that he heard on the international news yesterday that Mr Tomasin was acquitted and, when I confirm that he heard correctly, he says that Mr Angel must have been disappointed. And I tell him that yes, Mr Angel was very disappointed, especially as it was the first time he had lost a case. As Mr Ho signs me in, he asks me how I've been keeping—a delicate nod to my mental state—and if I had a good flight. When I tell him that I found it hard to sleep, he says the least he can do for such a good client as Mr Angel is upgrade us to one of their suites. The relief I feel that I won't have to go back to the room where I realised I had married a monster is so great I feel like kissing him.

Mr Ho insists on escorting me to my new room himself. It crosses my mind that he might wonder why we always stay in one of the smaller rooms when Jack is such an illustrious lawyer so I make sure to mention that my husband likes to maintain anonymity when we're on holiday rather than draw attention to himself by throwing money around. I don't put it quite like that but he gets the gist.

Once Mr Ho has left, I turn the television on and search for Sky News. Even in Asia, the Tomasin verdict is big news and, as they show Antony Tomasin addressing reporters as he came out of court the previous day, Jack appears in the background, besieged by journalists. Unable to watch any longer, I turn the television off quickly. I'm desperate for a shower, but there are two calls I need to make—one to Janice and the other to Jack, to tell them that I've arrived safely. Luckily, both are numbers that I know by heart—Jack's from when I first met him and Janice's because it's the most important number in the world. I look at my watch; it's three in the afternoon local time, which means it's nine in the morning in England. As the wife of Jack Angel, I make sure to get my priorities right and call him first. I have a momentary panic when I realise that anytime over the past year, he could have changed his number, so when I get through to his voicemail I feel weak with relief. I take a deep breath to steady myself and leave the sort of message a loving wife would leave, the sort of message I might have left had I been able to carry on living the dream.

'Hello, darling, it's me. I know you told me you might not pick up, but I was rather hoping you would—as you can tell, I'm missing you already. But maybe you're still in bed? Anyway, I've arrived safely and guess what? Mr Ho felt so sorry for me being on my own that he's upgraded us to a better room! Even so, I know I'm going to hate being here without you. Anyway, I hope the press aren't hounding you too much and that you're managing to get through all your paperwork. Don't work too hard and, if you've got a minute, please call me back, I'm in room 107, otherwise I'll try you again later. I love you, bye for now.'

I hang up and dial Janice's mobile. At this time on a Saturday morning, she and Millie should have finished breakfast and be on their way to the stables for Millie's riding lesson. When Janice doesn't answer immediately my heart pounds with fear, in case Jack has somehow managed to get to Millie after all. But eventually she does and, while I speak to her, I remember to mention that Esther and her children will be calling in to see Millie the next day. Then I speak to Millie and just knowing she is safe, at least for the time being, makes me feel better.

I walk into the bathroom. The shower stands in the corner, concealed behind opaque doors, which means I can't use it as there is always the possibility, however slight, that I may come out and find Jack standing on the other side of them. I look at the bath and work out that if I leave the door open, as well as that of the bedroom, I'll be able to see through to the sitting room and, so, the main door. Reassured, I fill the bath, strip off my clothes and lower myself tentatively into the hot water. As it rises up around my shoulders, the tension that engulfed me the moment I heard Jack step into the house at three o'clock the previous afternoon melts away and I begin to cry in huge racking sobs, which tear from my body at an alarming rate.

By the time I manage to pull myself together, the water is so cold I'm shivering. Climbing out, I wrap myself in one of the white towelling robes provided by the hotel and go into the bedroom. I'm desperately hungry, so I pick up the room-service menu. I know I'm going to have to leave my room at some point if I'm to carry on pretending that everything is all right but I can't, not yet. I order a club sandwich, but, when it arrives, I'm too frightened to open the door, even with the chain on, in case I find Jack standing there. Instead, I call for the tray to be left outside my room, which isn't much better because there's still the possibility that he'll be lurking in the corridor, waiting to bundle me back inside as soon as I open the door. Finding the courage to open the door wide enough to pull the tray into the room is a major triumph and I wish I'd thought of ordering a bottle of wine along with the sandwich so that I could celebrate. But I remind myself that there will be plenty of time to celebrate later, when it is all over, approximately five days from now, if my calculations are correct. Whether they are or not is something I have no way of knowing. At least, not yet.

When I've finished eating, I unpack my case, look at my watch. It's only five-thirty and because nobody would expect me to go down to dinner alone on my first night in the hotel, I feel justified in staying in my room for the rest of the day. Feeling suddenly exhausted, I lie down on the bed, not really expecting to be able to sleep. But I do and, when I next open my eyes and find that the room is in darkness, I leap out of bed, my heart thumping in my chest, and run around the room, turning on all the lights. I know I'm not going to be able to sleep again for fear of opening my eyes and finding Jack standing over me so I resign myself to spending a long night with only my thoughts for company.

When morning comes, I get dressed, pick up the phone and dial Jack's number.

'Hello, darling, I wasn't really expecting to get you because it's two in the morning in England so you must be fast asleep, but I thought I'd leave a message for you to listen to when you wake up. I meant to phone you before I went to sleep last night, but I lay down on the bed at six in the evening and only woke up ten minutes ago, which just goes to show how tired I was! I'm going down to breakfast in a minute but I've got no idea how I'm going to spend the rest of the day—I might go for a walk, but I'll probably just hang around the pool. Will you give me a ring when you wake up? You can always leave a message at the reception if I'm not in my room. I feel an awfully long way away from you—which I am, of course. Anyway, I love you and miss you, don't forget to phone me.'

I make my way down for breakfast. Mr Ho is on duty. He asks if I slept well and I tell him that I did. He suggests I eat out on the terrace and I cross the lobby, remembering all the times Jack walked me across it on the way to the dining room, his hand gripping my arm tightly while he whispered menaces in my ear.

Once outside, I help myself to fruit and pancakes and find a table in the corner, wondering if anyone else in the world has been as fooled by a man as I was. It seems strange that I'll never be able to tell anyone what I've been through, never be able to tell them about the monster I was married to, not if everything turns out as I hope it will.

I eat slowly, needing to pass the time and, as I eat, I realise that if I crane my neck I can see the balcony of the room on the sixth floor where I spent so many lonely hours. I sit there for over an hour, wishing I'd brought a book with me. Sitting on my own with nothing to distract me might look suspicious, as there can't be many people who go on holiday without taking a book with them except those that leave in a hurry. I seem to remember Jack walking me past a second-hand bookshop on our way to take photographs of the two of us having a wonderful time in Bangkok, so I leave the hotel and go in search of it. I find it easily; it's the sort of place I love, but I feel too conspicuous to linger so I buy a couple of books and return to the hotel, marvelling that I can feel relatively safe in a place that once held such horrors for me.

In my room, I change into a bikini and go down to the pool, arming myself with a book and a towel. As I climb out of the pool after a swim, I notice a couple of men looking in my direction and prepare to tell them, should they decide to come and talk to me, that my husband is arriving in two days' time. I eke out the time until three o'clock by reading my book and swimming, then leave the terrace and go up to my room where I leave a disappointed message on Jack's mobile.

'Jack, it's me. I was hoping you'd have phoned me by now, but you're probably still asleep, which can only be a good thing as I've been worrying that you're driving yourself into the ground working twenty-four hours a day. I've been at the pool all morning so I'm going to go for a walk now. I'll phone you when I get back. Love you.'

I wait in my room for an hour or so, then go down to the lobby and, with a quick wave to Mr Ho, who seems to work twenty-four hours a day, go out through the main doors. I walk around for a while, find myself in a market and spend some time buying silk scarves for Janice and Millie. I buy some postcards, search for a bar, order a non-alcoholic cocktail, read my book, write my cards and wonder how I'm going to be able to fill in the next couple of days.

I head back to the hotel and am immediately cornered by Mr Ho, who wants to know if I'm enjoying myself. I confide that I'm at a bit of a loss without Jack and ask him if I could perhaps book an excursion for the following day. He tells me about an overnight trip to ancient temples that some of the hotel guests are going on and asks me if I would be interested in joining them. It's the perfect solution, but it's important that I don't look too eager so I hum and haw a little and ask when exactly we'd be back, pointing out that Jack is due in on Wednesday morning. He promises that I'll be back at the hotel on Tuesday evening and, after a bit more hesitation, I let myself be persuaded. I add that because I'm going to have to get up extra early the next morning, I'll probably just have dinner in my room and he agrees that it's a good idea. I go up to my room and phone Jack once again.

'Hello darling, still no message from you so I can't help wondering if you've gone to Esther's for lunch—she said she'd invite you over at some point. I told her you'd probably be too busy but maybe you needed a break. Anyway, I just wanted to let you know that I've decided to go on an overnight trip to some temples, leaving early tomorrow morning—Mr Ho suggested it and at least it'll pass the time until you get here. I hate the thought of not being able to speak to you before

Tuesday evening, which will be Tuesday afternoon for you—
I'm definitely going to buy a mobile when we get back to England! But I'll phone you as soon as I get back to the hotel and
hopefully catch you before you leave for the airport. I thought
I might come and meet you off the flight, I know you said not
to, that you'll make your own way here, but maybe after being apart from me for four days you'll have changed your mind!
I can't wait to see you, you may as well know that I'm never
going away without you again no matter how much work you
have. Well, I'd better go and throw a few things together. Remember I love you very much. I'll speak to you Tuesday. Don't
work too hard!'

The next morning, I go on the trip and attach myself to a
lovely middle-aged couple who, when I explain that I'm on my
own because I'm waiting for my husband to come out and join
me, take me under their wing. I talk to them about Jack and
about the brilliant work he does on behalf of battered wives
with such conviction that I almost believe it myself. They
end up putting two and two together—because they've read
the papers—and I end up admitting that Jack Angel is indeed
my husband. Fortunately, they're discreet enough not to mention the Tomasin case although I can tell that they're itching
to. Instead, I tell them about Millie, about how much we're
looking forward to her coming to live with us and how grateful
I am to have such a wonderfully accepting husband. I tell
them about our house, about Millie's yellow bedroom and
about the party we gave her for her eighteenth birthday, just a
few weeks before. By the time we get back to the hotel, later on
Tuesday evening than expected, they've become firm friends
and, as we go off to our rooms, I accept their kind invitation
for Jack and me to have dinner with them once he arrives.

In my room, I look at my watch. It's almost eleven o'clock, so five in the afternoon in England. It's plausible that Jack could already have left for the airport so I phone his mobile and get through to his voicemail. This time I make sure to sound dismayed.

'Jack, it's me. I've just got back from the trip to the temples, later than expected, and I can't believe you're still not answering your phone. I hope it doesn't mean that you're still working because you should be leaving for the airport soon, unless you're already on your way. Could you phone me as soon as you get this message please, just to let me know that everything is on schedule for you leaving tonight? I know you told me you would be "incommunicado", but I expected to be able to speak to you at least once before you left! And I had hoped to find a message waiting for me on my phone here. I don't mean to nag, but I'm beginning to get a bit worried by your silence—I hope it doesn't mean that you don't want to tell me that you're not coming until Thursday, by any chance? Anyway, please phone me as soon as you get this message. Don't worry that I'll be asleep—I won't be!'

I wait for half an hour or so, try his number again and, when it goes through to his voicemail, I leave an 'it's me again, please phone me' message. Half an hour after that, I simply give a sigh of frustration before hanging up. Going over to my bag I take out Jack's business card and call his office. A receptionist answers and, without giving my name, I ask to be put through to Adam.

'Hello, Adam, it's Grace.'

'Grace! How are you? How's Thailand?'

'I'm fine and Thailand is as lovely as ever. I thought you might still be in the office—I'm not disturbing you, am I?'

'No, it's fine, I was in a meeting with a client, but he's just left, thank goodness. It's one of those cases that I don't particularly want to take on, but his wife is determined to take him to the cleaners and I can't help feeling sorry for him—not that I'm letting my emotions get in the way, of course,' he adds with a laugh.

'That certainly wouldn't be good for business,' I agree. 'Anyway, I won't keep you long, I just wondered if you saw Jack at all over the weekend, or at least spoke to him, because I haven't been able to get through to him and I'm beginning to get a bit worried. I know he told me that he wouldn't be answering his phone because of the press, but I thought he might pick up for me. Maybe he did for you?'

There's a bit of a silence. 'Are you saying that Jack is still in England?'

'Yes, until tonight, anyway. He's taking the evening flight, remember—well, at least I hope he is. He did say he might not be able to get here until Thursday, but I didn't think he really meant it. The trouble is, I can't get through to him.'

'Grace, I had no idea Jack was here, I thought he was in Thailand with you. I thought he left on Friday evening, after the case.'

'No, he made me come on ahead. He said he wanted to get all the paperwork out of the way first, that he couldn't bear the thought of having to face it all when he came back.'

'Well, I can understand that, I suppose. There's nothing worse than coming back from holiday and finding a backlog of work and it's always harder when it concerns a case that you've lost. I guess he must be feeling pretty low.'

'You could say that,' I admit. 'As a matter of fact, I've never seen him so down, which is why I wanted to stay with him.

But he said he preferred to be on his own, that if I was around it would take him longer to get through everything and then we'd both miss out on our holiday. So here I am.'

'Between you and me, I never understood why he took the case on in the first place.'

'Maybe he let his emotions get in the way,' I suggest. 'But the thing is, Adam, you must have known he was staying behind because didn't you offer to take him to the airport this evening?'

'When?'

'Well, on Friday, I presume, when he told you he was staying behind.'

'Sorry, Grace, I'm afraid I haven't spoken to Jack since Friday morning before he left for court, although I did leave a message on his voicemail commiserating with him over losing. Are you saying that you haven't heard from him since you left?'

'Yes. I wasn't too worried at first because he warned me he wouldn't be answering his phone and, anyway, I was away on an excursion for the last couple of days. But I expected him to have at least left a message on my phone here at the hotel to tell me that everything was on schedule for tonight. He may already have left for the airport—you know what traffic is like in rush hour—but I keep getting through to his voicemail. I know he won't answer the phone if he's driving but it's really frustrating.'

'Maybe he's forgotten to switch it back on again if it's been off since Friday.'

'Maybe. Listen, Adam, I won't take up any more of your time, I'm sure everything's fine.'

'Do you want me to phone around a few people and see if

they've spoken to him at all over the weekend? Would that put your mind at rest?'

Relief floods my voice. 'Yes, it would, definitely. You could try Esther—when she took me to the airport she said she'd invite Jack around sometime over the weekend.'

'Will do.'

'Thanks, Adam. How are Diane and the children, by the way?'

'They're all fine. Let me make those calls and I'll get back to you. Can you give me your number there?'

I read it out to him from the hotel notepad, which is lying on the bedside table, and sit down on the bed to wait. I try to read, but I find it difficult to concentrate. Half an hour or so later, Adam calls back to tell me that he hasn't found anybody who actually spoke to Jack over the weekend although several people saw him in the office before he left for court.

'I've also tried him several times myself, but I got his voicemail each time, as did Esther when she tried to get hold of him. But that doesn't mean anything—as I said, maybe he's just forgotten to switch it back on again.'

'I don't think he would have, especially as he must know that I'll be wanting to speak to him. And there's something else I thought of—why did he tell me that you'd offered to take him to the airport when you didn't?'

'Maybe he intended to ask me to then changed his mind. Look, don't worry, I'm sure everything is all right. I'm sure he'll be on that flight tonight.'

'Do you think that if I phone British Airways in a couple of hours they'll tell me whether or not he's checked in?'

'No, they won't, not unless it's an emergency. Passenger confidentiality and all that.'

'Then I guess I'll just have to wait until tomorrow morning,' I sigh.

'Well, when you see him, make sure you tell him off for worrying you. And tell him to send me a text to let me know he's arrived.'

'Then could you give me your mobile number?' He gives it to me and I jot it down. 'Thanks, Adam.'

Once again I have trouble sleeping. Early next morning, prettily dressed and beautifully made-up, I go down to the lobby. Mr Ho is once again at the reception desk. He guesses that I've come down to wait for Jack and tells me that I might have a long wait, as there are the queues at Passport Control to contend with plus the taxi ride from the airport. He suggests that I have breakfast, but I tell him that I prefer to wait for Jack, that he'll no doubt be hungry when he arrives.

I find a seat not too far away from the main door and settle down to wait. As time goes on, I look at my watch anxiously and, when it is evident that something is wrong, I go over to Mr Ho and ask him if he can find out if the London flight arrived on time. He checks on his computer and, when he tells me that the flight was in fact delayed and is due to land at any moment, I can't believe my luck, because I won't have to pretend panic for another couple of hours. Mr Ho smiles at the look of relief on my face and I admit that I was beginning to worry at Jack's non-appearance. I go back to waiting and Mr Ho brings me over a pot of tea to help pass the time.

When, almost two hours later, Jack still hasn't arrived, it's time to start feeling uneasy. I ask to use the phone at the reception desk and, as I dial Jack's number, I tell Mr Ho that although Jack had warned me he might only be able to take the Wednesday evening flight, I can't help feeling worried because he would have phoned to let me know. When I get through to his voicemail, my voice is shaky with tears of disappointment and frustration.

'Jack, where are you? I know the flight was delayed, but you should be here by now. I hope it doesn't mean that you're not arriving until tomorrow—if that's the case, you could have at least warned me. Have you any idea how worrying it is to be without any news from you for the last four days? Even if you didn't want to answer your phone you could have phoned me, you must have got all my messages. Please give me a ring, Jack, it's awful being stuck here not knowing what's happening—not that I'm not being well looked after,' I add hurriedly, aware that Mr Ho is listening, 'because I am, but I just want you here. Please phone and tell me what's happening—I'm in the lobby now, but I'll be going back up to my room, or you can leave a message with Mr Ho at reception. I love you.'

I hang up to find Mr Ho looking sympathetically at me. He suggests that I go through for breakfast and, when I tell him that I'm not hungry, he promises to call me if Jack phones, so I let him persuade me to have something to eat.

As I make my way to the terrace, I bump into Margaret and Richard, the couple I met the day before on the trip to the temples, and my eyes fill with tears of disappointment when I explain that Jack hasn't turned up. They tell me not to worry, pointing out that he had warned me he might be delayed, and insist that I spend the day with them. I tell them I'd rather stay in the hotel for the next couple of hours in case Jack phones or suddenly turns up, but that I'll join them in the afternoon if he doesn't.

I go up to my room and phone Adam. I'm relieved when he doesn't pick up as it suits me to leave a message letting him know that Jack wasn't on the flight. Later, I go down to join Margaret and Richard, the strain of not having heard from Jack clearly visible on my face, especially when I tell them that I've tried his mobile again several times without success. They are kindness itself and I'm glad to have them to take my mind off things. I punctuate the time I spend with them with fruitless calls to Jack's mobile, urging him to phone me.

In the evening, my new friends refuse to let me sit and mope alone so we have dinner together, where they talk brightly about how much they're looking forward to meeting Jack the following morning. I eventually get back to my room around midnight and find a message from Adam, saying he's sorry he missed my call and asking if I would like him to go over to the house to see if Jack is still there. I phone him back and tell him that yes, if he doesn't mind, but then we work out that if Jack is to catch the flight that evening, he will already have left for the airport. So I tell him not to bother and that I'll phone him the moment Jack arrives and we joke again about the telling-off he's going to get for worrying us all.

The next morning, Margaret and Richard keep me company while I wait for Jack to arrive from the airport so they are there to witness my distress when he doesn't turn up. At Margaret's suggestion, I try to find out from British Airways if Jack was on the flight, but they are unable to help me, so I phone the British Embassy. I explain everything to them and maybe because Jack's name is known, they tell me they'll see what they can do. When they phone back and confirm that Jack wasn't on the flight, I burst into tears. I manage to pull myself together long enough to tell them that he doesn't seem to be at home either, but, although they are sympathetic, they tell me there isn't a lot they can do at this stage. They suggest I phone friends and relations in England to see if they know where he is and I thank them and hang up.

With Margaret by my side, I call Adam and, my voice trembling with anxiety, tell him what has happened. He immediately offers to go straight round to the house and calls me back half an hour later to say that he's standing outside the gates, but that everything is shut up and nobody has answered the bell. So I worry that Jack has had an accident on the way to the airport and, although he reassures me, he says that he'll make some inquiries. I tell him that the British Embassy suggested I try to find out if anyone has spoken to him since I left and he offers to phone around for me.

While I wait for Adam to get back to me, Diane calls to reassure me and to tell me that Adam is doing all he can to track Jack down. We talk for a while and, after I've hung up, Margaret begins to ask me gentle questions and it dawns on me that she and Richard are wondering if there could be someone else in Jack's life, someone who he might have run off with. Horrified, I tell her that it had never occurred to me, because there had never been anything in his behaviour to suggest that there was, but that I suppose it's a possibility I'm going to have to consider.

The phone rings again.

'Grace?'

'Hello, Adam.' I make my voice hesitant, as if I'm dreading what he's going to tell me. 'Have you managed to find out anything?'

'Only that Jack hasn't been admitted to any of the hospitals I phoned, which is good news.'

'It is,' I agree, giving a sigh of relief.

'On the other hand, I phoned as many people as I could think of but no one seems to have heard from him, at least not over the last few days. So I'm afraid we're back to square one, really.'

I look at Margaret, who nods encouragingly. 'There's something I need to ask you, Adam,' I say.

'Go on.'

'Is it possible that Jack was having an affair, maybe with someone at the office?' My words come out in a rush.

'An affair? Jack?' Adam sounds shocked. 'No, of course not. He would never do anything like that. He barely looked at another woman before he met you and he certainly hasn't since. You must know that, Grace.'

Margaret, who gets the gist, gives my hand a squeeze. 'I do,' I say, chastened. 'It's just that I can't think of any other reason he would suddenly disappear without trace.'

'Can you think of any other friends he has, people that maybe I don't know?'

'Not really,' I say. 'Wait a minute, what about Moira and Giles, you know, the people who were at Millie's party. Maybe you could contact them. I don't have their number, though.'

'Leave it with me. What's their surname?'

'Kilburn-Hawes, I think.'

'I'll give them a ring and get back to you,' he promises.

He calls back half an hour later and, when he tells me that they haven't heard from Jack either, I become distraught. Nobody seems to know what to do. The general consensus— from Margaret, Richard, Adam and Diane—is that it's too early to launch a missing person's inquiry so they tell me that the best thing would be to try to get some sleep and see if Jack turns up the next morning.

He doesn't. The day passes in a blur as Mr Ho, Margaret, Richard and Adam take over. I tell them I want to go home, but they persuade me to stay for one more day in case Jack turns up, so I do. In the early afternoon—eight o'clock in the morning in England—Adam calls to say that he has spoken to the local police and that, with my permission, they'll be happy to break into the house to see if they can find anything to indicate where Jack might have gone.

They call me first and ask me to run through the last time I saw Jack and I tell them it was when Esther came to pick me up to take me to the airport, that he had waved me off from the study window. I explain that he hadn't been able to drive me to the airport himself because he'd had quite a large whisky when he'd come in from work and add that I hadn't particularly wanted to leave for Thailand by myself even though Jack had warned me, when the Tomasin case began to look as if it would overrun, that I might have to. They say they'll get back to me as soon as they can and I sit in my room and wait for them to phone with Margaret by my side, holding my hand. I know the news I'm waiting for is going to be a long time coming so after a while I tell Margaret that I'd like to try to sleep, and lie down on the bed.

I manage to sleep until the moment I've been waiting for since I arrived in Thailand finally comes. It begins with a knock on the door and, because I don't move, Margaret goes to answer it. I hear a man's voice and then Margaret comes over to the bed and, with a hand on my shoulder, gives me a little shake, telling me that there's someone to see me. As I sit up, I see her slip out of the room and I want to call her back, to tell her not to leave me, but he is already walking towards me so it's too late. My heart is beating so fast, my breathing so shallow that I don't dare look at him until I've managed to compose myself. With my eyes fixed firmly on the ground, it's his shoes I see first. They are made of good leather and are well polished, just as I would expect them to be. He says my name and, as my eyes travel upwards, I see that while his suit is dark, in keeping with the occasion, it's made of a lightweight fabric, because of the climate. My eyes reach his face; it is pleasant, but grave, just as it should be.

'Mrs Angel?' he says again.

'Yes?' There's a trace of anxiousness in my voice.

'My name is Alastair Strachan. I'm from the British Embassy.' He turns, and I see a young woman standing behind him. 'And this is Vivienne Dashmoor. I wonder if we could have a word?'

I jump to my feet. 'Is it to do with Jack, have you managed to find him?'

'Yes—or rather, the police in England have.'

Relief floods my face. 'Thank goodness for that! Where is he? Why wasn't he answering his phone? Is he on his way here?'

'Perhaps we could go and sit down?' the young woman suggests.

'Of course,' I say, ushering them through to the sitting room. I sit down on the sofa and they take the armchairs. 'So where is he?' I ask. 'I mean, is he on his way here?'

Mr Strachan clears his throat. 'I'm very sorry to have to tell you this, Mrs Angel, but I'm afraid that Mr Angel has been found dead.'

I stare at him, my eyes wide with shock. Confusion floods my face. 'I don't understand,' I stammer.

He shifts uncomfortably. 'I'm afraid your husband has been found dead, Mrs Angel.'

I shake my head vigorously. 'No, he can't be, he's coming here, to join me, he said he would. Where is he?' My voice trembles with emotion. 'I want to know where he is. Why isn't he here?'

'Mrs Angel, I know this is very difficult for you, but we need to ask you some questions,' the young lady says. 'Would you like us to fetch someone—your friend, perhaps?'

'Yes, yes.' I nod. 'Can you get Margaret, please?'

Mr Strachan goes to the door. I hear the murmur of voices and Margaret comes in. I see the shock on her face and I begin shaking uncontrollably. 'They're saying that Jack's dead,' I say. 'But he can't be, he can't be.'

'It's all right,' she murmurs, sitting down next to me and putting her arm around me. 'It's all right.'

'Perhaps we could have some tea brought up,' the young woman says, getting to her feet. She goes over to the phone and speaks to someone in reception.

'Did he have a car crash?' I ask Margaret, sounding bewildered. 'Is that what happened? Did Jack have a car crash on the way to the airport? Is that why he's not here?'

'I don't know,' she says quietly.

'He must have,' I go on, nodding with conviction. 'He must have been rushing to catch the flight, he must have left the house late and was driving too fast and had a crash. That's what happened, isn't it?'

Margaret glances at Mr Strachan. 'I don't know, I'm afraid.'

My teeth begin chattering. 'I'm cold.'

She jumps to her feet, glad of something to do. 'Would you like a jumper? Is there one in your wardrobe?'

'Yes, I think so, not a jumper, a cardigan, maybe. The bathrobe, can I have the bathrobe?'

'Yes, of course.' She goes into the bathroom, finds the bathrobe, comes back and puts it around my shoulders.

'Thank you,' I murmur gratefully.

'Is that better?' she asks.

'Yes. But Jack can't be dead, it must be a mistake, it has to be.'

She's saved from saying anything by a knock at the door. The young woman opens it and Mr Ho comes in, followed by a girl pushing a laden tea trolley.

'If I can be of further assistance, please let me know,' Mr Ho says quietly. I sense him looking at me as he leaves the room, but I keep my head bowed.

The young woman busies herself with the tea and asks me if I would like sugar.

'No, thank you.'

She places a cup and saucer in front of me and I pick up the cup, but I'm shaking so much some of the tea slops over the side and onto my hand. Scalded, I clatter the cup back down onto the saucer.

'Sorry,' I say. Tears fill my eyes. 'I'm sorry.'

'It's all right,' says Margaret hurriedly, taking a paper napkin and mopping my hand.

I make an effort to pull myself together. 'I'm sorry, I didn't catch your name,' I say to Mr Strachan.

'Alastair Strachan.'

'Mr Strachan, you say that my husband is dead.' I look at him for confirmation.

'Yes, I'm afraid so.'

'Then can you please tell me how he died? I mean, was it

quick, was anyone else hurt in the accident, where did it happen? I need to know, I need to know how it happened.'

'It wasn't a car accident, Mrs Angel.'

'Not a car accident?' I falter. 'Then how did he die?'

Mr Strachan looks uncomfortable. 'I'm afraid there's no easy way of saying this, Mrs Angel, but it seems that your husband took his own life.'

And I burst into tears.

PAST

Once I'd realised that I could get away with murder, I spent the rest of the night working out the details, thinking of ways to get Jack exactly where I needed him to be when the time came. Because my plan hinged on him losing the Tomasin case, I took a leaf out of his book and planned for every eventuality. I thought very carefully about what I would do if he won and, in the end, I decided that if he did I would drug him anyway and, while he was unconscious, phone the police. If I showed them the room in the basement, and the room where he kept me, maybe they would believe what I told them. In the event that I didn't manage to drug him before we left for the airport, I would somehow get the pills into him on the plane and try to get help once we arrived in Thailand. Neither solution was brilliant, but I didn't have any other options. Unless he lost. And, even then, there was no guarantee that he would bring up a glass of whisky to commiserate.

The next day, the day of the verdict, I spent the morning crushing the remaining pills into as fine a powder as I possibly could and hid it in a screw of toilet paper, which I pushed into my sleeve as I would a tissue. When I eventually heard the whir of the black gates opening and the crunch of the gravel as Jack drove up to the front door sometime in the middle of the afternoon, my heart began hammering so hard I was afraid it would burst out of my chest. The time had finally come. Whether he had won or lost, I was going to have to act.

He came into the hall, closed the front door and activated the shutters. I heard him open the cloakroom door, walk across the hall to the kitchen, followed by the familiar sounds of the freezer door opening and closing, the ice cubes being popped from the tray, the cupboard door opening and closing, the clink as the ice cubes were dropped into one glass—I held my breath—two glasses. His footsteps as he came up the stairs were heavy and told me all I needed to know. I began rubbing my left eye furiously so that by the time he unlocked the door it would be red and inflamed.

'Well?' I asked. 'How did it go?'

He held out a glass to me. 'We lost.'

'Lost?' I said, taking it. Without bothering to answer, he raised his glass to his lips and, scared he would knock the whole lot back before I'd had a chance to drug him, I jumped off the bed. 'I've had something in my eye all morning,' I explained, blinking rapidly. 'Could you have a look?'

'What?'

'Could you just look at my eye a moment? I think there must be a fly in there or something.'

As he peered into my eye, which I kept half shut, I worked the paper holding the powder from my sleeve and into the palm of my hand. 'So what happened?' I asked, unscrewing it as best I could with my fingers.

'Dena Anderson screwed me over,' he said bitterly. 'Can you open your eye a bit more?'

Keeping my movements small, I moved the glass I was holding in my other hand under the paper and shook the powder into it. 'I can't, it's too painful,' I told him, stirring the contents around with my finger. 'Can you do it? I'll hold your glass for you.'

With a sigh of annoyance, he handed me his glass and pulled my eye open using both hands. 'I can't see anything.'

'If I had a mirror, I'd be able to see for myself,' I grumbled. 'It doesn't matter, it'll probably work itself out.' He held out his hand for his glass and I gave him mine. 'What shall we drink to?'

'Revenge,' he said, grimly.

I raised the glass I was holding. 'To revenge, then.' I knocked half of the whisky back and was gratified to see him doing the same.

'Nobody makes a fool out of me. Antony Tomasin is going to suffer for this too.'

'But he was innocent,' I protested, wondering how I was going to keep him talking until the pills took effect.

'What has that got to do with it?' As he raised his glass to take another drink, I was alarmed to see tiny white specks floating in the whisky. 'Do you know what the best part of my job is?'

'No, what?' I said quickly.

'Sitting opposite all those battered women and imagining it was me who had beaten them up.' He knocked the rest of his glass back. 'And the photos, all those lovely photos of their injuries—I suppose you could call it one of the perks of the job.'

Incensed, I raised my glass and before I could stop myself, I had thrown the rest of my whisky in his face. His roar of anger, plus the knowledge that I had acted too soon, almost paralysed me. But as he lunged towards me, his eyes shut tight against the sting of the whisky, I took advantage of his momentary blindness and pushed him as hard as I could. As he stumbled awkwardly against the bed, the few seconds before he righted himself were all that I needed. Slamming the door behind me, I ran down the stairs to the hall below, looking urgently for somewhere to hide, because I couldn't let him catch me, not just yet. Upstairs, the door crashed back against the wall and as he came pounding down the stairs, I headed for the cloakroom and climbed into the wardrobe, hoping to buy myself a few precious minutes.

This time, there was no singsong in his voice as he called for me. Instead, he roared my name, promising such harm to me that I trembled from my hiding place behind the coats. Several minutes passed, and I imagined him in the sitting room, checking behind every piece of furniture. The waiting was unbearable but I knew that with every minute that passed, the chances of the pills taking effect increased.

At last, I heard the unmistakable sound of his footsteps

coming down the hall. My legs turned to jelly and as the cloakroom door opened, I found myself sliding to the floor. The silence that followed was terrifying; I knew he was there, outside the wardrobe and I knew he knew I was inside. But he seemed content to leave me to sweat, relishing no doubt in the fear emanating from every pore of my body.

I don't know when it occurred to me that the wardrobe might have a key, but the thought that at any moment he could turn it in the lock and imprison me there made it impossible for me to breathe. If I couldn't put the next part of my plan into action, there would be no saving Millie. Blind with panic, I flung myself against the doors. They burst open and I fell into a crumpled heap at Jack's feet.

His rage as he pulled me up by my hair was tangible, and afraid that he might harm me physically I began screaming for mercy, telling him I was sorry and begging him not to take me down to the basement, gabbling incoherently that I would do anything as long as he didn't lock me in there.

The mention of the basement had the desired effect. As he dragged me back along the hall I struggled so hard that he had no choice but to pick me up, and I let myself go limp so he would think I had given up. I used the time it took for him to carry me to the room he had prepared so carefully for Millie to focus on what I needed to do, so that when he tried to throw me down I held onto him as hard as I could. Enraged, he tried to shake me off and as he cursed me loudly, the slur in his voice was all that I needed. Still keeping hold of him, I allowed myself to slide down his body towards the floor, and when I reached his knees, I yanked them towards me as hard as I could. His legs buckled immediately and as he swayed above me, I used every ounce of strength I possessed to send him crashing to the floor. Stunned by the fall, his body heavy from the pills, he lay without moving for a few precious seconds and before he could recover, I fled the room, slamming the door behind me.

As I ran towards the stairs, I could hear him hammering on the door, yelling at me to let him out and the fury in his voice made me start sobbing with fright. Reaching the hall, I kicked the door that led to the basement with my foot, shutting it against the noise. Taking the stairs two at a time, I ran to my bedroom, retrieved the glasses from where we had thrown them and carried them down to the kitchen, trying to ignore Jack's desperate attempts to get out of the room below by focusing on what I needed to do. With shaking hands, I washed the glasses, dried them carefully and put them back in the cupboard.

Hurrying back upstairs, I went to my bedroom, straightened the bed, removed the shampoo, sliver of soap and towel from the bathroom and carried them into Jack's bathroom. Stripping off my pyjamas I put them in the laundry basket, went into the bedroom where my clothes were kept and got dressed quickly. I opened the wardrobe and took a couple of pairs of shoes from their boxes, some underwear and a dress, went back to the master bedroom and placed them around the room. On returning to the dressing room, I picked up the case that Jack had made me pack the night before and went downstairs.

I wasn't worried about getting out of the house—I didn't need a key to open the front door—but I was worried about how I was going to get to the airport without any money. I knew that Jack had probably hung the jacket he had worn that morning in the cloakroom, but I didn't want to rifle through his clothes for money and hoped I would come across some while I was looking for my passport and tickets. I opened the door of his study and turned on the light. When I saw both passports and tickets lying neatly on his desk, I almost cried with relief. There was an envelope beside them and, opening it, I found some baht. With the sleeve of my cardigan over my fingers, I slid open one of the drawers, but I couldn't find any money and I didn't dare rifle through the other drawers. Taking my ticket, passport and the baht with me, I went back into the hall and, because I couldn't get to the airport without money, I went into the cloakroom, found his jacket, opened his wallet as carefully as I could and took out four fifty pound notes. I was about to close his wallet when his business cards caught my eye and, remembering that at some point I would need to phone his office, I took one.

Realising that I had no idea what the time was, I went back to the kitchen and looked at the clock on the microwave. I was alarmed to see that it was already half past four, around the time I would need to leave for the airport on a Friday night for a check in at seven. In all my careful planning I hadn't actually thought about how I would get to the airport—I suppose I'd had a vague idea of taking a taxi—so it was galling to realise that I had no idea what number I should call to order one. Public transport was out—the nearest train station was a fifteen-minute walk away and I was loath to draw attention to myself by wheeling a heavy case along the road and anyway, I doubted it would get me there in time. Aware that I was wasting precious time, I went back into the hall and picked up the phone, wondering if such a thing as an operator still existed. As I stood there wondering what number I should dial, Esther's came into my head and, hardly daring to believe that I had remembered it correctly, I called her, praying that she would pick up.

'Hello?'

I took a deep breath. 'Esther, it's Grace. Am I disturbing you?'

'No, not at all. I was just listening to the radio actually—apparently, Antony Tomasin was acquitted.' She paused a moment as if she wasn't quite sure what to say. 'I guess Jack must be disappointed.'

My mind raced. 'Yes, I'm afraid he is rather.'

'Are you all right, Grace? You sound a bit upset.'

'It's Jack,' I admitted. 'He says he can't leave for Thailand tonight as he has too much paperwork to do. When he booked the tickets, he thought the case would be over long before now but because of the new evidence, about Dena Anderson having a lover, it overran.'

'You must be so disappointed! But you can always go later, can't you?'

'That's just it. Jack wants me to go tonight, as planned, and says he'll join me on Tuesday, once he's got everything sorted out. I've told him that I'd rather wait for him, but he says it's stupid to waste both tickets. He'll have to buy a new one for Tuesday, you see.'

'I take it you don't want to go without him.'

'No, of course I don't.' I gave a shaky laugh. 'But in the mood he's in, maybe it would be better. I'm meant to be phoning for a taxi to take me to the airport—he can't take me because he had a hefty whisky when he came in. The trouble is, I don't have a number for one and I don't dare disturb Jack in his study and ask him if I can use the computer to look for one, so I was wondering if you knew of a local firm.'

'Do you want me to take you? The children are already home from school and Rufus worked from home today, so it wouldn't be a problem.'

It was the last thing I wanted. 'It's very kind of you, but I can't ask you to drive to the airport on a Friday night,' I said hastily.

'I don't think it'll be that easy to get a taxi at such short notice. What time do you need to leave?'

'Well, as soon as possible, really,' I admitted reluctantly. 'I have to check in at seven.'

'Then you'd better let me take you.'

'I'd rather take a taxi. If you could just give me a number?'

'Look, I'll take you—it really isn't any trouble. Anyway, it'll get me out of the dreaded bath-time.'

'No, it's fine.'

'Why won't you let me help you, Grace?'

There was something about the way she said it that put me on my guard. 'I just think it's an awful imposition, that's all.'

'It isn't.' Her voice was firm. 'Have you got all your stuff ready?'

'Yes, we packed yesterday.'

'Then I'll just go and tell Rufus I'm taking you to the airport and I'll be straight over—say, fifteen minutes?'

'Great,' I told her. 'Thank you, Esther, I'll tell Jack.'

I put the phone down, appalled at what I had just agreed to. I couldn't even begin to imagine how I was going to be able to pretend to someone like Esther that everything was all right.

PRESENT

The air hostess leans towards me. 'We'll be arriving at Heathrow in about forty minutes,' she says quietly.

'Thank you.' I feel a sudden surge of panic and force myself to breathe calmly, because I can't afford to crack at this stage of the game. But the fact is, even though I've thought about nothing else since Margaret saw me through passport control at the airport in Bangkok almost twelve hours ago, I still have no idea how I'm going to play it when we finally land. Diane and Adam will be there to meet me and take me back to theirs so I need to think very carefully about what

I'm going to say to them about my last hours with Jack, because whatever I tell them I'll have to repeat to the police.

The seat-belt sign comes on and we begin our descent into Heathrow. I close my eyes and pray that I'll end up saying the right thing to Diane and Adam, especially as it is Adam who has been liaising with the police since Jack's body was found. I hope there aren't going to be any nasty surprises. I hope Adam isn't going to tell me that the police think Jack's death is suspicious. If he does, I don't know what I'll say. All I can do is play it by ear. The problem is, there are so many things I don't know.

The euphoria I felt when Mr Strachan told me that Jack had taken his own life—because it meant that my plan had worked and I had got away with murder—was quickly tempered by the fact that he'd used the word 'seems'. I didn't know whether he'd decided to be cautious off his own bat or if the police in England had intimated that there was room for doubt. If they had already started questioning people— work colleagues, friends—maybe they had come to the conclusion that Jack was an unlikely candidate for suicide. The police were bound to ask me if I knew why Jack had taken his own life and I would have to convince them that losing his first court case was reason enough. Maybe they would ask me if there'd been problems in our marriage, but if I admitted that there had been, even if I gave them all the details, they would surely consider murder, rather than suicide. And that is something I can't risk. Mr Strachan told me that Jack had died from an overdose, but he didn't give me any more details so I don't know where his body was actually found and I hadn't thought it appropriate to ask. But what if Jack had a way of getting out of the room in the basement, what if there was a switch hidden away somewhere that I hadn't found, what if, before actually succumbing, he'd made it up the stairs and into the hall? He might even have had time to write a note implicating me before he died.

Not knowing means I'm ill prepared for what is to come. Even if all went to plan and Jack was found in the basement, the police are bound to ask me why the room existed, what its purpose was, and I can't work out if it'll be in my interest to admit that I knew about it all along or deny all knowledge of it. If I admit that I knew about it, I'll have to make up some story about it being the place Jack used to go to before he went to court, to psyche himself up and remind himself of the worthy work he did as defender of battered wives. I'd rather deny all knowledge of it and profess shock that such a room could exist in our beautiful house—after all, as it was hidden away at the back of the basement it's feasible that I hadn't known about it. But then I'm faced with another di-lemma—if, for some reason, the police have fingerprinted the room, they might have found traces of my presence there. So maybe it would be better to tell the truth—but not the whole truth because if I portray Jack as anything other than the loving husband everybody thought he was, if I tell them the real purpose of the room, they might begin to wonder if I murdered him to protect Millie. And maybe a court would be sympathetic—or maybe they would make me out to be some kind of gold-digger who had killed my relatively new husband for his money. As we begin our descent into Heath-row, the importance of making the right decisions, of saying the right thing, weighs me down.

It takes a while to get through passport control. As I go through the double doors, I scan the faces of the people waiting, searching for the familiar faces of Adam and Diane. I'm so tense that I know I'll probably burst into tears of relief when I see them, which will be in keeping with my role as a bereaved wife. But when I see Esther waving at me, rather than Diane, a feeling of dread comes over me.

'I hope you don't mind,' she says, giving me a hug. 'I didn't have anything to do today so I offered to pick you up and take you to Diane's. I'm so sorry about Jack.'

'I still can't believe it,' I add, shaking my head in bewilderment, because the shock of seeing her waiting for me has dried up the tears I'd been hoping to shed. 'I still can't believe that he's dead.'

'It must have been such a shock for you,' she agrees, taking my case from me. 'Come on, let's find a café—I thought we'd go for a coffee before we start on the journey home.'

My heart sinks even further, because it's going to be so much harder to play the grieving widow in front of her rather than Diane. 'Wouldn't it be better to go straight back to Diane's? I'd like to speak to Adam and I need to get down to the police station. Adam says the detective looking after the case wants to talk to me.'

'We'll only get stuck in rush hour at this time of the morning, so we may as well have a coffee,' she says, heading towards the restaurant area. We find a café and she makes a beeline for a table in the middle of the room where we're surrounded by noisy schoolchildren. 'Sit down, I'll go and get the coffees. I won't be long.'

My instinct is to flee, but I know that I can't. If Esther has come to pick me up at the airport, if she has suggested coffee, it's because she wants to talk to me. I try not to panic but it's hard. What if she's guessed that I murdered Jack, what if there was something about my behaviour the day she drove me to the airport that aroused her suspicions? Is she going to tell me that she knows what I've done, is she going to threaten to tell the police, is she going to blackmail me? I watch her paying for our coffees and, as she heads back to where I'm waiting, I feel sick with nerves.

She sits down opposite me and places my coffee in front of me.

'Thank you.' I give her a watery smile.

'Grace, how much do you know about Jack's death?' she asks, opening her sachet of sugar and tipping it into her cup.

'What do you mean?' I stammer.

'I presume you know how he died?'

'Yes, he took an overdose.'

'He did,' she agrees. 'But that's not what killed him.'

'I don't understand.'

'It seems that he misjudged the amount of pills he would need and didn't take enough. So he didn't die—well, not from the overdose, anyway.'

I shake my head. 'I don't follow.'

'Well, because he didn't take enough pills to kill himself, he regained consciousness.'

'So, how did he die then?'

'From dehydration.'

I summon a look of shock to my face. 'Dehydration?'

'Yes, about four days after he took the overdose.'

'But if he wasn't dead, if he was still alive, why didn't he just go and get a drink of water if he needed one?'

'Because he couldn't. His body wasn't found in the main part of the house, you see. It was found in a room in the basement.'

'A room in the basement?'

'Yes. The worst thing is, it couldn't be opened from the inside, which meant he couldn't get out, even when thirst took hold.' She picks up her spoon and stirs her coffee. 'It seems that he tried to, though.'

'Poor Jack,' I say quietly. 'Poor, poor, Jack. I can't bear to think about how he must have suffered.'

'Did you have any inkling that he would do such a thing?'

'No, not at all. I would never have left him otherwise, I would never have gone to Thailand if I'd thought he was going to kill himself.'

'So how was he when he came back from court?'

'Well, he was disappointed about losing the case, of course.'

'It's just that it seems completely out of character for him to take his own life—at least, that's what people might think. So he was probably a bit more than disappointed, don't you think? I mean, wasn't it the first case he'd lost?'

'Yes, it was.'

'So he must have been devastated. Maybe he even told you that he felt his career was over. But you thought it was just something he'd said in the heat of the moment so you didn't really take any notice.' I stare at her. 'Isn't that what he said, Grace? Didn't he say that he thought his career was over?'

'Yes.' I nod slowly. 'He did say that.'

'So that must be why he wanted to kill himself—because he couldn't stand failure.'

'It must have been,' I agree.

'It also explains why he was so eager for you to leave. He wanted you out of the way so that he could take the pills—it seems that he took them not long after you left. Do you know where he got them from? I mean, did he sometimes take sleeping pills?'

'Sometimes,' I improvise. 'They weren't prescribed by a doctor or anything, he just bought them over the counter. They were the same ones that Millie was taking—I remember him asking Mrs Goodrich for the name of them.'

'The fact that he knew the door to the room in the basement couldn't be opened from the inside shows that he realised he might not have enough pills but was determined to kill himself,' she says. She takes a sip of her coffee. 'The police will almost certainly ask you about the room. You knew about it, didn't you, because Jack showed it to you?'

'Yes.'

She fiddles with her spoon. 'They'll also want to know what the room was for.' For the first time, she seems unsure of herself. 'It seems that it was painted red, even the floor and ceiling, and that the walls were hung with paintings of women who'd been brutally beaten.'

I hear the disbelief in her voice and I wait, I wait for her to tell me what I should say to the police. But she doesn't, because she has no explanation to offer me, and the silence stretches out between us. So I tell her what I came up with on the plane.

'Jack used the room as a kind of annexe,' I say. 'He showed it to me not long after we moved into the house. He said he found it useful to spend time there before he went to court, going through the files, looking at the photographic evidence. He said it took such an emotional toll on him that he found it difficult to prepare mentally in the house, which was why he had created a separate study in the basement.'

She nods approvingly. 'And the paintings?'

I feel a surge of panic—I had forgotten all about the portraits Jack had forced me to paint for him. Esther looks steadily at me, forcing me to focus.

'I didn't see any paintings. Jack must have hung them later.'

'I suppose he didn't show them to you because they were so graphic he didn't want to distress you.'

'Probably,' I agree. 'Jack was wonderfully caring that way.'

'They might ask if you knew the door couldn't be opened from the inside.'

'No. I only went down there once, so it wasn't something I would have noticed.' I look at her across the table, needing confirmation that it would be the right thing to say.

'Don't worry, Grace, the police are going to go easy on you. Remember, Jack told them you were mentally fragile so they know they have to be careful.' She pauses. 'Perhaps you should play on that a little.'

'How do you know all this—about how Jack died, where his body was found, the portraits, what the police are going to ask me?'

'Adam told me. It's going to be all over the papers tomorrow, so he thought you should be prepared.' She pauses a moment. 'He wanted to tell you himself but I told him that, as you and I were the last people to see Jack alive, I felt it should be me who came to get you at the airport.'

I stare at her. 'The last people to see Jack alive?' I falter.

'Yes. You know, last Friday, when I picked you up to take you to the airport. He waved goodbye to us after we'd put your case in the boot. He was at the study window, wasn't he?'

'Yes,' I say slowly. 'He was.'

'And, if I remember rightly, you told me that he didn't

come out to the gate to wait with you because he wanted to get straight down to work. But what I can't remember is whether he was wearing his jacket or not.'

'No—no, he wasn't. He wasn't wearing his tie either, he'd taken it off when he came back from court.'

'He waved us goodbye, and then he blew you a kiss.'

'Yes, yes he did.' The enormity of what she's doing, of what she's offering to do, hits me and I feel myself starting to shake. 'Thank you,' I whisper.

She reaches across the table and covers my hands with hers. 'It'll be all right, Grace, I promise.'

Tears well up from deep inside me. 'I don't understand— did Millie say something to you?' I mumble, aware that even if she had, even if Millie had told Esther that Jack had pushed her down the stairs, it wouldn't be reason enough for her to lie for me.

'Only that she didn't like George Clooney,' she smiles.

I look at her in bewilderment. 'Then why?'

She looks steadily back at me. 'What colour was Millie's room, Grace?'

I can barely get the word out. 'Red,' I tell her, my voice breaking. 'Millie's room was red.'

'That's what I thought,' she says softly.